W9-CXV-701

"AN ALMOST UNBEARABLE PITCH OF EX-CITEMENT AND ANGUISH . . . THE LAN-GUAGE ITSELF SEEMS ALMOST TO EXPLODE UNDER THE FIERCE PRESSURE OF EVENTS."
—*The New York Review of Books*

PAPER DOLL
A NEW NOVEL BY
Jim Shepard

"JIM SHEPARD HAS BRAVELY VENTURED INTO TERRITORY MINED BY JAMES JONES, NORMAN MAILER, AND, PARTICULARLY, JOSEPH HELLER. . . . [HE] MANAGES TO PULL IT OFF IN SPADES. . . . *PAPER DOLL* IS A FLIGHT WORTH BOOKING." —*USA Today*

"THIS IS NOT A PILOT'S EYE, OFFICER'S MESS NARRATIVE. NO SPENCER TRACYS OR CLARK GABLES. . . . IT IS AN AIR-GRUNT'S STORY, AND WHEN *PAPER DOLL* FLIES, ESPE-CIALLY IN THE FINAL SEQUENCE, THE READER GETS TO BURN WITH THE CREW."
—*Village Voice*

"WHITE-KNUCKLE ADVENTURE AND HEART-STOPPING DRAMA . . . RIVETING PAGES WHICH MAKE AIR BATTLE REAL IN A WAY YOU THOUGHT ONLY MOVIES COULD."
—*Kirkus Reviews*

ALSO BY JIM SHEPARD

Flights

QUANTITY SALES

Most Dell Books are available at special quantity discounts when purchased in bulk by corporations, organizations, and special-interest groups. Custom imprinting or excerpting can also be done to fit special needs. For details write: Dell Publishing Co., Inc., 666 Fifth Avenue, New York, NY 10103. Attn.: Special Sales Dept.

INDIVIDUAL SALES

Are there any Dell Books you want but cannot find in your local stores? If so, you can order them directly from us. You can get any Dell book in print. Simply include the book's title, author, and ISBN number, if you have it, along with a check or money order (no cash can be accepted) for the full retail price plus $1.50 to cover shipping and handling. Mail to: Dell Readers Service, P.O. Box 5057, Des Plaines, IL 60017.

PAPER DOLL

A NOVEL BY

Jim Shepard

A DELL BOOK

Published by
Dell Publishing
a division of The Bantam Doubleday Dell Publishing Group, Inc.
1 Dag Hammarskjold Plaza
New York, New York 10017

Grateful acknowledgment is made to the Edward B. Marks Music
Company for permission to reprint excerpts from "Paper Doll" by
Johnny Black © 1915 Edward B. Marks Music Company. Copyright renewed. Used by permission. All rights reserved.

Copyright © 1986 by Jim Shepard

All rights reserved under International
and Pan-American Copyright Conventions.

For information address: Alfred A. Knopf, Inc.,
New York, New York.

Dell ® TM 681510, Dell Publishing Co., Inc.

ISBN: 0-440-20076-8

Reprinted by arrangement with Alfred A. Knopf, Inc.

Printed in the United States of America

April 1988

10 9 8 7 6 5 4 3 2 1

OPM

for Sarah Fried

Acknowledgments

Most of this novel is based on verifiable fact. The characters in it are mine. Though care has been taken not to contradict historical testimony, I have not hesitated to invent whenever it seemed fictionally right to do so. While the overall situations and missions are as accurate as I could make them, *Paper Doll* and its fate remain wholly my invention.

I gratefully acknowledge my debt to the many people I've interviewed and the many texts I've consulted. I thank Joe Kusy, Lieutenant Colonel Juliann L. Kelly, U.S.A.F., Ken Kelly, Donald Lopez, Robert McIntosh, Colonel Richard Williamson and the staff of the 512th Antique Aircraft Restoration Group, Dover Air Force Base, Peter Chandler, Catherine Shine, Lenny Simon, Don McWilliams, Joe McCullough, Major Jim McGuire, Louis Kelley, and William Walton. Special thanks are due Albert Shepard and Betty Kelley, both of whom contributed far above and beyond the call of duty.

Besides original newspaper sources, I've made extensive use of information from *The Army Air Forces in World War II,* edited by W. F. Craven and J. L. Cate; *The Mighty Eighth,* by Roger Freeman; *One Last Look,* by Philip Kaplan and Rex Alan Smith; *The Pilot's Manual for the B-17 Flying Fortress; B-17 Parts Catalog for Type A-1B Turret; Ploesti,* by James Dugan and Carroll Stewart; *The Schweinfurt-Regensburg Mission,* by Martin Middlebrook; *The Fall of the Fortresses,* by Elmer Bendiner; *Piece of Cake,* by Derek Robinson; *Decision over Schweinfurt,* by Thomas Coffey; *The Good War,* by Studs Terkel; *Air Force Diary,* edited by James Straubel; *Impact: The Army Air Forces Confidential Picture History of World War II;* and *Air Force Combat Units of World War II,* by the U.S.A.F. Historical Division.

PART ONE

The Baby Train

THEY LAY ON THE HARDSTAND UNDER the wing of *Archangel,* more or less uncertain as to what they were supposed to be doing. Their commanding officer had been a car salesman from Pocatello, Idaho, and there was no acute sense around the base, yet, that the aircrews' ground time needed to be filled. The sun was warm and welcome on their legs. They'd just been playing with hoses and Lewis was letting his shirt dry on him. Bobby Bryant had spread his over a dismantled engine nacelle. Bean lay asleep on the grass with his head on a bag of doughnuts. His cheek and open mouth were turned to the bag, and the illusion was that of a swimmer taking a breath, or someone eating in a novel way.

They were new to all of this and fairly sure they had a good deal more to learn, but no one was going to ask for work. From what they could understand, the 8th Air Force was still in a disconcerting state of confusion.

Bobby Bryant was talking about back home, Providence, Rhode Island, and Lewis and Snowberry were lethargic enough to give him their attention, and Bean was asleep, so there was no one to interrupt him. He was encouraged.

His family had owned a series of dogs, all kept outside, all high-strung and aloof from Bobby—all his father's dogs, his mother liked to say. He remembered at five or six sitting in the hot sun with one of them, Toby, a small squat mongrel with German Shepherd somewhere in its bloodlines. Somehow he had reached for it and Toby had nipped his fingers, forearm, and bicep in a frenzy of irritation, and then had almost immediately resumed a sort of placidity. He'd been terrified of the dog after that, and the dog, as if to torment him, had developed a way of covertly lifting a lip in a silent snarl when only Bobby was looking. He did not risk his father's contempt by bringing it up.

They got the dogs through the mail—unflagging and omniscient hunting breeds promised from faraway kennels —and unfailingly the dogs arrived with some affliction—one eye ruined, a serious limp, odd lumps on the neck or chest— and a disposition soured by it.

They fell like Limeys at the Somme, his uncle who fancied military history liked to say. Toby was hit by a car. Corky tore off in full throat after a bird of some sort and plummeted, still baying, from a rocky outcropping. King died of an infection that made an eye swell up grotesquely. Someone poisoned Snapper, an animal of such epic nastiness that it had to be chained at all times. Neighborhood children, Bobby remembered, gathered at safe distances to watch it foam and tear with a chilling intensity at its chain and collar, in such awe of the animal's fury that they did nothing to tantalize it further, only watching day after day in hushed silence, as one might watch a volcanic eruption.

Tippi, Bobby's favorite, a smallish white and black animal with an inexplicably crushed ear, disappeared on one of his father's hunting trips and was never heard from again. The notion haunted Bobby that perhaps the dog had been hurt and left to fend for itself, and was even now dragging itself around the same stretch of forest in eastern Connecticut, its eyes wide with hunger.

All the dogs had frightened his sister Amy terribly— Toby had even stalked her when they were alone, its head low in wolfish concentration—and she kept as a talisman against them a gingham stuffed animal resembling a pork chop that her mother had made for her. She called it Miss Ebboo, introduced it only to Bobby, and lived in fear her father would find it.

"Miss Ebboo," Lewis said. It did not sound as if he was enjoying the story.

When he was a kid, Bryant went on, about seven, and the Depression had really hit, he remembered that it was clear to even the smallest kids in the neighborhood that there was something screwed up about the world the way they understood it and that a guy like his father or a neighbor could work hard and be good at something and still find out no one wanted him. He had told his sister then and there that he was going to be a pilot someday, flying around Texas and the ocean.

"Why don't you give it a rest for a while," Lewis said, and Bryant stopped talking. He closed his eyes to the sun and remembered St. Louis winning the World Series, cheating his Athletics. He remembered Capone going to jail, as if having just given up. He remembered his parents refusing to let him see *Frankenstein,* his mother herself in fact refusing to go, and his father taking it in one Saturday night alone without telling him, breaking his heart, and returning to pronounce it windy. He remembered his father leaning conspiratorially close and allowing, with a cruelty that still left Bryant breathless when he thought about it, that the monster was certain as ants something to see.

He remembered the world and his father shutting down possibility, and pilots—aero-men—as always the vivid exception. He resolved maybe then, thinking of the monster he still had not seen, the monster they wouldn't put on the advertising posters, that he was going to fly. The possibility of washing out was too terrible to entertain.

They lay spread out with the other crews beneath the wings of B-17F Flying Fortresses. They had been discussing with intermittent interest the possibility of the Wing's acquisition of impressive new B-17G Flying Fortresses. The interest in the G variant was not casual: it was supposed to feature a remote-controlled turret in the nose beneath the bombar-

dier's station, forming a kind of chin on the plane. The turret held two fifty-caliber Brownings and struck them all as
an enormous improvement over the single pivot-mounted
machine guns in the nose of their F. German interceptor
tactics for confronting the massed Fortresses had evolved
almost exclusively into head-on passes to take advantage of
the relative futility of the F's nose armament. And, as Lewis
liked to remind them, the relative futility of the F's gunners.
The tactics had become very successful. They thought about
the G's with a healthy and selfish dislike for any other crews
that might receive them first.

The first airplane Bryant had ever seen had crashed while he
was watching. It had been an old yellow De Havilland biplane, looping and sideslipping over Narragansett Bay, perhaps for the entertainment of the bathers on the surrounding
beaches. Bryant had been standing knee deep in a warmed
and reedy part of an inlet. The water around his legs lapped
and rippled quietly. The engine changed pitch and the biplane had trembled in mid-air, and while he watched, it
folded at the center as if on delicate hinges, collapsing upon
itself and twisting apologetically downward. Rowboats had
labored out to the point of the splash.

Their crew chief, an unpleasantly beefy twenty-four-year-old
named Tuliese, was standing on a rolling metal scaffold beside their plane, *Paper Doll*, a few hundred yards down the
flight line. He was painting a small vertical yellow bomb six
feet or so beneath the pilot's side window. The bomb de-
noted a mission flown, and now there were two on the plane.
Tuliese held the piece of sheet steel he used as a palette aloft
to block the sun while he worked. The flashing dazzled Bryant.

Snowberry was practicing his Crosby, nestled comfortably against some folded tarps the line crews used to protect
engines under repair. He introduced himself as Tech Three

Gordon Snowberry, Jr., somewhat proud of being the low-est-ranking crew member in *Paper Doll,* and made just about everyone who met him wonder at exactly what age the Army Air Forces decided someone was too young for service in the Air Corps. He was blond and small and did not shave, and was convinced his voice had a mellow resonance uncan-nily matching Bing Crosby's. He hoped to be a dentist when the war was over, and often pointed out while the men ate what Oh Henry!s and Baby Ruths could do to their molars. He liked to sketch, and had no aptitude for it. He enjoyed telling people about his past that he had just flat walked out of school and signed up to get in on this thing. He was a ball turret gunner, which was a job, Lewis liked to say, for small fanatics or pinheads, and he accepted with happy equanim-ity his position. He believed he was a good gunner. He had only been at it for two missions. A good friend of his with the unlikely name of Sneeb had been unlucky enough to be flying in the belly of a Fortress sustaining minor damage on the raid to Emden, flak shearing away a small piece of the rotating mechanism that allowed escape from the ball, and when the undercarriage had collapsed upon landing, the full weight of the sixty-five-thousand-pound Fortress had come down upon the ball turret, and Snowberry's friend. Speaking of it later, he had only been able to cry, his breath coming in small whoops. Bryant had been embarrassed to be present, and not much help.

Snowberry had settled in now, hands in his pockets, testing various scat phrases. He'd diversified recently to duets, a fact of which he was secretly proud, and he began both parts of "An Apple for the Teacher": "You're sophis-ticated. I think I'm naive." He softened his tone to affect the transition from Connie Boswell to Bing. Part of the key to Crosby was that certain insouciance.

Lewis opened an old forwarded newspaper he'd brought along to read in the sun and flapped it in Snowber-

ry's general direction. Snowberry lapsed into a more unobtrusive run: Buh buh buh bum, buh buh buh bum.

"Story here," Lewis said, "about an Army Trainer that
lost it and pancaked onto a funeral procession." Bryant
opened his eye a crack to see, but Lewis was folding the
paper, the *Dayton* something.

"Pilot error," Snowberry said.

"That One Check He Didn't Make," Bryant said.

"So the headline," Lewis said, "is *What Began As a
Funeral Ended in Tragedy.*"

They were quiet, thinking about it. "Can't deny it,"
Snowberry finally said.

"You know what I feel like?" Bean was awake. He
hadn't opened his eyes, though he looked considerably more
dignified with his mouth closed. He was *Paper Doll*'s radio
operator, and unpopular. He was fat around the face in a
way that seemed childish, and was instantly recognizable as
unathletic. He was already well known for his inability to
touch wriggly things. Squadron if not base opinion was that
he was insufficiently masculine.

"I feel like Mexican food," he said.

Bean had once confided to Bryant and Lewis that he
always kept thirty-five cents in mad money on his person, at
all times.

"Mexican food," Lewis said grimly.

"Lewis doesn't like Mexican food," Snowberry said.

Lewis bounced something small and light off Bean's
head. "You think they'd be swimming that river if the food
on their side was good?" he asked.

Whatever Lewis had thrown, Audie had gotten to and
was now eating. Audie was one of the base dogs, blind
enough that they'd often hear around the base the small-
scale collisions and yelps involving the dog and recently
moved equipment. When there was major movement going
on, the dog stayed in one spot, next to their Nissen hut. A

jeep had knocked her sprawling once, and the sound of the engines and brakes had made a lasting impression.

Bean tried to pet her, and she pulled away. Bryant had toyed with the idea upon first seeing her that here, finally, was his own puppy, but she had proven too stubbornly independent for that, disappearing for long stretches even as she seemed to recognize and acknowledge their kindness.

Bryant wondered aloud, gazing at her, when the G variants might come through.

"When they've used up all the F's," Lewis suggested.

"That's not very funny," Bean said.

"Shut up," Lewis said.

Bean apologized. He seemed to feel he was always saying something to irritate people and never knew why, and his method of handling it was to apologize frequently in general, hoping to suggest that he meant well.

Lewis stood and straddled a child's bike he had bought in the village. Or claimed he had bought in the village. He began pedaling in wobbly circles, his knees high and wide on the undersized frame, the front wheel nosing erratically about as he attempted to gain speed. He leaned dramatically over and, picking up velocity, scooped up a deflated Mae West with one hand.

"Where *is* everybody?" he asked. "We're supposed to be taking a picture here. Don't tell me I hosed down for nothing." He took a swipe with the Mae West at Bobby Bryant as he went by.

"They said they'd be here," Bryant said.

"You got somewhere to go?" Snowberry asked. Lewis swept past, trying to hook the soft noose of the Mae West collar around his head. He whapped Snowberry in the face.

"Lewis is the kind of guy," Snowberry said, "it said in the yearbook, 'Enjoys a good practical joke,' and what they meant was he likes to kick people's teeth out."

Lewis ran over his hand.

"You know, all you're doing," Snowberry said, "is making enemies of the very people on who your life may depend."

"I don't have enemies," Lewis said. "Though some of my friends could stand watching."

Snowberry said, "In my mind you're riding in a hole that's getting deeper and deeper."

Audie could hear the motion and sniffed the air nervously. She stood and stretched and curled deeper behind Snowberry into the tarpaulins.

"What a stupid dog," Lewis said, and swished the Mae West at her. Her ears curled back. "We get dog stories and blind dogs and every other thing. I'm sick of dogs."

"I like dogs," Bean said.

"What do *you* know?" Lewis asked. "I heard you once go 'Somebody get the door' during a Lionel Hampton solo."

"Dogs for sale," Snowberry crooned. "Appetizing young dogs for sale."

Lewis stopped riding. The rest of the crew was waving them down to *Paper Doll.* Tuliese had finished the bomb and was rolling the scaffolding away.

Their pilot, a first lieutenant named Gabriel, had arranged a photo session to promote crew *esprit de corps* and give everyone something to send home. Lewis was on his second tour and third crew and rarely tired of comparing the present group unfavorably to any other group in the ETO. On the way back from their first mission together he had angrily suggested changing the plane's name to *Chinese Fire Drill,* in honor of the overall coordination and performance of the ship's gunners.

Gabriel had a chart on which he'd figured the positioning for the photo, and he read it aloud: Kenneth A. Gabriel, Jr., pilot, Ellis Cooper, co-pilot, Willis Eddy, bombardier, Samuel Hirsch, navigator, standing, back row; Sebastian Piacenti and Lambert Ball, waist gunners, Harold Bean, radio operator, Robert Bryant, flight engineer, Gordon Snowberry, Jr., ball turret, and Lewis Peeters, tail gunner, kneeling, front row. While Gabriel read, they snickered at each other's names.

They lined up in that order and Bryant retrieved his shirt from the engine nacelle. Gabriel approved of their sloppiness in terms of the picture: it gave them that casual veterans' look.

He had talked another pilot, a guy named Charley Rice who flew *Boom Town,* into taking the picture. It was one of Rice's hobbies.

Rice had sauntered up while they were positioning themselves and had begun unfolding the camera tripod before them without comment.

"I figure you should frame it, Charley, so that you can see the name, too." Gabriel pointed at the name behind him on the nose of the plane.

Rice did not answer. He was trying to affix the box camera onto the tripod. It was apparently an arduous task.

They were not used to all being together with nothing to do, officers and men, and they waited awkwardly. Lewis said, "Bean told someone—and I'm quoting now—that Snowberry here, to get into the ball, has to 'curl into the fecal position.'"

"You've been reading my letters," Bean said, shocked.

"In a what position?" Willis Eddy asked. His toe nosed Bean's bag of doughnuts.

"He meant fetal," Gabriel explained. He made a circular motion with his hand, as if to hurry Rice's progress with the camera.

"I know that," Willis Eddy said. "I thought it was funny."

They waited and took special care with the kind of rumple they wanted to effect and calibrated their expressions and Rice still wasn't ready. He fumbled with a latch and sweated. Something gave a wicked snap and he seemed to have hurt a finger.

"That the right camera?" Lewis asked politely. "Some of those buggers are tricky."

From his kneeling position Bryant surveyed the row of profiles on both sides of him with some pride, imagining his father or mother or Lois seeing it. He imagined his mother saying, "That's the plane they fly, behind them," imagined his father grudgingly conceding that they looked like a pretty good bunch.

"Paper Do," Rice said, squinting down into the viewfinder. "What's that mean, you suppose?" Gabriel colored and moved the lines slightly to the right, to avoid blocking the painted name. Rice took four pictures and everyone put in orders.

"This one's for Jean, from all of us," Lewis said. They laughed. Jean was Snowberry's first girlfriend, a Brit from a nearby village, and she had dated a number of men on the base. Snowberry was sensitive about it. Lewis without his knowledge often compared her ability to say no to that of a particularly placid and acquiescent Red Cross doughnut girl known to all of them simply as Red Myrtle.

"Lewis," Snowberry said.

"She's a fine girl," Lewis said. "God knows."

Piacenti had once asked Lewis at chow if he thought of Jean as that kind of girl. Lewis had said he thought of her as a farm animal.

As they were leaving, he said to Bryant, "I got a dog story for you. We had a dog, Skeezix, we were going to take him to be fixed, my dad and me. Bit the shit out of me while we were rounding him up. I didn't punish him or anything, figured what the hell. The next day we picked him up and he looks at me with these wide eyes like 'Jesus Christ, this is the last time I fuck with you! Bite the guy's hand and he cuts your nuts off!' "

Bryant when he reflected on it later found the story haunting for the same reason Lewis found it funny: the notion of retribution out of all proportion.

* * *

He sat alone in the day room afterwards with some V-mail
from Lois. As Nissen huts went, this one was larger and
more dismal than most. He sat in a battered easy chair but
the corrugated metal walls made the whole thing feel like a
construction site. Higher up they were covered with pin-ups
no one liked enough to steal, and the pictures were torn and
dirty from constant pawing. There was a wooden table next
to his easy chair with a lamp on it and a tray of ancient
doughnuts. The undersides of the doughnuts were furred
with mold.

The day room had been set up for the aircrews' leisure,
and was looked upon by everyone as the nearest thing to a
last resort. Bryant spread the letter before him and concentrated on an image of Lois, his high school girlfriend. He
saw her on his parents' sofa, laughing at the radio. He reread
the letter.

*I guess it must seem strange to you sitting where you are
reading this thinking about me and where I am. I'm on Fox
near the water, where the railroad bridge goes over. It's a
beautiful day tho it's been raining lots lately. The war seems
very far away and very close at the same time. Everyone's very
excited and pulling and praying for you. Your uncle Tom says
you're probably an ace by now, and your father said he read
about a guy who shot his foot off cleaning his guns. (Can you
be an ace on a bomber?)*

*I'm glad you have a dog, because I think they're good
company. Even if you have to share them. It's too bad that the
dog can't see. I guess you're a Seeing-Eye person. Your father
says he didn't know you could have dogs. I didn't tell him
what you said about your friend taking a squirrel up in the
plane with him because I don't believe you and that's that.*

Lewis claimed that he had had a squirrel, Beezer,
trained to eat out of his hands—the little son of a bitch

would sit there like Arthur Treacher, he'd say—and that it
had flown two low-level missions with him toward the end of
his first tour. According to Lewis, at altitude the animal
skittered all through the fuselage, its feet sounding like light
hail on the aluminum. It showed up on the co-pilot's shoulder and nearly scared him to death. A rat! he'd screamed
over the interphone. Jesus Christ, we got rats! He'd been
reassured by the pilot and an amused bombardier that it was
no rat, judging by the tail, but he'd cursed throughout the
flight to the target that he'd wet himself because of the god-
damned thing and that it was probably eating through the
control cables right then, while he was talking. Ever see the
teeth on those bastards? he kept saying. They were all sitting
there laughing, he insisted over the interphone, and *pfffft*—
right through the cables, and into the drink the hard way.
They'd bombed some marshaling yards in Holland and
Beezer had never been seen again.

Beezer, Lewis liked to theorize, had done a flying one
and a half out of the bomb bay. Some Nazi manning an
antiaircraft battery got it right in the face. He would mimic
the plummeting Beezer, arms outspread, snarling. He speculated on the aerodynamics of the tail. He said, You think
anyone's going to know what he did? We're talking about
unsung heroes here.

So what's new?
There'a a young boy with the government that moved
into the third floor of the Duffy's (very mysterious) and every-
one's wondering what's up. All the girls are wild about him.
But you don't have anything to worry about as you KNOW.

Everyone we talk to is thrilled when we say we have a boy
in the service. The poor girls who don't are so left out. People
say that's our part—find a boy, write him letters, maybe even
get engaged. Mom says maybe they figure you'll fight even
harder and do a better job if you've got someone in mind
you're fighting for. How did I get on to that subject?

Bryant folded the letter and got up. He sighed, and went outside. Lewis was breaking plates over his head.

They made a curious and fragile wooden sound and separated easily into a rain of pieces, like clay pigeons. Snowberry was handing him plates from a tea service, and one by one he was breaking them over his head. Crockery pieces bounced and ticked off the pavement.

"Isn't it great?" Snowberry said. Bean and Piacenti were standing behind Lewis. "Lewis found all this stuff in the village. He got it all for nearly nothing. Some woman had lost her sons and was selling like everything she owned just right out in front of her house. Flipped. The neighbors were trying to talk her out of it and everything." He gestured at a small heap of plates and teapots, cups and platters. Lewis broke another and a piece ricocheted a startling distance. It struck Bryant again how young Snowberry was: the same age as Lois's little brother. He had a fleeting image of Lois's brother in a B-17, like a boy allowed to sit in the gunner's seat at a country fair.

"What's it all worth?" he asked.

"Who knows?" Snowberry said. "You think they give away good china for peanuts around here?"

"Old hell-for-leather Bryant," Lewis said. "He'd like to be a better gunner, but he knows what the bullets cost."

"Hey, I'm just asking," Bryant said. "You guys would piss on your mom's Sunday clothes."

"With Mom still in them," Lewis said. "She used to warn us about that."

"They sure break good, though, don't they?" Piacenti said. "Whatever they're made of."

"It's a funny gag," Bryant said.

"He did it to me, too," Bean said. "I thought he was gonna crack my skull."

"I am gonna crack your skull," Lewis said.

Bean shifted his weight uncomfortably from foot to foot. "I never know when he's kidding or not," he complained. Bean seemed to want to believe that the natural order of things was harmony, that conflict came from misunderstanding. His father had run for selectman with the slogan BEAN: IT'S LIKE BEING ELECTED YOURSELF.

"You gotta watch out, Bean," Piacenti said. "He's out to get you."

Bean nodded unhappily, half convinced.

Lewis did seem to have it in for Bean, and no one knew why. It was an instinctual thing, it appeared; pure schoolyard.

"I'm Bean's personal bogie," Lewis said. "His own bandit. In the cloud, out of the sun. Whenever he lets his guard down."

"I should talk to Lieutenant Gabriel," Bean said. "I don't see how we're supposed to work together."

Lewis shouted and jumped on him. Bean shrieked and Lewis drove them both into the crockery pile. The others laughed and a cup skittered edgewise like a top across the hardstand. Lewis held a teacup to the crown of Bean's head like a tiny dunce cap, and Bryant laughed, grateful to have been spared the humiliation.

"Leave him alone, Lewis," he said. As they shifted, the crockery made musical sounds beneath their weight. "Aren't we a little old for this?"

"Listen to George Arliss," Lewis snorted. "A year out of high school under his belt. And Strawberry, not even old enough to *have* a fight."

"I prefer other forms of contact, if that's what you mean," Snowberry said.

"I'm trying to toughen this crew up," Lewis said. "I know I'm doing the right thing. Bean knows that, even if you don't. Right?" He glared down at Bean.

"It's pretty clear to me," Bean said. Lewis got off him.

"You're the oldest," Bryant said. "You should set an example."

"I am," Lewis said. "I'm getting pretty tired of you

guys not picking it up." About them as a crew he often said,
The third time is no charm, boy, stressing the endless ways
they did not, as raw rookies, measure up to his first two
crews. He particularly had loved his original pilot, a man
named Sewell he described as an "ace tyro," who flew their
plane with a tender, sad care. "Some of these guys, they
wrestle and fight the thing," he liked to say. "Sewell, he
understood what I call Lewis's Law of Falling Tons of
Metal." Sewell had been killed in a manner Lewis did not
volunteer information on.

He pointed at Snowberry, whose mouth was slightly
open in childish concentration, as if he were going to sneeze.
"This is what I'm talking about," he said. He twiddled a cup
grimly. "We're going after the best air force in the world, on
their own ground. They don't have tours—you stay on till
you get killed. Makes for guys who are real good. And real
unhappy. Which makes them mean. They go head to head
with Gordon Snowberry, Jr., here."

"God help them," Snowberry said.

"We're the best Air Corps in the world," Piacenti said.
"Aren't we?"

"Yeah," Lewis said. "Listen, you fire eaters. I'm not
taking on Bean without help, next time. You and you are
going to help me." He pointed at Snowberry and Bryant.

"Come on, you guys," Bean said.

Lewis tucked in his shirt. A cup handle hung from his
belt loop. "My old football coach used to tell the defense,
'Boys, I want you to show up in groups of two or more and
arrive in a bad humor.' "

"You're not funny, Lewis," Bean said. "I hope you
know that."

"I appreciate the thought," Lewis said.

After he left, Bean stood amid the crockery uncertainly,
as if it had been his fault. He was an affable and quiet boy
who closed his eyes when chewing his food, and Bryant liked
him generally.

"Don't worry, Bean," he said. "He'll find someone else." He joined the rest of the crew, though, in being more or less satisfied that the abuse was centered mostly on Bean.

Snowberry said, "The thing about Lewis that's hard to keep in mind is that he doesn't have any good points."

"I know he's just kidding," Bean said. He seemed to doubt it.

At mess Bryant suggested to Lewis he lay off.

Lewis opened his mouth and displayed some masticated food and then looked away. Bryant felt that he'd disappointed him.

"What're you going to tell me?" Lewis asked. " 'Dislike May Split a Crew'?" It sounded harsher than Bryant would have liked, and he turned away, embarrassed. That had been pretty much what he had been planning to say.

"You think that's stupid?" he eventually said, trying to sound assertive. Lewis was on his second tour and the rest of the crew regarded that amount of experience and the decision to reenlist with nearly equal awe.

"He's not any good," Lewis said. "He's helpless as a gunner and as a radio op he couldn't pick up the BBC."

"He'll be all right," Bryant suggested.

"Look," Lewis said. "I'm flying with him. I can't teach him his job. I can teach him he's not all he should be."

"That's a nice thing to teach someone," Bryant said.

"I like to do it," Lewis said. "My pleasure."

Bryant felt chilled. He saw himself as no more competent than Bean was.

"Remember the kid from Idaho?" Lewis said. "Navigator? They figure now he thought he had the plane over the North Sea, by his figuring. Told the pilot to get down under the cloud, if he could, to look around. Only they were over Wales. Mountains."

"He got mixed up," Bryant said.

"Yes he did," Lewis said. "Anatomically."

Bryant ate, intimidated.

"Let me tell you something," Lewis said. "We don't have mistakes on *Paper Doll*. I don't allow them. I personally don't allow them. If Gabriel won't make a thing about this, I will. You make a mistake, it's your ass on a stick, and I'll put it there. And you look like you make plenty of mistakes." He turned his head, and Bryant after a pause stuck out his tongue. "We make a mistake, we're dead. Bean makes a mistake, we're dead. Ten people. You figure it out. Keep that in mind. There are no excuses. Some Nazi flies up our ass because I'm daydreaming in the tail, I'm going to get on the interphone and go, 'My goof'?"

Bryant had a headache, around the eyes. It seemed his training every step of the way, from high school all the way to England, had been inept and incomplete. His number one goal in high school had been to avoid humiliation—not excel, not learn, not stand out, simply avoid humiliation—and he was distressed to have learned that things hadn't changed in the Army. He was more frightened of Lewis than of the Germans, and Lewis knew it and used it. Bryant knew nothing. In high school history his senior year they had spent a week coloring in the countries of Europe—blue for France, black for Germany, cross-hatching for the conquered areas —and his Germany Proper had stretched from Normandy to Leningrad. His teacher had held the paper up to ridicule in front of the class. His high school English teacher had shown three weeks of sketches she'd done of the Acropolis and then had tested them on Greek tragedy, and he'd gotten a 17 as a score, on a scale of 1-100. At the bottom of the test he'd written, "Nice sketches," and she on the report card that went home that fall wrote, "Non-constructive and childish attitude." He'd seen her on the street a week before he left and she'd congratulated him on becoming an American Eagle, and he'd said, "Why don't you shut up?", wishing he'd had a wittier rejoinder.

Lewis took Bryant's roll and smoothed whitish margarine onto it with a finger. "Ah, we were as bad as you are," he said. "Worse. We were cockier. We used to shout, 'You'll be sor-ry!', at incoming crews. You get over that fast."

"Not funny," Bryant said.

Lewis leaned dangerously far back in his chair. "I'm in love with Gene Tierney," he said. "I've got it bad, and that ain't good. We've got this afternoon to kill. Any ideas?"

Bryant shook his head, and Lewis pulled a small assemblage of leather straps out of his pocket, and unfolded it. It looked like a small and complex muzzle.

After a moment of silence Lewis said, "It's a cat harness."

Bryant went on looking to indicate he needed more information.

"I'm thinking about organizing a cat throw," Lewis said. "You interested?"

Bobby Bryant shook his head. "I'm disgusted, is what I am," he said. "Really and truly."

"It's absolutely safe," Lewis said. "This design is based on our parachute design. Distributes the stress."

Bryant finished his milk. "Who says our parachutes distribute the stress?"

"You got me there," Lewis admitted.

"Why don't you do something normal?" Bryant asked. "Like read a magazine?"

"Or smell the flowers," Lewis said. "Or both at the same time."

"Well, don't tell Bean, whatever you do," Bryant said. Bean loved cats. It dawned on Bryant that that was the point.

Lewis said, "You just go read a book, Commander. Maybe this isn't your event."

They sat together under a huge hangar door and looked out at the steady drizzle. Ground school had been canceled and no one was forthcoming with any reasons why. The day had clouded up badly, as expected, and the sky was a depressing color. On nearby concrete engine block supports, water marks from the rain drooped like icing. Piacenti, Bean, Snowberry, and Bryant were rolling dice.

"This is what they call 'bright intervals,'" Piacenti complained.

Snowberry was picking at his scalp. "Now usually I hate bedbugs in my hair," he said. "But this one had that Certain Something."

They hadn't formulated a game and were simply noting who rolled higher numbers. It was not an interesting way of passing the time. Bean and Piacenti sat with their backs to the hardstand and behind them in the distance a small knot of men had formed around Lewis. Bean glanced over his shoulder and returned to the dice.

"What're they doing over there?" Piacenti asked.

Snowberry shrugged. A small flailing object was tossed upward, a thin cord twisting behind.

"Lewis is having a cat throw," Bryant said. He had decided he owed it to the cat.

Bean stood, without turning. "Was that a cat?" he asked.

The cat gained speed behind them, swinging now in a distant ellipsis around Lewis's head.

"He wants you to go over there," Snowberry said. "That's why he's doing it."

"Someone should do something," Bean said.

"Did you hear what I said?" Snowberry asked. "It's a trap."

"That's wrong. It's horrible," Bean said. He turned from them and took two steps out into the drizzle.

"Concentrate on what I'm saying," Snowberry said. "T-R-A-P."

Bean strode off.

Snowberry rolled the dice. "No hope," he said.

Bryant and Piacenti stood up, as well, and Snowberry looked up at them in surprise. He said, "All right, all right," and got to his feet. He added, "He showed me the harness. It *was* well designed."

They walked through the light rain in an echelon, like gunfighters. Bryant felt self-conscious and faintly silly.

Snowberry squinted ahead at Lewis. "Imagine," he said, "if he'd turned his genius to good, instead of evil."

The men were cheering in the chilly drizzle. Ahead, Lewis had given the cord a few sharp wristy turns and let fly, sailing the cat out over the tarmac. It flew with legs outspread, like extended landing gear. It landed with some force and scrabbled up, stunned. Lewis and the men made a show of calling off the distance, footstep by footstep, and Bean reached the cat first, bending over it with a tenderness evident even at Bryant's distance. Bean looked over at Lewis and the men with hostility and Bryant could see the cat's tail curling slowly and alertly behind his protective back.

As they closed in on the group, Lewis asked for the cat and Bean refused to give it. Lewis hit him in the face and he fell onto his back. The cat sprinted free and crouched nearby, indecisive with fright.

Snowberry and Piacenti tried to break it up, and someone from *Boom Town* jumped on Bryant's back. Bryant recognized him as a tech sergeant named Hallet and abruptly found himself twisting on the wet tarmac on his side, trying to free himself from an armlock. Hallet tore at his hair.

"Hey, you guys, an officer," someone said.

Gabriel broke it up with the shaky authority of a more or less new first lieutenant. Bryant pulled himself clear with a hot ear and a painful scalp and slapped Hallet's hand away. "What's the matter with you?" he said. "Are you crazy?"

He trooped them into the hangar, out of the rain. Bean's mouth was bloody and the blood bubbled onto his chin. Lewis rubbed a toothmark out of his knuckle. Bryant's ear was burning and he wondered what Hallet had done to it.

Gabriel confronted them with his hands on his hips. "So," he said. "Let me ask you: have any of you come across, in your experience, the phrase 'Dislike May Split a Crew'?"

Bryant gazed straight ahead. He could not look at Lewis.

Gabriel proceeded to dress them down. He was only a first lieutenant and not a very impressive one, though he meant well. Bryant thought about bacon.

He asked them if they thought he liked having to do this. "Is it that you don't have enough to do?" he said. "Do we have to fill up every minute to keep you out of trouble?" Boredom was getting to be the explanation accepted for any of the aircrews' actions that seemed unusually peculiar or pointless.

Bean and Lewis and Bryant spent the night guarding the fuel bowsers—huge, hulking, and filthy trucks that fueled the Fortresses before missions. The bowsers did not need to be guarded. The rain was a good deal more insistent. They stamped their feet endlessly in enormous shallow puddles and Bean hunched as though that would save some part of him from the wet, and touched his mouth tenderly with the tips of his fingers. He grumbled once that he got into trouble every time he associated with them, but otherwise the three of them remained silent, with the rain a steady rushing sound around them, and the chilled water sweeping down Bryant's back under his rain gear like a sluice.

Ground school was back on the next morning. The weather was awful and there'd be no flying for the third day in a row. No one was complaining.

Bryant had arrived early, with Willis Eddy and Bean. Aircrew filled the seats in the briefing hut without excess enthusiasm. There was always the vague and unspoken hope that at some point they'd pick up something useful. Those attending expected little, did not sit quietly or refrain from

cracking wise, as Snowberry called it, and remained stubbornly scattered throughout the room whatever the size of
the crowd. They chewed gum and tested postures which
might seem at once insolent and military. They yawned languidly. Someone nearby faintly tapped out what sounded
like Gene Krupa. Bryant noticed Sam Hirsch alone a few
seats ahead.

"What do you know about Hirsch?" he asked Willis
Eddy. He hadn't seen much of Hirsch, but he figured Eddy
and Hirsch, bombardier and navigator, crammed together in
the nose of the plane, might have had more contact. Eddy's
position was right up in front in the Plexiglas nose, over the
bombsight, and Hirsch was right behind his seat, at the navigator's table.

Eddy shrugged, uninterested. He looked over his shoulder as if hoping someone more intriguing might show. "Not
much," he finally said. "Doesn't say much. From Chicago, I
think."

"Who's he friends with?"

"Who knows?" Eddy was ready for a change of topic.
"I don't know much about Jewish guys. I guess, you know,
they keep to themselves, we keep to ourselves."

"What 'themselves'?" Bryant asked. "He's one guy."

"Look, whaddaya want from me?" Eddy said. "I don't
know anything about him."

"He's kinda quiet," Bean offered. "He seems like an
okay guy to me."

The three of them shifted for a better look and pondered the back of his head.

"Let's go sit with him," Bryant said. He hoped it didn't
sound too virtuous.

Eddy rolled his eyes.

Bryant and Bean moved up a few rows. Hirsch acknowledged them and returned his attention to the day's
instructor, who was pinning up some charts. They involved

black silhouettes of aircraft from various angles, with large single letters beneath them.

"How you doin'," Bryant said.

Hirsch nodded. "How you doin'." He nodded at Bean.

The instructor introduced himself to guffaws as Lieutenant Mipson. He called for general quiet. Someone in the back sang the first bars of "My Old Kentucky Home."

"I don't see much of you around," Bryant said.

"I don't see much of anyone around," Hirsch said.

Lieutenant Mipson sat, apparently relying on his dignity to provoke a general hush.

"Well, you should come along when we do things," Bryant said. "They're a pretty good bunch of guys."

Hirsch looked at him, and nodded.

A staff sergeant helped pull the screen down in front. It slid back up, and there was scattered laughter and applause.

"I've never known any Jewish guys," Bryant remarked, and wondered if he'd said the wrong thing. "I grew up in Rhode Island, and I didn't meet any."

Hirsch didn't respond.

"I hear there's a big one coming up, maybe, when the weather clears," Bryant said. "Maybe even Berlin." When the conversation flagged, rumors were a help. No one knew anything.

"I'm a Jew," Hirsch said. "We don't fight. We sit in the rear, going 'Here's five hundred. Keep attacking.'"

Bryant laughed. The lights went out. The screen to their right lit up for a second or two, flashing an aircraft silhouette, and went dark.

"Right. Any ideas?" Lieutenant Mipson called.

"An Me-110," someone called out.

"An Me-210," someone else said.

"A Bristol Beaufighter," a third voice called.

"I didn't even see it," Bryant whispered.

"An Me-110," Lieutenant Mipson said. The men hooted and laughed, delighted with the lilt in his voice. All

officers and desk warriors were continuously watched for
any signs of cowardice, hypocrisy, or effeminacy. "This?" he
said, and a plane flashed for what seemed less than a second.
Bryant had no idea.

There was a short silence. "Gene Tierney," someone
said. Everyone laughed. It was Lewis.

"Try it again." He flashed it once more, for a bit longer.

There was some coughing. "I was better off when I
wasn't looking," Bryant whispered.

"A Heinkel?" someone offered.

"What sort of Heinkel?" Mipson said into the darkness.

"An obscure one," Snowberry said from somewhere behind him.

"A 189," Mipson said.

"*That's* a 189?" Bryant asked.

"You, Sergeant." Mipson pointed to Bean. "What's
this?"

Bean gazed at the screen, his eyes like a rabbit's caught
in the headlights. "Sir?" he said. "A Dornier?"

"A Mosquito," Mipson said. "About as wrong as you
can be, Sergeant."

From the back someone made the sound effects of skidding tires, smashing glass.

Lieutenant Mipson announced a spot quiz, with some
weariness. "Ten planes for two seconds apiece," he said.
"Take out papers and number them from one to ten."

The lights came back on, and it was noisy out of all
proportion to the task supposedly being performed. They
numbered their papers, and waited. Bryant's column of
numbers strode off to the left as it descended. The lights
went off again. Men made kissing noises.

"One," Mipson said. A Focke Wulf 190 appeared on the
screen.

There were boos and hisses. "Gene Tierney," Lewis
called from the back.

"Quiet," Mipson scolded.

Another went up. A Dornier something, Bryant knew.
217? He glanced at Hirsch's page in the gloom.

Another. An Me-109. The men cheered the most famil-
iar silhouette in the Luftwaffe.

Seven more went by. Bryant figured he'd gotten five.
They were gone so fast. The lights were back on, and they
were stretching and trying to look at each other's papers.

"Now the chart," Mipson said. He went from A to Q
with his pointer. Then they did lookalikes from confusing
angles. Bryant mistook a Spitfire for a Messerschmitt.

They filed out peeved at their ignorance and angry with
this kind of desk fighting anyway. Beside the door was a
morale poster, a drawing of a Focke Wulf 190, probably the
best of the German interceptors, with its broad snout comically exaggerated, its squared wings shortened and absurd.
The caption read *Who's Afraid of the Big Bad Wulf?* Beneath it someone had written, *We are.* Following that was a
row of signatures, running off the paper and a good ways
down the wall. Lewis Peeters was the first name on the list.
He'd also drawn in, in some detail, the Focke Wulf's underwing cannon.

AFTER THE AFTERNOON SESSION BRYANT AND HIRSCH
waited for Snowberry and Lewis to file out. Hirsch seemed
reluctant to wait. Bryant called the two of them over when
they emerged, but when they arrived he discovered he had
no real idea of what to say. They stood in a foursome awkwardly. Hirsch was an officer, a second looey himself, which
made things more difficult. They were tech sergeants.

Lewis tested and worried a loop of string, the movement of his hands relaxed and intricate. Snowberry regarded
the process, then Hirsch, with interest. Lewis said, "Lieutenant, maybe you can answer a question Strawberry here is
having trouble with. You've seen us in action as a crew.
Think we have a chance of getting through the doors of the

mess without hurting ourselves? What do you think of what
we got here? A wop at one of the waist guns, this Long
Islander in the top turret, and Strawberry, who should be
thirteen next April, in the belly."

"Rhode Island," Bryant said.

Hirsch gave the matter some thought. "Seems an all
right group," he said. He sounded wary.

"And then the lieutenant here," Lewis said.

Hirsch gave him a tight smile. "I have to go," he said.

Bryant watched him leave. "What'd you do that for?"
he asked.

Lewis said, "Bryant, sometimes you are so rock stupid
that it makes us want to sit down and cry for the Army."

"What? What'd I do?" Bryant asked.

Lewis repeated his question, adding a little more whine.
The effect was not flattering. He said to Bryant, "Remember
you said you wanted advice before, from an old hand? Well,
here's the advice: Don't make plans." He repocketed his
string and left with Snowberry without issuing an invitation
to follow. Bryant straightened his belt and tried to appear as
though he had a reason for standing alone where he was,
feeling like someone just in from overseas, without a buddy
in the world.

He sulked the balance of the afternoon. He sat near the
hedges on the perimeter, under the overhang of a small
house which served as an information booth and guard hut.
The mist glazed his boots and the dry area beneath the overhang resembled a small beach. He had more mail, from
Robin, so the sulking was easier to pull off. As far as he
could make out, though, he was unnoticed where he was,
and his irritation in all likelihood remained unrecorded. Half
the squadron was up practicing assembly and cooperation
with escort fighters, and the rumble above the cloud cover
was constant and exciting.

Robin was Robin Lea, an Englishwoman who lived

with her mother two villages over. She was in training as a
Civil Defense clerk. They'd seen each other four times and
she'd charmed and fascinated Bryant each time. She had
spoken to him persuasively about the failures of appease-
ment and the sorts of insects they'd find, were they to dig up
the earth ridging the hedgerows. She was kind and patient
with what he felt to be his stupidity. He had confided to her
his fears of inadequacy and she had assured him that many
of his friends, Lewis included, probably felt that way too,
and that it was most likely a reflection of his growing knowledge. He had danced with her the third time they'd been
together and she'd worn a green silk dress that had flexed
and shimmered with light. He thought she was very beautiful.

Lewis and Snowberry were mainly interested before
meeting her in finding out if she had what it took. He'd done
his best to describe her and had finally settled on compari-
sons and had left them with the suggestion that she was a
"heavier Gene Tierney." It had gotten a big laugh. They'd
never forgotten, and Lewis's adoption of Gene Tierney as his
pin-up love afterwards had not been a coincidence.

Bryant had protested their laughter, and Lewis had responded that he didn't like the sound of that "heavier."
"You can tell us," he had said mildly, with paternal sympathy. "Is she a lard-ass? Is that the problem?"

"In England, the term is 'overlarge,'" Snowberry said.
"As in, 'That freight car is overlarge.'"

"Aw, the hell with that," Lewis had said, wrapping an
arm around him. "Looks aren't important."

Snowberry and Piacenti had hooted and wondered
aloud if Lewis liked boys.

Lewis said, "What we need to know before we give our
blessing is this: has she got a good heart? Will she take care
of him?"

"He says she looks like Gene Tierney," Snowberry said.

"He's right," Lewis said. "She'll take care of him."

They had been watching a dull three-legged race organized by the special events, or morale, officer. He was a
gawky and shy Iowan so useless his duties had since been
unofficially assumed by Stormy, the weather officer. Snowberry had gone from finger to finger on his outspread hand
ticking off his reasoning. "Here we've got a good crew, a
Christian crew, a stable crew, and what happens? Cheating,
fornication: Could the Axis Have Planned It Better?"

Bryant had protested, feeling the color coming into his
face. Piacenti had looked dubious. He had asked Bryant if
Bryant had told Lois about their "just seeing each other."
Bryant had hemmed and hawed.

"There it is," Snowberry had said. "We know what Bryant wants and we're all disgusted. Why don't we just come
out and say it?"

"C'mon," Bryant said. "I don't know what to do. We
haven't done anything. I don't even know if I should keep
seeing her."

Lewis wondered aloud just who was in the driver's seat.

"This is stupid," Bryant said.

They had cheered for their team in the three-legged
race, Lambert Ball and Willis Eddy, who were trundling
along the course dead last. "Bigger question," Lewis had
said. "Is it just the hots? Is the Brit better? Now didn't he
compare what's her name—Lulu—"

"Lois—"

"Lois—to someone else, for us? Another movie star?
Before he met Gene Tierney?"

"Yes he did," Snowberry said. Snowberry had always
claimed to be the smartest kid in his high school, and at
times like these Bryant could imagine it: the wise-ass kid,
always ahead of the teachers. "Remember? Jean Arthur, he
said."

"She does, sort of," Bryant said miserably.

"I've seen her picture," Snowberry reminded them. "I
think he means Chester Arthur."

"How about Sergeant Bryant?" Lewis said. "Two movie stars, not one. And he claims he's got troubles. You're wasting our time. And taking advice from those who truly need it."

"Who's Chester Arthur?" Piacenti asked.

"So one knows about the other but not the other way around," Snowberry said, summarizing. "Well, it's the Army way. Though you're not going to meet *my* sister."

"Look," Piacenti had finally said, irritated and trying to bring a little common sense to bear on the subject, "so you got a girl back home and a girl here. I don't see the news. Some girls, you know." He made a motion with his fist. "Other girls you marry."

"It's not like that," Bryant murmured.

"It's not like that," Piacenti repeated. He looked at Bryant as if he'd messed himself. "Look: what's so difficult? I got a fork, I use it for meat. I got a spoon, I use it for soup. How complicated you want to make this?"

"Everybody repeats everything I say," Bryant said.

"Listen to *Il Duce,* there," Lewis said. "He made the trains run on time."

Bryant's sulk had petered out without attracting much attention. Everyone was staying inside because of the drizzle. A small boy peered around the side of the hedge delineating the base perimeter. "Hello," the boy said.

Bryant said hello. He thought, Why is he standing in the rain?

"Are you working?" the boy said. He was round-faced, with light hair. "Are you planning a bombing mission?"

"They're all planned," Bryant said. "Now I'm reading letters."

The boy hesitated. "That's very nice," he eventually said.

Bryant opened Robin's letter. "What's your name?" he

asked. The boy was wearing black shorts so large his knees were covered. He was scratching a leg with his shoe.

"Colin," he said. Bryant made a show of starting to read. "Are you from Texas?"

Bryant shook his head. "Rhode Island."

"I'm afraid I don't know where that is," the boy said after a while. The mist fused his light hair together at the ends and darkened it. Bryant pulled Robin's letter from the envelope and counted the pages.

"Do you know anyone from Texas?" Colin asked.

"I may," Bryant said. "I'm not sure."

The boy was apparently working his courage toward something. Bryant waited a moment before beginning to read.

Dear Bobby,

Your letter made me happy and sad—happy because it recalled you so vividly to mind, and sad for the same reason. You are too far away. You have a worrisome occupation. I am alone, save Mother. Those are enough reasons to be sad for now, I think.

Mother's visiting her eldest sister, my aunt Susan, for the week, and I'm rattling around the place alone (save the geese). In my training program there's some sort of confused reorganization going on, or consolidation, so I'm perfectly idle this week and the next two. Mother has suggested that there are many things I could do in town. I'm trying right now somewhat unsuccessfully to persuade myself that I am not afraid of spiders in the bath or baby bats in the shed. If I want to live in the country so much, I tell myself, I have to get used to the night creatures and night noises of a house.

The house: the house is a lot of work as well as pleasure. I have barely any time at all for my painting. There is little that doesn't need help, from the garden to the roof slates. Another thing I can do with this time to myself. I'm trying to do as much myself as I can. Mother should be spared a good

*deal, if possible, and if you and Gordon are able to come up
and take advantage of our local Civil Defence muddle (Jean,
by the way, informs me that Gordon claims to be absolutely
certain about visiting), I won't want the four of us to spend
our time tidying up. Today I painted the iron lattice garden
gate and those nails you were gracious enough to admire are
now largely a very inelegant black. Which makes me wonder
if painted nails belong in the countryside. I fear not. Weren't
you the one who claimed to be incapable of imagining me in a
farmhouse?*

*When you come, your imagination will be given a push.
The house dates from 1791. The farm part was years ago split
up, though there's still a good bit of land left. I'm afraid it
won't seem very American to you and Gordon—cold stone
walls and big rattling windows that let the wind in (in the
mornings outside it's cold and damp, now, and inside it's
colder and slightly less damp). It's dull this summer, but very
pretty. There are cracks all about the house and the stone is
crumbling but it's far from disaster. The garden is full of old
twisted apple and beech trees and one cherry tree which has
grown from a pip I planted when I was five. There are for-
sythia and bluebells and roses and primroses—all untame, all
very lovely. In a corner of the garden we found an enormous
man-hole (eight feet by six feet and carefully lined with stone)
which we romantically claim to have been Cardinal
Newman's hideout when the Protestants were after him.*

"Any gum, chum?" the boy said. He was still gazing at
Bryant, still standing in the same spot near the hedge.

"Excuse me?" Bryant said.

The boy looked crestfallen. "Then you don't know it,"
he said. "I told him you wouldn't."

Bryant waited, and the boy removed his hands from the
hedge and withdrew them behind his back. "My friend Keir
told me if you asked Americans that way, they gave you
chewing gum. He said you found it amusing."

Bryant fished some gum from his pocket. "He was right," he said. He leaned forward and handed the gum around the side of the hedge.

"Thank you very much, Sergeant," the boy said.

"Well, you tell Keir he was right on the beam."

"I will," Colin said. "And I hope you remain alive, Sergeant. I have to go now, I'm afraid. Thank you for the chewing gum."

He waved, and Bryant returned the wave. He watched the boy cross the open grassy area bordering the base and disappear, finally, down the lane.

"I hope you remain alive?" he repeated to himself. He shook his head.

After scrubbing floors and washing windows and repairing mattresses and sewing curtains I was quite fatigued with the indoors and ready for the garden. I asked my neighbour who around here knew about gardens, and the Hampdens arrived.

Lucky me. The Hampdens owned and ran a small plant and feed shop and have retired, it seems, to my back garden. Mr. H. was rather suspicious of my free time, but he's come around, I think. They've provided some expertise, aid, and company, and we spent the last two days gardening in some fairly heavy rain. Again, not very American, I suspect, but something one does, gardening in England. It's beginning, they tell me, to resemble a real English garden—with the variety and colour. You scoff, I'm sure. I'm not certain I know what makes an English garden (Mr. Hampden likes to say a watering can, some fertilizer, and three hundred years): the rock beds, the beautifully level and rich grass, the sense of age, of hidden surprises.

I've been trying to learn the botanical names for the new plants: this morning I pointed out a delicate one at my feet and said "Arabis," proudly, for I suspected I was right. "Arabis variegata," said Mrs. Hampden. "Variegata," I said,

*as though that were obvious. "Is that Latin?" "No, dear," she
said. "English." The dictionary says from the Latin* variegare.

*Mother, and the gardens, and the Hampdens, are almost
enough. But almost is not it, is it?*

*I'm well. I'm fairly happy. I hope you are well. I hope
you are safe. I'm very much looking forward to your visit.
Mother has said there's plenty of room for Jean and Gordon,
so you shouldn't worry.*

*The enclosed, perhaps, I should explain. It comes from
my realisation that only watercolours can match some English colours. Though this—my first attempt with flowers
since thirteen—conveys only a bit of what I'm trying to send.
Please take care of yourself. I hope to see you soon.*

Robin.

In the envelope—Bryant had missed it at first—was a
piece of cardboard, with a watercolor of a spray of small
starburst-like flowers of an intense blue, over green stalks
and dark brown earth. It was labeled *Endymion nonscriptus
(English Bluebell)*.

That night he lay in the Nissen hut on his bunk, the enlisted
men's quarters cramped enough that an outspread arm
would touch Snowberry, sleeping soundly to his left. There
was a mission on for the next morning, though the weather
was again problematic. Apparently someone was tired of
waiting.

He dreamed of Training, of Basic and Gunnery, and he
woke and lay still, his friends' quiet breathing filling the
space around him. Snowberry's breathing had a slight
wheeziness to it that always inspired inappropriate tenderness in him, as though he were listening to an infant son
with the croup. The metal canopy of the Nissen roof above
made random and hushed sounds in the wind. The air was
close. The blanket beneath his nose had a flat, airless smell,
and beyond it the darkness was chilled. Bean's socks were

somewhere nearby. Outside the rain was returning, the soft rush on the aluminum light and uneven. He imagined the canvas flaps on the fuel bowsers, billowing and wet in the darkness.

He remembered field-stripping the fifty-caliber Brownings day after day at Harlingen in the dreamy Texas sun. In only shorts and boots, on a square piece of olive canvas dusty and patinaed with grit. The gun was heavy and difficult to manipulate, smooth with oil. There were cocking levers and bolt assemblies, firing pins and sears, belonging to a system of order which had to be retrieved once broken down, and Bryant had always been the slowest, the clumsiest. He mashed fingers and skinned palms repeatedly wrestling with oil buffer body spring locks. The procedures were difficult to hurry, though the stripping and reassembly were being timed. In the intense heat there was an unpleasant, dreamlike effect of having to do something rapid and intricate while submerged in warm water. Men he knew slightly and would never know again were spread in distant rows on the canvas squares across the baking and flat earth. The impression was that of a series of desolate, individual picnics. On good days shirts were piled and tied sheik-like on heads, and the rotating, depressing, releasing, and the click and clatter of interlocking metal components coming apart proceeded with a more ordered if still-hesitant smoothness.

There was one instructor, a Sergeant Favale, whom he remembered with fondness. Favale was a heavy-set Italian who'd been through two whole tours and seemed almost thirty, and had always had for Bryant a sly and kindly manner to go with an impossibly coarse sense of humor. Favale had guided him through the field strip drills, always benevolently late to start the stopwatch, with long and pointless dirty stories that he now understood had been intended to help him relax. Bryant remembered the surreal discomfort of having to endure the drills blindfolded and wearing flying gloves, oversized and lined with sheepskin, that soaked up their sweat and swaddled their arms in the heat like great floppy weights, while Favale reported his sense of what ways of dying most flyboys preferred. Bryant had fumbled and lost parts and Favale had ticked off flak, anoxia, shellfire, burning. He remembered clearly the exhilaration of finishing and ending the frustration, tearing off his blindfold and gloves to grin sweatily up at a happy Favale, the two of them looking around at others still working blind with their over-sized and swaddled hands, like prisoners of a mysterious sect. A hopelessly frustrated boy, still blindfolded, had called out to him across the spread tarps, "What way do you want to die, Sergeant?", and Favale had said, "Boys, the only way: I want to melt and drain out my prick." The tarps had rocked with laughter, and Bryant remembered the moment, blindfolded and laughing boys all around him slap-ping their thighs with gloves like enormous weighty potholders.

He remembered Favale as having pins and plates every-where in his body, everyone knew, having been wounded over France, all two tours of missions done. He remembered Favale's small fat figure in the late afternoon on the thirty-caliber range, a lunar plain with stumplike mounts in a lonely line, the instructor off firing absently by himself, the tracers a curving hot arc under the sun, bouncing and trem-bling where they intercepted the target.

He woke again in the night from a dream in which Snow-berry and some Germans had been pointing at the nose of *Paper Doll* and laughing.

Gabriel had pulled rank for the name in Gander. The final choice—he remembered *Miss Behave* and *Wrecking Ball* as other finalists—had been explained to him in a com-plex and confusing way and was lost to memory. A series of in-jokes had been involved. He hadn't been unhappy with the name, though he remained slightly uncomfortable with the suggestion of flimsiness. But that was part of the bravado, he understood: with the Flying Fortress, word was you could fly into a cliff and need only to replace the Plexiglas afterwards. You could joke in those terms.

He remembered standing outside their cold and low Nissen hut and Snowberry's noncommital attitude toward the winning name. Snowberry had crouched beside him against the cold wind, stroking the greens and grays of the lichen and pronouncing the words for the new plane, *Paper Doll,* and this new place, *Gander,* slowly, exaggerating the enunciation.

All of them but Lewis had met as a crew weeks earlier, in Florida. Lewis had joined them in Britain, much later, a replacement for a boy named Fichtner who'd been the original tail gunner, a pale boy from Missouri with white spindly hands who told them only that he was a musician, and cleared his throat with a quiet precision that annoyed everyone. He had seemed anything but their idea of a Southerner, and they had been frankly relieved to discover he'd gone AWOL one morning soon after their arrival in Britain. There was an official notion of crew compatibility as the basis for assignments, and if they were in a group with a guy like that, Piacenti had wondered aloud one night, eyeing Bean as well, what did that say about them?

They'd imagined themselves arriving by train from all parts of the country to come together as a permanent crew, a lean and single-minded fighting force. As they got to know each other, the suspicion grew that there had been a series of unobtrusive mistakes, that the selection process had involved dice or cutting decks of cards. The immediate blood bonds they had heard about seemed something for other crews, and they got to know each other slowly. Other crews seemed more confident, more raunchy—their slang for anything casually masculine—more competent.

Florida struck Bryant as the way he would have imagined a casual penal colony. They slept on raised wooden platforms screened on four sides with canvas traps. Bryant assumed a steady stream of lethal nightlife passed routinely beneath the boards and listened for every scuttle. Bean hectored them into the night about the horrors of the insects' size and persistence, and distinguished himself as well by being maddeningly clumsy around the zippered door, his embarrassed and muted struggles when returning from the latrine letting in clouds of mosquitoes which sang and tortured Bryant in the humid darkness until he found himself spending hours resolving to kill Bean and stuff his mouth and ears with insects.

The field looked as though it had been leveled in an afternoon. Half-crushed spider lilies with thick white stamens and stinging nettles grew and bloomed at oblique angles, and stagnant puddles filled the bulldozer tracks, giving off at dusk still more mosquitoes. Palmetto swamps bordered the asphalt runways. While they waited for their first Fortresses, they stayed out of the sun and flipped gravel at posing lizards and gazed at the groups of brown and ugly B-24's spread along the aprons like giant dragonflies in the waves of heat. They sweated through their shirts by seven each morning and talked with enthusiasm of their good fortune in drawing Fortresses. When the Fortresses finally appeared, they delighted in comparing the two heavy bombers: the Forts, like swept-back and low racers with their noses in the air, alongside the hopelessly boxy Liberators, each with all the military aplomb of an old flying boat. They liked to say that the Liberators were the crates the Fortresses had been shipped in. When the time came, they flew two unremarkable orientation flights in a tired old E variant, their first B-17.

Bryant had risen early the morning of that first flight and had gone over the plane nose to tail with the ground crew chief as the sole flight engineer for the first time, feeling fraudulent and redoing and botching checks, whispering to himself. He had waited, later, until Gabriel was seated in the cockpit and gazing at him pointedly before officially pro-

nouncing the engines ready, in a voice so constricted with
fear over the interphone that Snowberry had later compared
it to Andy Devine's. The four old Wright Cyclone engines,
decommissioned after fifty or so missions over God knew
where in France and Holland, performed with efficiency, and
by the end of the flight his checks had become routine. His
confidence had grown. He had imagined his fellow crew
members admiring his steady professionalism, and then had
discovered that Gabriel had been having the crew chief
double-check the important systems.

They had flown without warning from the Floridian
heat to the Newfoundland cold. Fichtner had sat on the gray
and cold rocks of Gander like a seabird. They'd flown from
Florida to Texas to Iowa to Newfoundland and he was dis-
oriented by the changes. The crew had treated him as they
might have treated a strange dog in camp that was behaving
erratically. They spent much of their time waiting for assign-
ment to a bomb group, pulling chairs around the stove of
their Nissen hut. The stove had thrown off heat so feebly
they had nicknamed it "the Icebox" and had all urinated on
it together the day their orders had come through.

Besides Fichtner, only Bryant and Snowberry spent any
appreciable time outside. The sky was gray and roiling and
close, and clouds moved aggressively offshore, flapping
windsocks and causing splashed mud to spatter dismally and
unpredictably. Gulls cried and sideslipped over Fichtner,
who spent whole half days off by himself, perched above
rocks washed black by the swells.

They had sat in small groups the night of their transatlantic
flight, Bryant talking quietly with Snowberry. The water was
black and vast over the rocks beyond the airstrip. Seabirds
huddled near the leeward sides of the huts like pigeons, their
feathers puffed against the cold. The support staffs had gone
ahead by boat, and the aircrews would make the flights
alone, under cover of darkness. They felt isolated and closer,

not only as a squadron but as a crew. Reticent girls in blue
Red Cross uniforms at a makeshift canteen served them a
sad and metallic tea while they waited. All of their gear,
stowed in huge green duffels, had been piled in the nose, and
they were waiting for a cold front to pass. The wind was
high and the sky low and opaque and they could hear the
sea. Ice glazed *Paper Doll*'s rubber tires like doughnuts.
Hirsch and Gabriel and Cooper worked the charts and reck-
onings, and rechecked agreed-upon headings by flashlight,
their murmurs reassuring.

On takeoff he remembered clearly the sensation of the
plane gathering speed in the darkness in its rush down the
runway, and the gentle shift in his stomach as the Fortress
lifted into the air, banking around to the north. He climbed
into his station in the top turret for the view and saw the
lights of the field behind and below them, turning slowly
away, and the red lights of the Fortresses ahead of them,
lifting into the cloud cover. They climbed until they broke
through the clouds like something emerging from the sea,
and the half moon illuminated the entire world.

Far ahead they could see the other 17's. He stayed in
the top turret, his weight back on the turret's padded sling.
His goggles were up on his forehead and the elastic strap
bunched the crown of his soft, sheepskin-lined headgear.
Cooper and Gabriel threw shadows in the yellow glow of the
cockpit before him, and the enormous wings extended out
beyond him dark and reassuring on both sides.

The stars were brilliant and foreign and extended undi-
minished to the cloud line. Every so often Hirsch's head
appeared in the glow of the smallish astrodome in front of
the cockpit, taking a fix with the sextant. The plane tipped
and rocked smoothly. His toes curled and flexed in the
sheepskin linings. St. Elmo's fire shimmered and glowed fur-
tively around the wingtips and propellers. Hirsch intruded
on the interphone in a low voice to give new headings.

Still hours from first light or landfall in Ireland, Bryant

had felt completely happy in a world all those back home
could never know. Below, everyone but pilots and navigator
slept, deep in sheepskin jackets with collars up, curled
around parachutes and duffels. Above, Bobby Bryant rode
high in the cold dark air in his glass bubble under the stars
and watched *Paper Doll* all around him sweeping toward
Ireland, across the darkness, skimming the fluid and onrush-
ing ceiling below, the smoothed and ever-changing clouds a
ghostly topography.

THEY WOKE HIM WITH A FLASHLIGHT, the glare harsh in
the darkness. Men were making startled and angry sounds
and the orderly on wake-up duty was going from bed to bed
uncovering faces and giving blanketed legs a hard shove. He
called the briefing time, 0330, in a clear and tired voice,
without malice. The lights flicked on and off. Men cursed
and thrashed under bedding and someone down the line of
steel bunks, dreaming or awake, called Sylvie, Sylvie, don't
you go away now.

Bryant stretched, miserable. Bean lay as if stunned.
Lewis sat on the side of his bunk with his feet on the floor
and his hands on his face. Bryant could feel the shock of the
cold on Lewis's soles. Metal lockers were slamming and
johns flushing. Snowberry was calling, "Oh, Mama, can't we
fight in the daytime?"

Piacenti went by with a towel over his head, fumbling
with his kit. The far end of the hut remained dark and quiet,
the other crew, not flying today, ordered and still, as if
breathing or movement might give them away, children hoping the heavy snowfall has canceled school. The last time,
too, this crew had not gone when they had, and Bryant
remembered one of the guys off the hook guffawing like a
loon in the dark.

They were angry and quiet at the latrine, annoying one
another in the limited space around the sinks. They stood in

their underwear and flying boots, warming their feet in the sheepskin lining and shuffling from mirror to can. Only Snowberry was somewhat cheery, remarking on the cold. Bean blinked repeatedly and tottered around like someone coming out of anesthetic.

Bryant dressed slowly, shivering, with razors still ringing faintly on the sinks in the uneven light. Beside him Bean was having trouble with the knot of his tie. When he finished, the knot was badly shaped and off-center and he pulled on a thick Army issue sweater, a dismal pea green in the electric light. Around his neck he crossed and recrossed a silk scarf—his lone Red Baron gesture—stitched from a salvaged parachute. He grinned.

An Order of Dressing had been stenciled on the wall near them:

1. Underclothing.
2. Uniform.
3. Trousers (folded inside boots).
4. Jacket (slightly open at top).
5. Boots (outside trousers).
6. Oxygen mask (lines clear).
7. Hood (skirt inside jacket).
8. Gloves.

A number of parodies were outlined beneath it. Snowberry's Order of Defecating was a general favorite, but Bryant did not resent any system of checks, however ridiculous. He patted the pockets of his overalls to reassure himself that what he had carefully packed the night before still remained, and joined the crowd shuffling outside to clamber onto the open backs of the trucks for the drive to the mess hall. They sat with legs hanging and swaying from the back, quieted by the hiss and spray of the mud from the trucks' tires. It was misting and the mud seemed more difficult than usual for the trucks and drivers. Someone closer to the cab mentioned the possibility of a scrub, and Lewis told him to shut the fuck up. At this point going and not going were both miserable prospects; a scrub meant the long emotional unwinding, all of this for nothing, and no progress toward the magic total of twenty-five missions which established a tour. And speaking about a scrub was sure to produce one.

At the extended breakfast tables they were served coffee which tasted faintly alkaline in warm, thick mugs. And toast and powdered GI eggs cut into squares and topped with a small floweret of grated cheese. The color and texture were unappetizing. Bryant ate without speaking. Bean looked ill and rubbed his neck tenderly. Piacenti ate all of his food and drank all of his coffee and sat quietly with his hands on both sides of his plate.

It was still dark when they filed into the briefing room, an oversized Nissen hut. They sat on narrow wooden folding chairs, feeling gradually more frightened and more excited. There was a low platform before them facing the rows of chairs, lit by theatrical spotlights hung from a steel beam overhead. Near the front it was very hot and near the rear it was cold. The middle seats were in demand. A staff sergeant from *Plum Seed* held a brown and white puppy slack in his arms, the puppy's ears curled back in apprehension. Bryant thought briefly of Audie, who'd taken to sleeping in the backs of jeeps in the motor pool. Once she'd been discovered by two captains only after they'd reached London, when they'd tried to pile their dates into the back. Some of the guys called her Stowaway Canine.

The CO spoke briefly of the dangers of collision after takeoff and during assembly in such weather, and reported that the chances of mid-air collision had been assessed as two planes in a thousand. Someone from the back excused himself and wondered aloud if the CO had any idea which two.

They crowded before their lockers and tumbled the final layers of outerwear—lined leather jackets and pants—

into piles that shifted together at their feet. Oxygen hoses coiled into sleeves and interphone cords snagged on gloves. They sorted hurriedly through their equipment as though *Paper Doll* were priming to leave without them, and wore and carried everything to more waiting jeeps. They overloaded the jeeps until they looked, in the gloom, to be a convoy of college pranksters, and rode to the revetments and *Paper Doll* in the dark, Lewis swinging way out on a running board, bouncing with each jolt in the darkness. They called out as they passed their plane and the driver executed a flamboyant turn and jerked to a stop. They piled out, dumping their equipment into heaps, and the truck shifted gears and roared off, its light jouncing through the mist toward the other 17's farther down the line.

Tuliese was poking carefully around beneath the number two engine. The sky was paling to the east and it was beginning to feel like morning. They gathered around Hirsch expectantly, and he went over in subdued detail the navigational data, just when and how they would end up where. Bryant ran through his series of checks with Gabriel and Cooper, gazing at his own panel and over their shoulders into the cockpit at the rows of lit-up information. Beyond the cockpit the nearby windsocks emerged like ghosts and flapped energetically, and water tracked and veined the Plexiglas. They were going to scrub, Gabriel theorized disconsolately. They were so socked in they couldn't even see the tower. Bryant climbed to his perch in the dorsal turret and looked around. He could make out only the dull glow and occasional flashes from *I Should Care,* less than a plane length away. "If they send the flares up, we won't see them anyway," he murmured to himself.

Another jeep swung by and stopped and a voice from it called out a fifteen-minute delay. "Do you register, pilot?" the voice said.

"Chew my thing, Sergeant," Gabriel called from the cockpit.

"Thank you, sir," the voice said. "We don't chew things."

With the extra time Bryant ran through additional power plant checks with Tuliese, who seemed unusually defensive and unhappy, and with nothing further to do left the plane and crouched next to Snowberry, who had long since made himself comfortable on a small pile of parachutes. He was surprised to feel how tired he was already.

Stormy, the weather officer, came by on foot, with extra boxes of candy in his new unofficial role as morale officer. He was an earnest and gently funny man, who took his inability to predict the weather with any accuracy seriously, and they liked him. He seemed to genuinely wish he could fly with them, and to genuinely worry about them. He had instituted the tradition of the Living Safety Deposit Box with their crew and the crew of *I Should Care,* holding on to their valuables during a mission. Valuables turned out to the aircrews to mean only watches and letters, and Stormy had just come from *I Should Care* and had eight watches on his arm. The pilot and the navigator kept theirs. Bryant peeled his from his wrist, and handed it over. Snowberry did the same. They declined the Baby Ruths with thanks.

They could hear other jeeps, and headlights illuminated parts of *Seraphim* and *I Should Care* and swept toward them. One of the jeeps hit a bump and the beams jerked upward and down, as though fencing with the darkness.

"Lewis borrowed Tuliese's jeep," Snowberry commented. He was eating peanut brittle from his flight rations. "More ammo."

The jeep roared up and jerked around with a rakish and dangerous tip. Lewis climbed out and started unloading boxes and loose belts of fifty-caliber ammunition.

"You're going to kill somebody driving like that," Cooper called from somewhere off in the darkness.

"I'm paid to kill somebody," Lewis said. The cooling jeep made ticking and shuddering sounds.

"Is all that authorized, Lewis?" Stormy said, and Lewis told him to have sex with his mother.

"Back there in the tail I just want me, my flak vest, the armor plate, and all these fifty-caliber gewgaws," he said.

They helped him ferry awkward and spiraling belts into the tail, and coiled them into every conceivable space, in and out of the storage boxes. When they had finished, Lewis gave them each an extra belt for their stations.

"There's a reason you're not supposed to do this, you know," Snowberry said. "The tail's gonna be so heavy we're gonna end up leaving you behind."

"That's fine, too," Lewis said. "One way or the other, I'll get by." He called to Tuliese and flipped the jeep keys in the crew chief's general direction. They rang on the tarmac and Tuliese was left to hunt around in a crouch, moving in slow arcs like someone sweeping mines.

They waited in a small group, squatting and sitting. The B-17's around them were becoming clearer and the runways faintly luminous. Various figures moved about.

"I'm going to write a war book someday, I think," Bryant said. He thought again of his high school English teacher with her sketches of the Parthenon, and her assessment of him. His holster rode up the small of his back. "Only in this one no one's going to get killed."

Neither Lewis nor Snowberry chose to respond. Stormy wished them well and left. Cooper and Gabriel paced by, gazing worriedly down the runway.

Lewis shifted audibly on his pile of equipment. "You write a war book and no one gets killed," he said. "I don't know what you got, but it isn't a war book."

Snowberry sang disconnected bits of a Crosby song to himself, his voice too low to carry.

Piacenti was in the plane looking for something with a flashlight, like a prowler. He climbed out of the waist hatch and stood over them with his hands on his hips. "There're bugs or something in the waist," he reported. Mist drifted from his words. "Hornets."

"Hornets," Lewis said. "In England." He sounded profoundly unhappy.

"Tell Bean," Snowberry said. "He's the bug man."

"Check it out," Bryant suggested softly. "See what they are."

"Your ass," Piacenti said. "I'm not going in there." He blew on his hands.

Lewis said, "Isn't this something? We're ready to get killed, but not get stung by hornets."

Hushed noises floating over from *I Should Care* sounded like someone straightening tool boxes, double-checking gear, doing something recommended and orderly and useful.

"My parents had this cabin once, on the Jersey shore," Lewis said. Snowberry hummed softly. Bryant studied the morning light on the undersides of the clouds, annoyed with the prospect of a long story at this point and finding it difficult to listen. He was growing more convinced that a scrub was a near certainty.

"We used to run around over some back acres," Lewis said, "us kids. Once, in the middle of these bushes, thick bushes, surrounded by trees, we found this '34 Nash—green with green upholstery—just sitting there, with no roads out and no roads in and no way on God's earth it could have gotten there. Perfect condition. There were leaves and stuff on it, of course. All the windows rolled up. Trees all around it, and these were big trees."

It was clear enough now to make out the doors and Plexiglas canopies and turrets, and Willis Eddy in the bombardier's station up front sneezed violently.

"I'll tell you," Lewis said. "No way of figuring it. We're being tested every day, boy."

Piacenti snorted. "Somebody gonna do something

about these things?" he asked. He was peering tentatively into the waist, his weight on his heels.

"Maybe it was a bootlegger's car, or something," Snowberry suggested. It was the first indication he had been listening. "Some gangster left it there for the getaway. Al Capone."

Why don't they cancel it if they're going to cancel it? Bryant thought. Instead of making us all sit around here like idiots.

"That's the thing; there wasn't anywhere to get," Lewis said, standing and flexing a leg in front of him. "It was like the trees grew up after the car got there."

He went in after the hornets, Piacenti following and Snowberry covering their rear. The plane was brightening and detail took on clarity. The fifteen-minute wait had long since passed. While they were inside the fuselage, shifting gear around in the search for the insects like someone rummaging through a closet, notification came to stand down, that the mission had been scrubbed. Bryant made futile and angry jerking motions with his hands down into the gravel and thought, How is Lewis going to get all that ammo back? He hated everything for being harder than it needed to be and sat with his legs spread before him like a child, winging loose gravel and small stones and whatever else his hands swept up from the tarmac at the gray space beneath the body of *Paper Doll*.

LATER IN THE AFTERNOON THE SUN came out to mock the entire enterprise, giving the ruts everywhere beside the hardstands and around the base buildings a dusty instability. Snowberry found him beneath a tree, watching the smallish clouds of dust drift from trafficked areas in the distance.

"Tuliese is working on the ball," Snowberry said. He had chocolate or dirt on his chin. "You wanna come look?"

Bryant got up, officially interested, as flight engineer,

with all mechanical problems having to do with *Paper Doll.*
They crossed long empty warm-up areas. Some of the crew
of *Geezil II* were playing football with a rugby ball. Bryant
could hear one staff sergeant—Baird?—shouting *Yah, yah,
yah* as he sprinted wide to turn the corner. His duds were
greasy and worn in the seat.

Tuliese was on one knee, leaning precariously beneath
the ball turret, tools fanned out beside him in the shade of
the fuselage. On the back of his fatigues he had stenciled
May Your Ass Never End Up on a Drumhead. The clip and
case ejector chutes for the turret were disassembled and
curled neatly inside one another on the grass.

"It's the hydraulic line," Tuliese said, instead of hello.
"With this turret, it's always the hydraulic line." He had
hung rags of various sizes from the barrels of the machine
guns. Bryant thought of the Italian clotheslines in North
Providence.

Tuliese knew what he was doing, and their working
relationship was such that Bryant was asked only to contrib-
ute his presence much of the time, to testify to the importance of what was going on. Snowberry, more in the dark
than he was, and with more at stake in this case, this being
his turret, poked closely at the nozzle assembly and offered
odd and tangential suggestions. Tuliese accepted them the
way he might have a child's, and Bryant recalled a *Saturday
Evening Post* cover, a tow-headed boy offering incongruous
tools to help with Dad's Hudson.

"I heard this horrible story from Billy Mitts," Snowberry said. "Belly gunner in the 100th. You hear it?"

Bryant shook his head. There were a lot of ball turret
stories going around.

"This guy was in a Liberator that went down short of
the field in Long Stratton—did one of those numbers
through a thicket, ended up in big pieces all over some guy's
estate. The belly gunner came out of it without a scratch."

Bryant nodded. "That's a great story," he said.

"Listen, listen," Snowberry said. "This guy, he gets out, it turns out, he's the only one there. He's calling and calling, and crawls around the pieces, no bodies, no nothing. Turns out everybody bailed out. They gave the order and his interphone must've been shot out. He'd come all the way in and crashed alone."

Tuliese snorted to indicate that the idea appealed to him. He was feeding a new length of flexible hydraulic line onto an accepting nozzle.

"I can't get over that," Snowberry said. "It gives me the jeebies just thinking about it."

"Listen," Bryant said. "The word ever comes to jump, I'll make sure you're in the know. My mother's honor."

"Just leave a note for him, Sarge," Tuliese said. "Plane goes down, it's every man for himself."

"Come on, Tuliese," Bryant said. "He doesn't think it's funny."

Tuliese looked at him without sympathy. Sweat stains under his arms connected at his sternum. Word was he hadn't changed his undershirt since landfall in England.

"Why not?" he said. "He thinks everything else is."

Lewis and Snowberry enjoyed speculating on Tuliese's family's political orientation, as they did with Piacenti. Tuliese asserted that his family was American, having come over from Genoa years ago. Lewis and Snowberry called them the Blackshirts.

"Hey, come on," Snowberry said. "Imagine coming in alone like that?"

"You think that's bad," Tuliese said. "You oughta ask Peeters about that poor son of a bitch in *Cheyenne Lady*. Ott. Dick Ott."

"Is this the guy in the tail?" Bryant asked. He hated when the conversations took this you-think-that's-bad direction.

"Ott? The wacko guy?" Snowberry asked.

Hydraulic fluid squirted from the line connection across

Tuliese's arms. "This guy, don't ask me why he isn't off making pencils right now. He was on a ship called *Flying Bison,* they're not even over the Channel yet, barely at altitude, and something goes wrong with the oxygen to the waist gunner. He passes out. Pilot goes looking for air and drops them eight thousand feet but panics and pulls out too fast, and the control cables go, and then the whole starboard wing."

Many of Tuliese's stories carried a cautionary component involving reckless pilots damaging well-maintained aircraft, with fatal and grotesque results.

"The wing root pulls the bomb bay doors off, they shear back through the fuselage, and tear off the tail. Ott's in it alone, ass over teakettle at twenty-four thousand feet. It's spinning like one of those seed pods gone nuts. The windows won't give and the centrifugal force is pinning him against the seat. He finally kicks his way around to face the opening and tries to squeeze by the seat assembly. And gets his shoulders caught on the armor plate."

They sat rapt, listening to a story they'd heard before. The only sounds were those of Tuliese's tools.

"He must've been at a thousand feet he finally got clear, got his chute open, hit with a helluva crack, broke both legs. Rest of the plane came down in the same field, like a brick. Nobody else made it."

"Lewis told me that story," Bryant murmured.

"This guy is still flying." Tuliese said it as though it had a terminal eloquence about the mental state of flyboys. "He screams at night and sometimes, a guy told me, they find him moving his bed so it's at a right angle to the other beds. Me, I'd think I was Napoleon at that point."

He sat back on his haunches and farted with some finality, surveying the turret.

"Who told you that?" Snowberry said. "About the beds."

"Guy who bunks with him. Same crew. Pissbag Martin."

Snowberry and Bryant nodded, accepting the source. Martin had been named for his inability to control his bladder in combat. He was pretty well known, bladder aside, for being one of the calmest and more accurate gunners in the Group. Lewis had said, in their presence, "At least he *scares* 'em every now and then."

Tuliese repacked his tools and left without mentioning whether or not the turret was now fully operational. After he'd left, they sat with their backs to *Paper Doll*'s tail wheel, the aileron over their heads an enormous low ceiling, like a boy's hideout.

"Did you know I hadda stretch myself to get into the Air Corps?" Snowberry asked.

Bryant looked at him. He'd swallowed some of Snowberry's stories before and had been made to look foolish, the slow kid who caught on last, or last before Bean. "What're you feeding me?" he said.

"No lie. They said I was too short. I rigged some cable between two poles and hung there, two full weeks, on and off. I had bags of sand on my feet."

It was possible. Bryant couldn't read his expression. "Weren't you worried you'd stretch your arms?" he asked.

Snowberry nodded, ready for that. "I hoisted myself up and hung with the cable under my armpits," he said.

Bryant said, "Are you going to tell me you think bags of sand made you taller?"

"All I know is, I'm in now," Snowberry said comfortably. "And I wasn't before."

Bryant thought, He's pulling my leg, and resented it. While Snowberry made contented squeaking noises with his cheek on his gum, he thought back to Gunnery Training, missing skeet, missing towed targets, missing first with the .22, then with the shotguns, then the thirty calibers, the fifties. He didn't fully remember how many of his test scores

Favale had fudged for him. He thought about his position and the level of ability he had demonstrated and grew frightened and unhappy with his secret, sitting under the expanse of tail. He was both anxious and relieved that no one understood how poorly trained he was.

"It's a funny war," Snowberry said.

Bryant thought he understood what Snowberry meant. He had tried to write to Lois about it, but didn't have the words to express his sense of the boredom and tension together, the unreality of the whole thing, and the fear.

"It seems like nothing's happening, you know?" Snowberry said. "And everything's happening."

Bryant agreed. "It's like you just sit around, or you're like Famous Walter," he said.

Famous Walter had become famous, unhappily, as the Two Hour Replacement: having just arrived at the base he'd sat down to mess, been told he was needed as a last-minute replacement in the tail of *Banshee,* and had been killed by flak over Hanover. All they'd gotten in the mess was his first name. Someone else had finished his Spam.

Snowberry clunked his flying boots together at the toes. They were oversized enough to be his father's. "God, I wanted to be a fighter pilot," he said. "I thought they were the end. Girls die for fighter pilots. They only get wounded for us."

"I was a Lindy nut," Bryant said. "Were you a Lindbergh nut? He came and gave a speech in Providence and they sold little hats. I think it was about staying out of the war, but what did we care? It was Lindy."

"Oh, boy," Snowberry said. "I must've made two thousand *Spirit of St. Louis*'s from those wooden Popsicle sticks. House was knee deep in *Spirit of St. Louis*'s."

"I used to play toy soldiers," Bryant said. "The cardboard kind, with the wood bases. I had a little lead *Spirit of St. Louis,* used to fly over, strafe the soldiers. I used to have

the guys go, 'Look out! It's Lindy! Aaah!' No one stood up
to the airplanes. Everyone did a lot of running and dying."

"Like now," Snowberry said. "The Krauts: 'Bryant and
Snowberry! Aaah!' "

They laughed. Bryant had a vision of flak crews in Germany chafing at the insult, crossing hairs over the belly of
Paper Doll, and sobered.

"You're all right, Bobby," Snowberry said. "Lewis is
tops, but . . ." he trailed off.

Bryant was grateful and slightly embarrassed, unsure
what he was getting at. He cleared his throat.

"Anyway, I keep, like, a diary," Snowberry said.

"I saw you working on it," Bryant said.

"I know you read a lot and stuff." Bryant read magazines in the day room. "I want to send some parts home to
my folks, the best stuff. They're always telling me to write
and I never know what to say."

"That's nice, a diary," Bryant said. The idea didn't ap-
peal to him.

"Here, you can look at it," Snowberry suggested. He
pulled it out of his back pocket. It was a smallish softcover.
Bryant started to hand it back and protested it was private,
but Snowberry assured him that it was all right, they were
buddies, so Bryant was forced to open it.

The cover featured in red ink a battle-weary GI who'd
apparently stopped to write beside a makeshift roadside sign.
The sign said *My War Diary.* The book was already half full.

The margins were crammed with additions and helpful
drawings and diagrams—how the arc of the tracers helped
him lead a target in gunnery, what approaches he was re-
sponsible for defending from the belly. There was a cutaway
drawing of *Paper Doll,* outlining the crew positions, entitled
Our Plane.

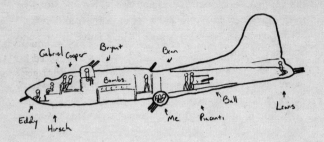

He flipped to the back, the morning's entry.

Hi again. Another f-ing(!) scrub. It's terrible and now we're all juiced up with nowhere to go. It always clears up later but by then it's too late and everyone's a real pain to be around. Lewis you can't even go near. Trying to guess the weather is awful hard. And harder, I guess, for the weather-man (!) We call our base weather officer Stormy. Lewis says he uses a weejee (?) board. He's a nice guy, though. It's real bad for morale, a scrub: we fly eight missions on the ground for every one in the air, and it's bad to get up and think you're going to be a day closer to the end of your tour and then find out it's all blooie.

He paged back to July and Training. There was a small sketch of a latrine with flies and curving lines above it.

I stink, though I'm getting better, everybody says so. I whipsaw everything like I'm using a garden hose and I squeeze off bursts that are too long. My training officer told me he was going to ration me, but he can't, of course. I have to be through in the next week and a half or it's washeroonie. I don't think I'll wash, though. On the flexibles me and an-other guy named Flynn flying tandem cut a tow target clear in half this morning, and that's good work! The tow plane even had it dipping and weaving, like real Jerries.

I still like the idea of being a dentist. I talked to the guy who examined me at the induction center and he said I'd be looking at big money and mucho opportunity after the war and the government would help out in terms of school like I couldn't believe. Mom's nuts about the idea, of course, and wouldn't she be surprised to hear we agree on something. Mom said Liz said I'd never do it because I'd have to wash my hands. Ha. Ha.

Snowberry was gazing lazily ahead, humming "When the Blue of the Night Meets the Gold of the Day."

Bryant said, "You never said you had a sister."

Snowberry looked at him. "That's right," he said. "I didn't."

Bryant closed the book and stretched, his finger holding the place.

"Keep reading," Snowberry said. "It gets better."

I remember before Dad died we'd go camping out at Port Jefferson. Somebody owned the land and Dad didn't care, though I never wanted to have a fire, I thought they'd come and start shooting. We went for my birthday once. I loved the woods and stuff. There were never any stores or lights and you didn't have so much noise. We saw a shooting star. Dad said on my tenth birthday I saw a shooting star and on my first birthday I saw Babe Ruth clout number forty-six on his way to sixty, and he didn't think if I lived to be a hundred I'd ever see the like of either again. Though of course I don't remember the home run.

Bryant did some quick figuring, and confirmed Snowberry's age as seventeen. He was underage, something everyone suspected and joked about.

He thought again with regret about how rarely he was able to remember the kind of father and son stories Snowberry always told, recognizing with a pang Snowberry's references to the private jokes that seemed the code of a happy family. His only memory of a camping trip had involved a weekend in Block Island with his father. His father had always called it in an unpleasant way Our Only Night Out. He had had to go to the bathroom late the first night and had stumbled out of his bedroll and up the dune ridge. Above him, the night was coming down in curtains, silver and red and purple. He hadn't been able to think of the word for it, and had called to his father, who'd come hurrying up the dune and then had stopped short and said, "The northern lights. For God's sake." But he had wrapped an arm around him.

He remembered it as their happiest time together, maybe their only happy time together. He remembered that they had fished and hadn't caught anything, and that his father had said, "The buggers are unionized." His father had pulled from an old pack some bread and a roll of provolone cheese that he called guinea cheese, and then had gone down to the cove sheltered by the dune ridge and had collected saltwater snails in a pan, a small black figure against the wavering light off the water. The snails had looked like little rounded black pebbles, and he had cooked them in saltwater and split them with Bryant. They had had twenty or so apiece, and had eaten them out of their shells with a pin. They had been terrible.

The next night they had had corn dogs and bluefish. They hung netting against mosquitoes on a crisscrossing pole thing he'd rigged up, on a wide flat sandy stretch at the bottom of the dunes on the west side of the island, away from the cliffs. His father had congratulated him on the netting arrangement. They sat at the water's edge on huge driftwood twisted smooth into horror movie shapes and gutted the blues, the raspberry and clearish fish organs washing

away in the rippling dark water. His father had popped a
blue's eye and it had floated a while in a strange blank way
before sinking. His father had dipped the fish in some warm
beer he'd carried in, and some corn meal, and they fried it
over a fire they dug low in a sandy pit. His father had drunk
quietly and consistently from a flask and Bryant could smell
the rye on his breath. He remembered the rye and fish and
saltwater smell. He remembered sleeping looking up
through his netting and poles with all the mosquitoes locked
out and the stars beyond.

"Pretty good, isn't it?" Snowberry said. Bryant still had
his diary open, though he'd been on one page for a good
while. He nodded, and flipped around.

He remembered the sound of the water and the little
waves from the boats tied up in the bay. They could hear the
boards and planks creaking a long way off. In the morning
they were wet and the fog made the water disappear. He
remembered the speckled metal cup with the big ACE stenciled cryptically on it, and the heat of the coffee with no milk
through the cup to his hands. He remembered the stray dog
that had snuffled around while the sun was still pink and low
and everything was wet and cold and the dog's nose snorting
in the morning air. Its back leg was badly hurt and it nosed
and sniffed them but wouldn't let his father get near to help.
"Poor son of a bitch," his father had said, and he remembered thinking that the dog was going to die.

That night the projector broke down. Bryant and Snowberry
took a reel of *Buck Privates* from the can and unspooled part
of it, holding an open-mouthed Lou Costello up to the light.
On another reel they found June Allyson, in color besides.

"They must've mixed up the reels," Bryant said. "Too
bad the projector broke."

"Some of these guys wouldn't've even blinked," Snowberry said.

They had remained in the darkened briefing room after

everyone else had drifted away. Snowberry looked farther down the reel for more June Allyson, whom he called Prince Valiant. He was starting a good-sized tangle of celluloid at his feet. He crooned softly to himself.

Poor Stormy, who'd arranged all of this, sent a tech sergeant off to Supply for a manual. They needed one, the projectionist had theorized, since it evidently wasn't with the machine. Most of the men had already left in disgust or boredom. The lamp for the machine was still on and light flickered on the sheet hung as a screen. There was nothing to do.

Lewis was sprawled between two folding chairs, flipping through something. Piacenti and Pissbag Martin were playing blackjack on a fifty-gallon drum labeled, mysteriously, USARC.

Bryant straddled a chair and asked Lewis what he was reading.

"Gabriel's pilot's manual," he said.

The others looked up from the card game.

"He won't miss it," Lewis said off-handedly. "He only studies it twenty-three hours a day. This is his hour off."

"Lemme see," Snowberry said. "What's it say?"

"It says you should get to know your crew," Lewis said. "Their strengths and weaknesses." Snowberry was making shadow animals with his fingers in front of the projector lens. "Listen to this: 'Of all branches of the Service, the Air Corps must act with the least precedent, the least tradition.'"

Snowberry looked over at him. "That's not a pilot's manual," he said.

Bryant looked closer. "It's something called *Bombs Away*," he said.

"It's a book Bean brought with him," Lewis said. "The kind they give kids in school about the Army." He continued reading. "'Nearly all the tactics and formations of infantry have been tested over ten thousand years. Even tanks, though they operate at a high rate of speed, make use of tactics which were developed first by chariot and then by cavalry. But the Air Corps has no centuries of trial and error to study; it must feel its way, making its errors and correcting them.' "

"Oh, God," Snowberry said. They laughed. Hirsch and Willis Eddy wandered back in, and sat beside Bryant. Lewis flipped the manual to Snowberry, who turned a page and went on aloud:

" 'The pilot and co-pilot must fly the ship, that is true, but they take their directions from the navigator, for he knows where they are and where they are going and how to get there.' "

"Where are we, Hirsch?" Lewis asked.

"England," Hirsch said.

" 'Arriving at the target, the bombardier must take command, for it is he who must drop the bombs on the target safely.' "

"This just confirms what I been saying all along," Willis Eddy said. He was a big, slow-moving boy who liked to say he reminded people of Gary Cooper. "You're all just here to get me to the target safely."

"Eddy here was hell with the practice bombs," Pissbag Martin said.

Eddy shrugged. He cultivated the impression that he was hard to rattle. "My instructor used to say, 'Dropping your eggs on a dime from twenty thousand feet is easy. Think of this simple analogy.' "

"What is this Southern drawl stuff?" Snowberry asked. "Who're you supposed to be, Henry Fonda?"

"He used to say," Eddy continued, "it was like getting on a bike, riding it past a thimble, and dropping grains of rice into the thimble."

"Pretty big thimble, in your case," Lewis said.

Bryant thought it might be time for some *esprit de corps.* He said, "The whole wing dropped early on that mis-

sion. Willis wasn't lead bombardier." Eddy's bombs, with
everyone else's, had been dropped short on *Paper Doll*'s
most recent mission. Eddy was unperturbed and didn't seem
to feel he needed defending.

Snowberry flapped the book to show he was going to go
on reading. " 'All during flight,' " he read, " 'the engineer
commands the engines and sees that they continue to func-
tion well.' " Bryant felt himself reddening, but no one commented. " 'The radio man is the voice and ears of the plane,
keeping contact with squadron and base.' "

"You know, it bothers me that I'm a member of an
important team alongside the fat kid who never got into
games at the playground," Lewis said.

" 'And all the time the aerial gunners are charged with
the defense of the ship. On the sharpness of their eyes and
the accuracy of their aim the safety of the whole crew de-
pends.' "

Lewis snorted.

Snowberry said, "Aren't you the Hottentot! Are we so
bad?"

Marksmanship was a sore point with Lewis. He said,
"We're not the Tennessee riflemen up there, if you were wondering." He had been spending time with them lately on
deflection shooting, and not having much success. They had
only had time to learn, and relied upon, what the Air Corps
officially termed the Zone System. The Zone System was
defined as pointing at the offending object, leading it a little,
and filling the sky with bullets.

"I think the boys're doing fine," Willis Eddy drawled.

"The only way to get through this," Lewis said, "I figure, is to make the Heinies look for a bigger pushover. You
have to turn yourself into some kind of risk."

"Hell, these guys can't shoot," Pissbag Martin said.
"The guns're there so they can show they're pissed off at
being attacked."

"Sometimes I do get the idea we're just sort of feeling

our way, here," Snowberry admitted. "It's like one day I just woke up operational."

"I don't know how Billy Barty could shoot straight from that ball turret," Eddy said. "Twisted up looking down through your legs and all that hooey."

Pissbag Martin shook his head. "I don't go anywhere at twenty-five thousand feet you can't take your parachute."

"What if we do like you say, Lewis?" Bryant asked. He was thinking while they had been talking that he was going to be up all night again, dreaming of a sky filled with Germans. "What if we do like you say, and then get it?"

"We have a saying for that," Lewis said. "We say, 'Tough shit.'"

They were quiet. "Hit me," Pissbag Martin said, and Piacenti flipped a card onto his two.

"Ah, if God had wanted us to shoot down Germans, he would've kept us guys out of gunnery," Snowberry said.

"'A boy who can hit a clay pigeon on a skeet range can knock a Messerschmitt out of the air,'" Bryant said. "The instruction manual used to say that."

"Jesus God," Lewis said.

Piacenti tried to shuffle one-handed and spilled cards all over his lap. He said, "My mother said there was a thing in the paper back home that said that for a guy's mother to wear the pin of the Air Forces is to tell everybody that she's produced a son far above average mentally and physically."

They were quiet again. A chair squeaked and he collected the cards into a messy pile.

"It's true," he said. "She clipped it out."

Snowberry tossed *Bombs Away* back to Lewis. "We're getting to be too negative," he said. "They're the ones on the run. We're going after them in their backyard now. I read somewhere somebody said, Napoleon, I think, said that the logical end of defensive warfare is capitulation." He repeated it. "I like that phrase," he said.

"Napoleon was short of Focke Wulfs," Lewis said.

Pissbag Martin stood and stretched and told them peevishly that he had to go. They could see he thought they were talking too much.

The card game broke up, and Piacenti and Eddy and Snowberry left with Martin. Stormy returned, disappointed that things hadn't worked out and blaming himself, and turned off the projector lamp. He boxed the projector and pulled the tacks supporting the sheet screen.

While they watched him work, Lewis said, "My father worked as a porter out of Chicago for a few years. I ever tell you that? White porter."

Bryant shook his head. "You told me you lived in Dayton," he said.

"We did. He told me once they were coming into a station in Louisiana, bayou country, and it was completely dark. Woman was getting off alone. He'd estimate the station stop—a dirt road—and signal the conductor. He really wants to impress this woman, beautiful West Virginian. She's oohing and aahing he can see anything at all in this pitch black. He waits and waits and then calls for the stop, and when he throws out the stepdown box, there's this little splash, and then nothing. All they can see in the dark are these little bubbles."

He laughed. "I always loved that story," he said.

Stormy laughed too, distractedly, and gave them the word that something was on the next morning, folding the sheet apologetically and becoming more awkward at their lack of response, as they stayed where they were, each of them quiet and alone now in the darkened briefing room.

The next morning they were part of a forty-plane raid which was to join a larger force headed for Kiel. They had heard that RAF meteorologists were reporting the frequent lows that had covered northwestern Europe for the last two months were giving way to highs, and that Bomber Command intended to take advantage of the upcoming weather in a big way. Lewis had remarked grimly that they might have their next twenty-three missions in twenty-three days, it sounded like.

They never got to Kiel. They never got airborne. Whatever the lows or highs, whatever Stormy's weak and maddening optimism, at 0600 the sun had not risen high enough to dispel the early morning ground mists, and the bombers ran up their engines one behind the other on the flight line with their olive tails rising above the mist like the dorsal fins of sharks. From his turret Bryant could intermittently see *Quarterback,* the plane ahead of them. Farther down the runway, the seventh aircraft in line had an engine fail during takeoff and went off the field and into the woods, through the perimeter hedge. The running lights on its tail winked through the fog. Crash trucks began rolling and the B-17's in line behind became confused. The eighth ship, *Miss Quachita,* had already started its run, but stopped halfway down, Bryant learned later, having either heard the radio command to cease takeoff or having seen the red warning flares fired by Flying Control. *Miss Quachita*'s pilot, a quiet boy from Birmingham, turned it around and brought it back up the runway. Coming down the runway full tilt was the ninth ship, *Cheyenne Lady,* with Dick Ott in the tail and Pissbag Martin in the nose as bombardier. It was carrying sixteen five-hundred-pound bombs stacked in columns in its midsection and its throttles were wide open. They collided head on, and the detonation snapped *Paper Doll* two or three feet back on the hardstand, jerking Bryant violently around in his takeoff harness. Martin and Ott and eighteen others were killed instantly, and the pilot and co-pilot of the plane immediately following were savaged by their disintegrating windshield. The column of fire billowed up like an enormous flare, the burned-off mist haloing around it. The runway and its hardbase were torn apart and took five days and nights to repair.

Morale for those five days hit some sort of all-time low. Someone had reported finding a piece of Dick Ott's flight jacket, where he had stenciled a small white parachute to commemorate the escape from the severed tail, and the crews found the irony hateful. Hirsch kept to himself more than ever. Bean continued to annoy them and now seemed distracted and morose. When he did speak, it was often to make lists for the listener of what he had just been doing. Lewis seemed to want nothing to do with any of them, Piacenti wrote long letters home he then destroyed, and Snowberry sat with his journal, rereading more than writing. They flew practice missions and sat through training sessions sullenly.

Bryant spent his free stretches watching repairs of the runway, or watching Audie sprint from the hedge to the information hut at the outer reaches of the airfield. The dog tirelessly ranged after low-swooping birds with smallish V-shaped tails and chocolate and orange markings. "What are those?" he called to Lewis. "Sparrows?" Lewis was sitting on some stacked rubber tires, penciling notes on a fifty-caliber breakdown sheet.

"Sparrows," Lewis scoffed. "Me-109's. It's a relief to know you're up there in that upper turret, boy."

Bryant flinched but felt encouraged that Lewis had responded. He walked over to the tires. Toward the fence Audie slipped in a wide turn and sprawled on her chin.

"I had a dog once," Lewis remarked. "Looked a lot like Fido out there. We lost him on a trip to a combination car wash and country kitchen. I'm trying to teach Bean a little shooting," he said, switching subjects without a pause. "In case he's gotta fill in. He's all right with a radio, I guess. But Ge-od, with anything else . . ." He shook his head. "If his IQ drops any more, we'll be watering him."

"You should stop riding everyone, Lewis," Bryant said.

"We're doing all right." But he was depressed and wasn't sure he believed it.

"You guys," Lewis said, "got the best substitute for nerve. Stupidity. Cooper," he said. "Know how he got ready for this? Pulling trailers around Arizona, thirty-five dollars a shot. Ball used to catch rats in his family's farm in Pennsylvania. His father gave him ten cents for every rat he got in the barn. Now he makes eighty-five a week and flight pay. You know? You guys can't learn this stuff in five weeks." He used the nail of his small finger to clean between his teeth. "You should've grown up with guns. Didn't your father ever give you a .22? Didn't you ever want to kill anything?"

"It was hard," Bryant said, apologetic. "I lived in Providence."

Lewis made a defeated gesture. "So, you know. There's lots of things you could be doing. And they got you here doing this. With my ass depending on it."

Audie trotted by and hunched to defecate, edging forward as she did so.

"Why'd you reenlist, Lewis?" Bryant said. He had asked before and Lewis had refused to answer.

"Flight pay." Lewis rubbed his face. "Why else?"

"No, really. Why?"

"You got something better?" He guffawed. "The girls. I don't know." When Bryant didn't look away, he continued irritably. "You ever check out the other services? Let me tell you something. I did. I transferred in. I was in the infantry. In the early days they said you could transfer into flight training, but I heard the physical for the Air Corps was a killer booger so I figured I'd flunk. 'Eyes of an eagle,' and all that. One day we went on maneuvers about twenty-five miles out into the scrub and it rained and then it was about 110. My shoulders, my crotch, my feet, everything was killing me. They started to show us how to disperse in the event of a strafing attack. And this plane flew over and made a couple of passes at us. And I thought, Well this guy didn't get up at

0400, he didn't march twenty-five miles, he's not lying in this shit, and he's gonna go back and have a nice lunch. Tonight he gets a pillow and the sack and I get the chiggers. That was the end of that."

Bryant was silent, reflecting on his good fortune.

"Hey, we're commuters. They live at the war. And who doesn't want to be an American Eagle? You think Robin'd have the hots if you were some dogface GI?"

"But you reenlisted. You could've been an instructor," Bryant said. But he couldn't imagine that, either: he remembered Favale, alone on that baked range in the sun.

"Ah, I was staff sergeant. I would have outranked the guys who'd been there for months. That would have been a mess."

"You could've gone home," Bryant said.

"Home," Lewis said. "Yeah."

They were silent. Bulldozers labored and roared to push earth into the great hole in the far runway. Huge rolls of thick linked metal sheeting were stacked nearby, structural support for the concrete. "I want to do this," Lewis said. "Half of everybody I know from my first tour is dead or missing. I want to kill some of *their* friends."

He was angry. "I'm a wrecker. Think about it that way. My question always is, what's its Fuck-Over Tolerance? How long does it have to be sprayed? How accurately? Does it come apart big or just drop like a dog in heat? I'm checking out everything. 109's, 190's. 110's catch 'em right and the wings go like oak seeds. Coming back on the deck I'll spritz a roadside shrine, or a barn. Sheep keel right over. Cows pop like mosquitoes."

"They're just helpless animals," Bryant said. He wondered why he felt surprised.

Lewis looked at him appraisingly. "I don't know what I expect," he said unhappily. "Most of you gremlins don't even shave." He scrolled sweaty residue into visible dirt on his arm. "Look. I don't know what other guys think, but for me what this is all about is precision. Get good at something. You get good, and you try not to go ass over flak happy. You come through for the nine guys you're stuck with."

He gaped to mock Bryant's expression, and shook his head. "Guys in the 351st named one of their planes *The Baby Train.* I know what they were getting at, boy."

"The way you talk it sounds like it's every man or every crew for themselves," Bryant said.

Lewis spat with a satisfying arc. "I don't know anything about politics, if that's where you're heading."

"We're fighting because of what they've done to Europe," Bryant said, a little shocked despite himself. "What they've done to everybody."

"That's good to know," Lewis said. "It doesn't help me shoot any straighter. It sure as shit hasn't helped you."

Bryant could see, over where Audie had been, Hirsch walking the hedge, hand in the green. "Everyone's so mopey," he said. "It's pretty bad, morale."

Lewis had stopped talking. Then he said, "I knew a guy in high school, used to play football, used to run back punts. Very good at it. I got a picture of him, once, doing it, and I remember his eyes. They were like silver dollars, seeing everything, guys all around him. You need that—super-vision, that nose for trouble. Sort of like wide-angle seeing. All the guys I know still around have that. Don't worry about shooting. Worry about that. Just help us see."

"I can do that," Bryant said. "And shoot people down."

Lewis nodded. He seemed to have given up. They listened to the rumble of the bomber streams returning from Kiel to the other bases, the bases without their devastated runway.

That night Bryant dreamed of his grandmother, an old Irishwoman who'd gone erratic from drink, and a mental condition the doctors weren't able to diagnose. She kept flasks in with the linens, he remembered, and behind the big bags of dog food in the nether reaches of the pantry. Bryant and his little cousin had been staying over at her house in Woburn—Bryant was ten, nine?—and the door had flown open and she had stood before them blocking the light from the hall, an enormous silhouette. She held aloft what could have been a whisk. "Who're you?" she'd demanded. "What're you doing in my house?"

"We're your grandchildren," Bryant had said, in terror. His younger cousin had whimpered, either at the whisk or at not being recognized, and their grandmother had remained like that, a frightening dark shape, watching them as they lay still with their eyes and noses above the protecting line of the covers.

The dream stayed with him through the roust-up and he stood before the mirrors over a sink in the latrine frightened of his grandmother and half asleep. Beside him Lewis was shaving with special care, feeling his jawline continually, and smoothly reshaving areas that offered resistance. The aircrews had discovered that even slight beard growth caused the oxygen masks to leak around the edges. Snowberry was shaving as well, scuffing away unnecessarily at areas Lewis was fond of comparing to a baby's ass.

Hirsch already had on a tie and an olive sweater against the chill and was filling his coverall pockets with pencils. It made sense to Bryant as he washed his face: he could imagine the terror of having to navigate home without a pencil. Hirsch patted each pocket, thigh, forearm, breast, and hip, and patted them again, absently. He carried his holstered pistol like a box of pastries.

Bryant tramped to the mess hall feeling more or less outside of himself, a novice actor. The men beside him walked as comically overburdened as Okies fleeing the dust bowl. A boxy jeep crossed through the mist some yards away, pulling connected low wagons each of which carried two clumsy and smallish two-hundred-fifty-pound bombs.

Ordnance crews were loading late in some instances. The winch sounds of the bombs being shackled in columns into the bomb bays drifted over to them. Armament crews were checking the gun stations within the bombers, and turrets whirred and whined faintly. He could make out men on the wing of *I'se a Muggin'* struggling with the canvas engine covers, cursing and sliding on the slippery metal.

It had rained but it seemed possible the mists were lifting. Puddles along the tarmac shone like mercury. They had combat eggs—real eggs—this mission morning, and spirits picked up because of it. Most of the men were smoking, and the air over the tables, Lewis said, looked like Akron on a bad day. Lewis and Willis Eddy were still talking about the promised B-17 G's. The G offered the additional armament of a nose turret, but Gabriel and Cooper had heard that the double chin created considerable drag, and that in the event of the loss of one engine, keeping up with the flight would be impossible. Straggling behind was suicide. Willis Eddy's gunnery scores, besides, were abjectly low, and as bombardier he'd be operating the nose turret. They felt a little better about still not having G's. They all preferred the greater assurance that they could hide in the pack to the extra guns.

"What happened to the biscuits?" Snowberry complained. "The only thing I liked was the biscuits."

"No biscuits on game days," Lewis said. "No beans, either. The gas expands at high altitude. Guys fart like rifle shots. Take a balloon half filled up to twenty thousand feet, it's filled. Take it to thirty thousand, boom."

Snowberry looked at his eggs with distaste.

They were checked into the briefing room by MP's with white leggings filthy from the mud. The gunners sat in a line on benches facing the curtained mission board and immediately checked the yarn pulleys alongside it. A good deal was missing. As they noticed, they became even less happy. The more yarn was missing, the more was on the map and the longer the trip.

They were shoulder to shoulder in the soft and heavy flight jackets, and the smells after the morning air were eye-watering: Kreml hair oil, shaving lotion, sweat, cigarettes. Wet dog, toward the back. "This place is always pure arm-pit," Snowberry groused.

Lewis leaned across them and gestured toward the cur-tain. "I love this. Big security production. In a few minutes we find out what the Nazis've known all week." Men around them coughed and stomped their feet as though to keep warm, and hushed their voices in anticipation like a parody of a theater audience.

The CO entered on schedule and they stood in a noisy mass. He had them sit down again—Lewis blew out his breath heavily, exasperated at the suspense—and nodded to the intelligence officer, who pulled the curtain. The red yarn line ran to Hamburg, and an adjacent enlargement showed U-boat yards.

There were scattered boos. Someone in the back held up a civilian gas conservation sign: *Is This Trip Really Neces-sary?*

The overhead projector flashed diagrams and photos of the U-boat yards. Intelligence laid out the route, and the expected reaction from fighters and flak. The officer had written, "Outlying Flak Batteries Dwarfish by Compari-son," the "Dwarfish" hyphenated at the end of the board, and someone from the back asked in all sincerity, "What's a Dwar Fish?"

"Don't worry about the flak," Snowberry whispered to Bryant. "Official word is that it's only a deterrent."

"I'm still trying to figure that one out," Lewis said.

Operations and Planning provided some last-minute op-erational data, and Stormy talked about the expected weather changes to and from the city. He drew large billowy cumulus clouds on his own chalkboard to illustrate the ex-pected 20,000-foot ceiling.

They were reminded not to underestimate the enemy, a

bit of advice they found as gratuitous as anything they had heard since their induction. The gunners were reminded to harmonize at 250 yards, and to remember the bullet streams would converge at that distance and then begin to diverge.

The crews were glum and attentive. They always half hoped for unimportant targets, targets which would not stir the Germans into anything more than their usual hostility.

The CO announced the time and they all set their minute hands to it, and he called "Hack!" and they started their watches again.

"Good luck," he said. "Remember what's at stake."

"What?" someone asked.

The group broke up, navigators heading off in one direction, bombardiers and radio ops to pick up their information sheets, the gunners to the flight line lockers. Piacenti, Ball, Lewis, Snowberry, and Bryant walked in a line carrying parachutes and flak vests to the armament shop to pick up their guns. They piled everything into two jeeps and rode to *Paper Doll* minutes ahead of everyone else.

The guns were slid into their steel frames and locked in the stowed position for takeoff. The turrets were turned to face the rear. The five of them stood beside the plane, checking the layers of gear and waiting for the rest of the crew. Bryant hunched near the enplaning hatch on the fog-colored underside and dandled his finger around the connecting ring of his oxygen hose. Lewis went off into the mist a few feet and urinated through the circle of his thumb and forefinger.

Gabriel arrived with everyone else and gathered the group in a circle for some final instructions. He talked about the need to communicate on the bogies but to otherwise stay off the interphone. He cautioned Snowberry and Bryant to keep alert for fighters at twelve o'clock high and low, and said some of the scuttlebutt was there'd be a big diversionary raid which might tie up a lot of interceptors to the south. Snowberry was wearing a button he'd gotten from the New York World's Fair, which read *I Have Seen the Future*. Ga-

briel peered at it, and asked if there were any questions. His
cap had been pummeled and soaked in water to affect the
fifty-mission crush, and when he moved, his unconnected
oxygen hose and interphone cable flapped and gestured.

No one else spoke. They lined up to enplane.

"Do the bear dance, Bean," Snowberry said, and Bean
startled Bryant by hopping from one foot to another, back
and forth, looking for all the world in his heavy gear and
flight suit like a dancing bear. They had all seen this before,
and laughed affectionately. Bryant had not. He felt suddenly
he was outside even this group. When had Bean started a
bear routine? Who had encouraged it?

Piacenti, climbing in ahead of him, turned and displayed an old orange warning tag from the Norden bombsight, and grinned. He slipped it inside his flight jacket and
clambered up into the hatch.

Bryant hesitated before the opening, having missed the
point.

"Do-it-yourself superstition," Lambert Ball said behind
him. "Can't beat it."

They individually ran their preflight checklists from
their dark stations, calling in over the interphone. Bryant
stood at the flight engineer's panel and then at Gabriel and
Cooper's shoulders, double-checking their run-through.

They waited. A full hour passed. Bryant felt as if he
were wearing a constricting and damp pile of laundry.
"Stormy, if you're wrong, we're gonna kick your fucking
ass," Lewis murmured over the interphone. They heard rain
patter lightly on the fuselage and everybody groaned.

"Isn't this weather something?" Piacenti cried. He
sounded stuffed up. "Sun for the tail and rain for the nose."
Their chatty informality over the interphone was not official
operating procedure, but among the crews a certain amount
of radio sloppiness was considered masculine.

Bryant climbed into the padded sling in the dorsal turret for a look around. Across the tarmac he could see shining water, broken by birds.

Above them a green flare arced rapidly and crookedly away and immediately the cockpit was furious with activity, Gabriel taking Cooper quickly through the checklist: Alarm bell/Checked, Master switches/On, Carburetor filter/Open, and Bryant slipped back to his panel to check the engine status. From there Gabriel ordered him back to the bomb bay to the manual shut-off valves of the hydraulic system, so they could check the hydraulic pressure. "No hydraulic pressure, we're back to Lewis's Law of Falling Tons of Metal," Gabriel liked to say. Lewis's Law of Falling Tons of Metal was simple: the B-17, Lewis said, was not lighter than air, and when it came down for the wrong reason, it came down hard.

He could hear the whine of the inertia starter in the wing and the engines caught and fired, and the plane shook with the sound and the concentrated horsepower and Tuliese yanked the chocks away. They began to inch forward. His last glimpse up through the dorsal Plexiglas before resuming his takeoff position behind the pilot was of the mist lifting obligingly like a gray theater curtain.

They taxied behind the other Forts, a long parade of dull green ships, along the perimeter track to the end of one of the short runways, and waited, locking the tail wheel. Four thousand or so feet away were hedges, and a low fence. The planes were nose to tail, foreshortened enough from Bryant's vantage point to seem an awesome and comic traffic jam.

The ship ahead of them throttled up, hesitated, and began to roll, the grass on both sides of the tarmac flattened by the propeller wash, and gravel and bits of paper flashed up to make gritty sounds against the windshield.

It disappeared into the haze throwing up big wings of spray and they followed its lights, edging up and to the side. Gabriel set the brakes and advanced the throttles all the way. The engine sound created a physical overpressure on the ears and the plane strained and shivered against its locked wheels. Bryant kept an eye on the oil pressure and rpm's. Gabriel's hand played over the brake release knob as if refining the drama, and then he released the brakes.

They did not rush forward, they never did, and Bryant hated the disappointment of the fully loaded 17 simply rolling slowly forward after all that straining and racket. He hunched and unhunched his shoulders hoping to affect the acceleration. The tarmac began to wheel by and Cooper called the airspeed in increments of ten, his calls coming more quickly, and Bryant caught a glimpse of a black-and-white-checkered runway control van disappearing along a side panel window and began to feel the great pull of acceleration on his shoulders, and at Cooper's call of 90, 100, the engines' sound changed, and they could feel the tail come up, and at 120 Gabriel pulled them off the ground, the hedges and fence rolling softly past the nose, and they bucked and swayed but gained power and swept high over some trees.

They broke out of cloud near their assembly altitude, and Bean gave a fix on the radio beacon of their assembly plane. All around them B-17's were popping from the clouds trailing mist and carving into the blue sky above, looking for their colored squadron flares. Group leader ships at higher altitudes were firing yellow and green flares in graceful parabolas. Each squadron circled in its section of sky waiting for completion, a horizon of small groups at play, and Bryant watched in wonder from his turret the planes sweeping by opposite and above in a dance of leviathans. Their squadron, Pig Squadron, consisted of two vees of three planes each, with their vee fifty feet ahead and below as the lead vee. With two other squadrons they formed an extended vee, and soon a fourth squadron filled the slot behind them to complete a diamond. They matched with another group after forty-five minutes of laborious circling and maneuvering, and finally came out of a long wide sweep and headed toward the Channel together with a staggered and shaky precision. Above and behind him he could see *Boom Town* and *Geezil II*, their belly turrets already cautiously turning.

The Channel eased brightly beneath them and he could see the bulge of East Anglia receding beyond *Paper Doll*'s huge tail. He could not make out any evidence of their expected fighter escort. He imagined hundreds of Luftwaffe pilots over Holland and northwestern Germany scrambling for their sleek monsters, and clouds of silhouettes from his aircraft spotter charts rising to meet him, Plexiglas canopies glittering over the fuselages with the heartlessness of the eyes of insects.

He double-checked the seal on his oxygen mask, the heavy gloves giving him little feel for what he was doing. Lewis and Piacenti were clearing and testing the guns, and the plane shook, and already he could pick up the ugly cordite smell through his mask. He felt the tremor of Snowberry firing beneath him, and cleared his own guns, pointed away from the aircraft above, and squeezed the thumb triggers on the hand grips that controlled the azimuth and elevation of the guns, and the twin fifty calibers on either side bucked and fired visible tracers with a lazy, drooping sweep. Then everything was silent against the steady background of engines and slipstream. Smoke puffs trailed from the guns of *Boom Town* and *Geezil II*.

He swung the turret around at medium speed, the gun barrels tracking the horizon smoothly. The ease of the electronically operated controls reminded him of a ride at a fair. Track the Jerries, five cents, he thought.

"Shouldn't we turn back?" Piacenti called in. "My gun's not working."

"What do you care?" Lewis said. "When do you ever do anything with it?"

They rendezvoused with their expected escort, RAF Spitfires. The Spitfires waggled their wings out of range to show off their markings before approaching, a precaution against trigger-happy Yanks. They roared ahead to the front of the formation, their razored contrail streams like scratches on the ice of the sky.

They continued to ride. The altocumulus and cirrus high above them were sheeted and pebbled like the silvery lining of a shell. His electric suit and sheepskin jacket and pants kept him unevenly warm, but the air was bitterest winter, 40 below zero at altitude. Bryant worried about his suit shorting out from sweat or urine and had heard enough frostbite stories. The air came in blasts through the openings for the gun barrels, and for comfort's sake he found himself turning away from *Paper Doll*'s nose. His eyes and temples ached under the goggles and strap.

The interphone crackled and Snowberry's voice came over low, singing. "I'm dreaming of a White Christmas," he crooned. Contrails began to unfurl from the bombers above them like long streams of white spun sugar, or cottony bandages unrolling endlessly from the engines. They reminded him of enormous wakes from motorboats. The effect with a large bomber group was spectacular. The spectacle was lamentable, considering their position. "When we're up that high and putting out that kind of contrail signature, I think Rommel in North Africa can see us coming," Gabriel had once told him glumly. Ice had formed on the upper seal of Bryant's mask, and there were smallish crystals on his goggles. "Where the treetops glisten/And children listen," Snowberry sang.

"Can it," Gabriel said.

Bryant struggled with his mask. It was dark and cold and smelled heavily of rubber, and condensation inside it was dripping down his neck and freezing. He thought of the water freezing in the rubber hose, of oxygen starvation, and his hands shook. Every so often Cooper called them to check in, for that reason. It was Lewis's private terror that in the tail he'd only be reached too late.

They were over the Dutch coast. There were little thumps and pings occasionally, and Bryant watched smallish clouds with interest as they appeared and drifted backward through the formations.

"It'll be easier over the target," Eddy said over the interphone. "Without these little clouds."

"Little clouds, my butt," Gabriel said. "That's flak, you idiot."

Bryant gave a start. They could feel the delicate musical sound of the light shrapnel. The plane lurched and straightened out.

"That one s.o.b.," Lewis said. "He's set up right at the end of the Zuyder Zee. I can see his flashes."

A burst shook *Geezil II* above them, the ship rocking and sideslipping.

"He is hot," Lewis said. "Dick Ott used to call him Daniel Boone. Up yours, pal." They could hear him chatter his guns out at the ground below, uselessly.

There was a minor commotion.

"Piacenti's sick," Ball commented. "We put it in a box, and left it in the bomb bay."

"War is hell," Snowberry said. "They shoulda thought about this when they invaded Poland."

"What's the matter, *Duce?*" Lewis asked. "Nervous in the service?"

The plane lurched again dramatically and Bryant felt a momentary terror that they'd been hit. "Wop Barf Kayoes Ack Ack," Lewis said. "What a story."

The Dutch coast was disappearing behind them and Bryant was beginning to feel a good deal more excited and frightened. Wherever their fighter escort had been, it was around now turning back.

" 'You fiddle with my shrimp and then you turn me down,' " Lewis sang. " 'You know I can't do nothin' till my shrimp's unwound.' "

"All right, can it," Gabriel said. "I mean it."

Bryant could see the cirrus clouds as ice crystals at this
height, rippled and thin and extending for hundreds of
miles. Around the tail the flight's white contrail streams
converged in a vanishing point like a burst of illumination.

"God a mighty," he murmured. He felt a peculiar and
foolish excitement and a pride in where he was and what he
felt was about to happen.

Hirsch called in their position quietly. They were now
all looking for fighters, 540 men in 54 airplanes. Bryant
swiveled the turret slowly, searching through the polished
perspex for the dots. He tried to concentrate, fighting the
cold and the plane's shaking and the erratic ghost flecks
from the defects of his own eye. He tested a speck's integrity
by immediately shifting his eye; if the speck shifted with it, it
was phony, a momentary unreliability. Bad peepers, Lewis
said, killed more people than bad anything else.

Bryant slipped a flight glove off, and touched the gun triggers lightly. The cold metal seared him and he jerked his
hand back and fumbled with his glove. He went on watching, his fingers burning with a steady and painful pulse.
Cooper called another oxygen check. While they ran
through it, each station calling in, Bryant sang to himself the
lyrics of "Paper Doll" as some sort of talisman: "When I get
home at night,/She will be waiting . . ."

Lucky Me! and *Milk Run* had closed on either side and
wallowed nearer, wingtips already alarmingly close to *Paper
Doll*'s. He could see the dorsal gunner in *Lucky Me!* peering
up to the east, a bunched scarf flashing white beneath his
chin. They were closing the combat box, making it tighter to
concentrate the defensive fire. Above him *Geezil II* floated
down closer, the bubble of its ball turret still rotating slowly.

"Bandits! Bandits!" Lewis called. "Comin' through past
me! What the Christ are you guys lookin' at?"

Two planes at two o'clock, someone else yelled. Four at
two-thirty.

Bryant swiveled the turret around to the front right, his guns tracking over the outboard Wright Cyclone, and six or eight fighters flashed by underwing, gone before he could register them.

The flak was everywhere around them, billowing in round puffs with strings of larger shrapnel trailing downward like legs. He was sweating, he realized, spinning the guns in an attempt to follow the action, his ears filled with bandits being called in and curses.

He spun to face front and angled the guns up to catch an echelon of four fighters coming down across and through the flight, their wings winking light even at that distance. They began taking on features instantaneously and he could see colors, insignia, letters, radio masts, yellow noses, then they flashed past—Me-109's, he understood. He turned the turret again, his gloves light on the controls, and a fighter leaped at him like an apparition, impossibly close, shocking him immobile, and was gone. Its squared wing seemed to have passed through his turret. The burnt powder smell was thick even through the oxygen mask: everyone else was firing, and *Paper Doll* was trembling with the power of the recoils. A Messerschmitt spiraled by the nose with pieces tumbling back from its wings.

The air burst right before them, it seemed, just above Hirsch and Eddy in the nose, and he could see red fire within the black cauliflower shape and the air jarred like water in a bowl. The shrapnel rang over the plane like someone hitting it with steel pipes and Bryant shook on his sling until the world came back to level in a long slow sway. He found himself looking through the Plexiglas at another echelon coming around again and finally came to, in some way, and swept his guns around and up and framed in the glass of his gunsight a fighter's blinking wings as it grew toward him. The fighter was shooting at them, he could see, and the hits sounded around him like thunder and hail on his father's tin shed, and he became aware of Gabriel screaming at him over the interphone to open up, for somebody to check on Bryant. The German's tracers flipped and curved by and he hunched his shoulders in the turret instinctively. His thumbs squeezed and the guns deafened him and wrenched with recoil, and tracer streams wove out and toward the fighter which was already gone, flashing its half-S curve beneath them to loop back for another pass. He could hear and feel Snowberry below firing after him, and Lewis.

One Fortress from the flight was trailing smoke from two engines, and falling back. He couldn't identify it, and didn't have time. Even at that distance he saw holes stitch by magic in a line across the wing and upper fuselage, and the plane staggered in the air. Its gear fell, and it sheared away and slipped beneath his line of sight.

Another echelon came through, and everyone fired forward, Snowberry's and Eddy's and his own tracers braiding and coiling out toward the fighters, and he raced the turret around firing as they roared past in an attempt to track them.

He swept the turret the opposite way, feeling overloaded, overwhelmed. On the interphone Cooper called out bandits reforming ahead, Piacenti tracked one for Lewis, Ball was yelling something. Snowberry said, "My parents'll kill me. I get killed now, my parents'll kill me."

A parachute went diagonally by, the man pulled at a crazy angle by the squadron's prop wash.

Cooper and Hirsch announced the start of the initial point of the bomb run. From there to the main point of impact they'd be on automatic pilot, coupled to Eddy's Norden bombsight, flying straight and level. The usual comparison was to metal ducks in a fairground gallery. Ahead of them the flak was concentrated into a barrage box in the area the flak gunners knew the formation would have to fly through. Bryant had heard it referred to as iron cumulus and now he saw it. The shells were all exploding at the same altitude—their altitude—and the detonations merged to form a low black anvil. The first planes of the flight were already pushing into it and he stared in wonder at their apparent survival even as the bursts approached and surrounded *Paper Doll*.

The plane shook and stayed level. The bursts were everywhere. They seemed to be standing still, not moving at all. The fighters had sheared off to let the flak take over. Eddy continually called Steady, Steady, until Bryant wanted to kill him. Beneath him he could hear Snowberry firing his guns in rage and frustration at flak gunners 20,000 feet below. Above him the bomb bay doors of *Geezil II* and *Boom Town* were opening, the inside racks and dark bomb shapes slowly becoming visible. He could hear the doors below him swinging open as well and felt the extra drag on the ship.

A burst over the tail blinded him and tore away metal in finger-like strips. He found himself refocusing on the now tattered vertical stabilizer and he heard someone yelling they were hit over the interphone. "It's Lewis! It's Lewis!" Snowberry yelled. "Lewis is hit!"

"I'm hit," Lewis said.

"What do you want me to do?" Gabriel said. "Park it? Somebody check him out."

Bryant slipped from his seat, trying to get stable footing below.

"Bombs away," Eddy called. The plane bucked upward from the release of the weight, and Bryant found himself on his side.

"Bombs're gone, it's all yours, Lieutenant," Eddy said, and the plane lurched as Gabriel retook flying control and wrenched it out of its level path, and Bryant fell again, onto his hands and knees. He struggled back through the catwalk over the open bomb bay to the radio room, and then to the waist position, leaning against the severity of the plane's bank, past a curious Ball, and stopped when Piacenti emerged from the hatchway to the tail and made an open palm and thumbs up.

Back in the dorsal seat he reconnected his interphone to a flood of voices. Cooper told Lewis to hang on, they'd be home soon.

"I'm fine," Lewis said. "Just doing my best to bleed to death back here."

The fighters were back on the return flight, but in diminished numbers and intensity, it seemed to Bryant. Two spiraled through the formation just above him in perfect choreography, flashing their powder blue undersides and black crosses at him before looping out of sight.

What pilots these Germans were! He tracked and fired at them like someone throwing stones at sparrows. Even as he fired he felt reduced by their elusiveness and invulnerability, and found the impersonal nature of their menace unsettling and fascinating. They concentrated on the rear of the flight, and he fired industriously and fruitlessly at a few echelons streaking past until Eddy reported fighter escort coming back to meet them and the last Germans wove away behind them and dipped into clouds and were gone, leaving the horizon beyond their contrails clean, the sky bare.

They began descending over the Channel. Bryant felt exhilarated and lucky and thought briefly about the unknown plane he'd seen falling back. "You're right, Doctor," Snowberry said, his interphone making him sound like Walter Winchell. "We never should have called it 'a silly native superstition.'" The interphone became noisy with comments, everyone asking if anyone had seen what they had seen. When the plane dropped below 12,000 feet they were able to get off the oxygen and felt better and safer breathing freely. Bryant went back to the waist, where Lewis was sitting up, wrapped in blankets. Another blanket was folded behind his head as a pillow. He looked okay, more or less. Snowberry was tucking him in and Ball and Piacenti were working awkwardly around them, stowing the waist guns inside.

Bryant hunched nearer. Lewis shrugged. "No prob-lem," he said. "You should see my flak vest, though."

"Are you comfortable?" Bryant asked.

Lewis nodded. "I make a nice living," he said.

There was a crashing and loud metal sounds and the plane banked violently to the left, tumbling everyone to-gether in a heap, and they scrambled up to Bean's screams that there were bandits, bandits, and the plane continued such violent evasive action that Bryant pinballed his way back to his station, slamming knees and elbows trying to climb back into his turret, and when he finally pulled himself onto his seat by the gun handles they were rollercoastering low over the treetops, the scattered flight around them at various altitudes also weaving and turning. Behind them a pillar of black smoke grew upward in a staggered column and at nine o'clock someone's 17 was trailing fire steadily, and they all watched as it sailed into a gently rising hill like a skater gliding into a wall. The concussion gave their plane an extra bit of lift.

Piacenti was cursing in a violent stream, badly fright-ened, and still trying to unshackle the guns. Bryant spied four black shapes high above them heading back to Ger-many. "Ju88's," he said over the interphone. "Six o'clock high withdrawing." They were jet black and appeared harm-less and unreal, right off the silhouette charts.

Another Fortress came in short of the field. They flew over it and the crew was still piling out, and it looked as if everyone was unhurt. Of the twelve planes that had taken off that morning, nine returned, with *Paper Doll* one of the last. Gabriel fired flares on his approach to signal wounded aboard, and the meat wagon trundled out to their nose be-fore they'd come to a full stop, but Lewis climbed out of the waist himself, showing off the hole punched in his flak vest and the spent 20mm incendiary shell that had done it. Ev-eryone wanted to see, and his luck was at once considered to be potentially legendary. Beneath his vest the meat of his

pectorals had been sheared up a bit, he reported, but it was
pretty shallow, and he chose not to ride in the meat wagon.
He walked along with them holding the incendiary in his fist
happier than Bryant had ever seen him. "Imagine this scar
with the girls," he said. Even more cheering, they all understood, was the seemingly incontrovertible evidence this represented that he led a charmed life, and they flew with him.

Paper Doll's engines went on ticking and hissing and
pinging as they cooled, smelling strongly of diesel. The knees
were torn on Snowberry's flight suit, sheepskin gaping out.
"You look like you were hit, too, Sergeant," Cooper said.

Snowberry shrugged. "Yes, sir. No room. The bolt
mechanisms in the guns tear my knees. This is the third pair.
The requisition people hate me."

Their elation for Lewis wore off, and they all suddenly
felt exhausted. They stood around empty and silent as if at a
horrible party. Trucks carried them to debriefing rooms.
They each were allowed a shot of whiskey from the bar and
then they argued with each other over what they had seen
and what they had done, still awkward in their flying gear,
everyone angry and relieved and not giving ground on their
version, while the intelligence officers looked and listened
and tried to piece together one plausible narrative from all
the information.

PART TWO

The Glass Mountain

AFTER THEY'D BEEN ABLE TO EAT Bryant found himself back at the plane, restless despite his exhaustion, and he watched Lewis and Gabriel carry out a holes count, clambering over the plane's upper surfaces and calling out the jagged machine-gun and cannon-fire holes. Tuliese stood below them, his arms crossed.

Lewis stood erect on the stabilizer and counted with his fingers. "We could drain noodles through our tail, Lieutenant," he said.

Tuliese found a few more holes forward near Snowberry's turret. "Lieutenant, what the hell you been doin' to my ship?" he complained.

"You got off easy, Sergeant," Gabriel said. "I heard *Archangel* may be Category E, from the Ju88's." Category E meant wrecked beyond repair, unsalvageable.

"I heard the pilot of *Archangel* was so mad about being jumped that he wouldn't get out of his plane after he brought it in, sir," Lewis said. "That true?"

Gabriel said it was. "Gus Truncone. He says cannon shells caved in the whole right side of his cockpit. Looks like a single-seater now."

Lewis climbed down from the tail. "Is the co-pilot hurt?"

"No," Gabriel said. "He's dead."

They were silent, watching Gabriel make his own check.

"And his best buddy was on *Home for Dinner,* listed as missing."

"Missing," Bryant said, angry with the vagueness. They turned to look at him. "Like he took a wrong turn at the mess after breakfast."

Gabriel nodded. "That's about it," he said. "Isn't it?"

Later the crew gathered around *Paper Doll* for another photo, crowding around Lewis, who held his battered flak jacket aloft with one hand and the remains of the incendiary shell in the other like a small prize fish. They were all there, uneasy and apprehensive, to celebrate Lewis's good fortune, all but Cooper, who it was reported had gotten the shakes soon after debriefing, and Piacenti, who had wandered away from the plane before the photo session had been organized, and sat up across the way on the hardstand, watching them.

After chow they walked to The Hoops, the village pub. It rose two stories with a quaint lean and Bean was forever getting over the fact that it had a thatched roof.

Hirsch had not been invited, and Bryant was starting to get used to the idea. Snowberry returned to their table with a large red tray full of the oversized English pints. "The way they water them down, it's a normal beer, all told," Piacenti said.

"Great story my old man wrote me," Lewis said. He downed a third of Bean's beer and passed it to him. "This guy who lives next to my old man, 4F bastard, right?"

"He's home makin' the rounds of the skirts while we sit here like chumps," Piacenti said. He seemed to be considering whether or not to work up a good anger about it.

"What was wrong with him?" Bean asked. Nearly everything was wrong with Bean, and here he was in the Air Corps, on a B-17.

"How should I know?" Lewis said. "I think he told them he had a trick knee or something."

"Yeah, and I know the trick," Bryant complained.

Lewis sipped from his beer and folded his arms primly. "Whenever you guys're ready, I'll finish my story," he said.

"We're not ready," Snowberry said. He gazed over at the bar. "Why don't we tell those guys we're going to be facing screaming death tomorrow, and that we should have the darts?"

"Go ahead, Lewis," Bryant said.

Lewis topped off his beer with Snowberry's while Snowberry stared in ostentatious boredom toward the bar.

"This guy's wife tells him the sink's acting up. She's on him all day about it. He says he'll look at it."

"I'd look at it," Piacenti said. "She'd be lookin' at this." He made a fist.

"After she goes out, he looks at it and figures he doesn't know what he's doing. He goes next door and gets this friend of my old man's, a retired plumber, real old guy. The old guy is wearing overalls just like the husband. He climbs under the sink and goes at it. 4F goes down the cellar to get tools. The wife comes back. She sees the old guy under the sink and thinks it's her husband. When she goes by she gives him one of these." He made a goosing motion with his hand. "Poor old son of a bitch jumps like he's shot, cracks his head on the sink, knocks himself out. He's out cold. Bleeding from the noggin. She sees it's not her husband, and the blood, and starts screaming. 4F runs upstairs, they drag the neighbor out, but they can't wake him up. They call the ambulance. Ambulance guys put him on a stretcher. They live in a top-floor apartment. The ambulance guys hear the story and they're laughing so hard they drop this poor old geezer down the stairs."

Piacenti sputtered beer over the table.

"He breaks his hip. He wakes up in the hospital his head stitched up, seeing two of everything, and a broken hip. He told my old man the last thing he remembered was reaching for the wrench and a hand grabbed his crotch."

They all felt the best part of the story was all the trouble caused someone who had avoided the Army. Through his laughter Bryant said, "Imagine what the old man told people who came to see him?"

Snowberry pulled his garrison cap over his head like a bandage. "Well, my neighbor's wife stuck her hand up my ass, see, and . . ."

Bean was watching them and smiling, the way he watched the radio.

"Funny, huh, Bean?" Lewis asked. He mimicked Bean's expression. "Bean's only here because his sweetie stood him up."

"Her dog died," Bean said, in her defense.

"Her dog died?" Bryant asked.

"She stood me up for a dog's funeral," he said ruefully. They observed a short silence, out of respect.

"You're better off without her," Snowberry said. "She was built like a fuel bowser."

"Have you seen her? I've seen her," Piacenti said. The head of his beer gave his expressions a foamy emphasis. "Dark rooms are awful good for her."

"You guys shouldn't say that," Bean murmured. "She's nice."

Piacenti went for another round and got into an argument with someone at the bar over the darts. Lewis and Snowberry went over to see what they could do.

Bean gave Bryant a wincing smile and they sat opposite each other with their hands folded.

"You think about women a lot?" Bean asked.

"Women?" Bryant said.

"You think about Robin? And Lois?" He added the last question with some embarrassment.

"All the time," Bryant said.

"I do too, with Cynthia," Bean said. Cynthia was his English girlfriend. He seemed to believe he'd uncovered something unexpected. "You think you'll marry Robin? I'm only asking out of curiosity."

"I don't know," Bryant said. He wished he'd gone over to the bar, where Lewis had collected four of the six darts and was negotiating with a stubborn-looking fat man with a flat tweed hat for the final two. The fat man was shaking his head emphatically.

"You think you'll marry Lois?" Bean was nudging his empty pint in various directions with his index finger.

"I don't know," Bryant said.

Bean didn't respond, and Bryant understood that what he had meant to be bravado had sounded to Bean simply evasive.

The negotiators returned with beer and without darts.

"You're better off, Bean," Lewis continued. "Kids, mortgage, it's not for you. You're Mister Wild Oats."

"You know," Bean said, "it's funny how quick here you start doing things you wouldn't do at home."

"You mean like swearing, getting squiffed, grassing?" Lewis said. Grassing was their term for having sex with the local girls outside of the Nissen huts on the grassy areas bordering the revetments.

"I guess," Bean said uncertainly.

"Part of fighting a war," Lewis said. "Ask Bryant."

"Oh, shut up," Bryant said.

"Women sap the resolve of our fighting forces," Lewis confided. "Right now she's all Mary Pickford. Right, Bean? But once she gets you alone—table for two, summer night, you can't trust her. They get to working on you and they leave you gasping for air. That's been my experience."

Snowberry laughed.

"Gasping for air?" Bean asked.

"What I'm saying is, you gotta take some and leave some," Lewis said. "Like Bryant here."

"How would you like a knuckle sandwich?" Bryant asked.

Lewis held up his beer to protect himself.

"Gasping for air?" Bean said.

"You know what I heard?" Piacenti said. "I heard our wing has the highest VD rate in the whole ETO."

"I heard that, too," Snowberry confirmed. "Is that something, or what? Talk about men."

"Listen to Sergeant First Aid Station," Lewis scoffed. They laughed. Prophylactic stations were being called First Aid Stations in deference to the local Brit sensibility.

"You guys can laugh," Bean said with distaste. "Some of you put your—private parts where I wouldn't put my boot."

The table sat stunned, and then whooped with laughter.

"There may be hope for you yet, Bean," Lewis said.

The darts came available and they stepped up to the bar, sloshing beer on the floor and each other. Lewis threw one dart nearly dead center and four into the wall. The Englishmen at the bar roared with laughter. "So you're a gunner, mate?" one called.

"Jealous of the uniform," Lewis said. "I get it all the time." He took aim with his final dart. "Focke Wulf," he said. "Coming up through our contrails." It stuck on the outside perimeter of the board.

"Hope it's a big wingspan," Piacenti commented. They all took turns, keeping track of the points. On close calls they argued the scoring. Bean sat at the bar and smiled apologetically for the noise. Things degenerated until the throwers were lunging and stabbing the board, while the others tried to wrestle them away from it. They pulled the board down from the wall and the barkeep came out from behind the bar and sent them back to their tables like children. They ordered another round as a concession and the barkeep brought it, looking at each sternly as he set the pints before them.

They sipped a while in silence. Lewis's nose was bleeding, and he was stanching it with a bar napkin.

"Nazis can *fly,* can't they?" Snowberry said. It was the

first mention of the morning. Bryant agreed he'd seen some awfully great flying.

"Except that we don't want them flying," Lewis said, napkin to his nose. "We want them dead."

Bryant felt himself blushing. He glanced at Lewis but couldn't tell if he'd been referring to Bryant's lateness in firing during the first attacks.

"We gave 'em a little something to think about," Piacenti said.

Lewis snorted. "If that's so, they're thinking with big grins on their faces," he said.

Bryant stood up. He was frightened and ashamed of his performance. "You know, Lewis, we're really getting tired of your negative attitude," he said. "You don't think we have a chance, fine. You don't have any ambition, fine."

Lewis took the napkin away from his nose. The blood had formed a bright red oval. "My ambition," he said, "is to die in my spare time. My ambition is to get something useful into your head so you won't die the know-nothing asshole you are now."

Bryant was shaking. "I'll be outside," he said.

"Just great, asshole," Lewis said. He reached for his beer. "I'll be in here."

Bryant stormed out and paced the street in front of the bar, rehearsing what would occur when Lewis emerged. It began to drizzle, and he stood under an overhang. After half an hour he weighed going back in, and decided he had more pride than that, and began the long walk alone back to the base.

When Snowberry finally came in that night, Bryant asked what had happened after he left, and Snowberry related that they'd had a smash 'em up game of pub bowling, using the pint glasses, and had mucked it up with some of the locals. Even Bean had pitched in, although he'd been more or less forced to. He sighed happily, and Bryant again was aware of being left out. "You shoulda been there,"

Snowberry murmured. "We are beyond a doubt the most destructive group of young men in history, in or out of pubs."

"Did he say anything about my not coming back?" Bryant whispered in the dark. "Gordon." But Snowberry was asleep on his back with his mouth open, snoring, and from a nearby bunk Lambert Ball grumbled that God, it was like sleeping in a stockyard.

Bryant spent the next morning going over *Paper Doll* with Tuliese and after lunch settled under the wing to read letters. Lewis had not spoken to him since the night before and he found himself overaware of any movement to or from the Nissen huts.

Piacenti and Ball were fencing with the detached whip antennas from two jeeps. They called En garde! and made gruesome stabbing noises. Bryant ignored them and they went on with their stamping and lunging.

A letter from Robin had come the day of the mission and V-mail from Lois had come that morning. In addition there was a letter from the village that he didn't recognize. He thrilled a bit to the notion of a secret admirer and opened that one first.

> *Dear Sergeant Robert Bryant,*
> *I hope this letter reaches you as it represents my regards. My mother suggested I might write you and thank you for your gift of gum and send support for your difficult task which we are all in together. I sincerely hope you are well and have not been hurt by German action.*
> *Yours,*
> *Colin Best.*

On the back of the envelope Colin had drawn a bulbous B-17 with overprominent gun positions, all unerringly spitting dotted lines out to broken and tumbling smaller planes marked with black crosses. From one a stick figure with a pumpkin head fell spread-eagled and grimacing. *Happy Shooting!* it said underneath.

He sniffed Robin's letter. It smelled like paper. He opened it. She had compressed her penmanship carefully, to fit more on the page.

Dear Bobby,

Eight a.m. in the damp garden this morning I innocently happened upon eight ravaged gooseberry bushes. In a strange way the sight was frightening. They had been gnawed bare and completely stripped, leaving only branches budding leaf skeletons. What a sight!—like a cartoon post-locust scene. Only twelve hours earlier, or less, the bushes had been healthy, leaved, and berried. We're at a loss. Birds? They don't eat the leaves and pips (they had stripped every cherry from the just-ripe cherry tree only the night before last, leaves untouched and messy pips strewn over the stones below). Clearly this unknown gooseberry lover had an appetite—the odd remaining leaf actually seemed to show teeth marks.

Other things. Mrs. H (the retired gardening expert I spoke of) was feeling down the other night—no word of a missing son in Africa—so I suggested a country walk. "I do so love the country," she said. We walked for perhaps an hour, randomly, round unexplored areas just outside the village. We walked past great expanses of watercress growing in shallow flooded beds. She talked about how she missed her Derek and I talked about you. We walked past trimmed hedgerows, some sleepy sheep, big manors I suggested we'd one day have as our own. I could see she was very curious about Americans but reluctant to ask. She said that she had heard Americans were quite uncontrollable in public places but that she imagined a good deal of that was just talk and that she felt sure my young man would hardly be—and here she looked for the word—a cowboy. I told her how we had met, of your graciousness and our talk concerning the usefulness of the Red Cross. She

*asked if you were very free with gifts and I said you were
generous but not like some. I told her as well that you might
have the opportunity to meet.*

*Will we? Will you be able to arrange the leave? Write or
ring up when you can. Mother says she'll be the strictest of
chaperones but I have plotted walks and activities certain to
drive her back to her garden. Do you like to swim?*

Robin.

He reread the letter, folded it crookedly back into its
envelope, and opened the half-sized V-mail from Lois. Boy,
what a Class A rat, he thought. He felt harder and pleas-
ingly more like a soldier.

V-mail was photographed and reduced to save space
and weight, and Lois had taped a factory newsletter over
half her sheet. It was *The Minesweeper,* out of Groton, Connecticut. He frowned. What was she doing in Groton, Connecticut? The title was surrounded by anchor chains and the
words *Let's Win an "E" in '43.* She had written over the top
margin, *Mama, what did you do in the war? Were you a Wave
or a Waac? No, dear, I just hid things for other people to find,
and found things others had hidden.* He didn't understand at
first, and then the newsletter's title came back to him, and he
chuckled. The headline was *They Call Her "Frivolous Sal,"*
and beneath it were a group of women standing before a
clapboard wall, squinting and smiling uncertainly at the
camera. There was a thick caption.

*Call 'em Frivolous Sal if you care to, but if you do you're
as wrong as Tojo or "that funny little man in the dirty rain-
coat," Herr Schicklgruber. The girls pictured above are em-
ployed in this yard—in the electrical shop, the copper shop,
Navy warehouse and tool rooms. They're doing their stuff!*

*Reading from Left to Right: Ilene Reavis, electric shop;
Jerrie McManamy, cable room; Naomi Lundgren, electric
shop; Betty Kelley, Navy warehouse; Alma Woolridge, copper*

shop; Dorothy Schnellhardt, copper shop. Second row: Evelyn Everett, electric shop; Joanie Swift, electric warehouse; Irene Erickson, electric shop; Louise Erickson, warehouse; Wilma Jacobsen, machine shop tool room. Third row: Marge Dotts, copper shop; Lois Simon, Navy warehouse; Amanda Duffy, Navy warehouse; Gladys Roeder, tool room; Martine Loomer, copper shop.

Lois's name and job had been circled and an arrow had been drawn to her head in the photo.

Hi! Surprise! We've moved down to Groton and yours truly is now a Rosie! Can you believe it? I was scared at first but I'm really getting the hang of things and making new friends. I'm making thirty-five dollars a week! And I'm saving nearly everything, what with the rationing anyway. I've been pitching in at the USO, too. I haven't got a minute to myself, it seems. I'm also plane spotting. Can you believe it? Naomi and I sit there with our little radio and work the grave-yard shift Tuesdays and Saturdays. We haven't seen too many planes. I keep waiting to see your B-17F. With its distinctive tail assembly I can tell it from a B-24 or B-25, so I'll know it when I see it.

Everyone here is following the war the best they can. The newspapers leave so much out. I guess they have to. It sounds like things are really starting to go well for the Air Corps. Even though I know how terrible this war is, there is such an excitement in the air! I lie on my bed after a fourteen-hour day and I look over at my old Sonja Henie doll and I feel like it must have been a thousand years ago.

Bryant stroked the page with some fondness, trying to put a finger on a certain part of her.

Some of the servicemen throw notes out of the train windows or leave notes near the coffee machines at the USO.

*They're not mash notes or anything; they say things like
"Girls please write," and then the name and address. I've
starting writing a few—one in Fort Ord, California—and
they've been perfect gentlemen. One even wished you all the
luck in the world.*

*That's all for now. I'm so tired my hand is wiggling. I
miss you. Write when you are able.*

All my love,

Lois.

"Let's go, spruce up," Gabriel told him. "The crew of
Paper Doll is going to be interviewed by *Impact* magazine."

Gabriel was circling the base collecting everyone and
left Hirsch and Bryant in the day room.

Hirsch winced. "Great title, isn't it?"

"Don't wander off," Gabriel called from the door.
"And try not to have something hanging out of your nose
when the guy's talking to you."

They sat down opposite one another. The silence was
awkward. Bryant had an impulse to talk about the night
before at The Hoops but stopped himself.

Hirsch pulled over the current copy of *Impact* and
leafed through it. " '11th AF Reconnoiters, Bombs, Strafes
in Attu Action,' " he read. He showed Bryant the photo, a
double-pager displaying nothing but snow-covered mountains with unappetizing black rock showing through on the
slopes.

"What're we looking at?" Bryant asked.

Hirsch leaned closer. " 'Reconnaissance photo located
position of a unit of our scouts (see arrow) which came over-
land from Blind Cove on May 11.' "

He pointed to the arrow, which indicated a white expanse.

Bryant peered closely at it. "Those are the scouts,
huh?"

" 'They were to join the attack at Massacre Bay, but are shown here turning left too soon.' "

"I'll say," Bryant said.

Hirsch sat back, bored. "Maybe they're tunneling," he said.

Bryant sneezed. "I guess they're attacking that white area over there," he said.

Hirsch shrugged. "Or this white area over here." He shook his head. "Imagine fighting in a place like that?"

They nodded soberly together at their good fortune.

Hirsch ran a fingertip lightly back and forth over his eyebrow, an unobtrusive nervous habit. " 'Sousse Study Shows What Bombs Accomplish,' " he read.

Bryant waited. "What's that?" he finally said.

Hirsch read silently for a moment. Then he said, "I guess we just captured this, and now they're looking at what our bombing really did, instead of just high-altitude photo interpretation."

Bryant brought his chair around and together they studied the photos. The images were largely unintelligible and they relied on the captions.

Damage to 300–400-ton ship is confined to bridge super-structure, one read.

Bomb damage negligible but a direct hit on the star-board side of this ship aft of the funnel set fire to its oil cargo. Bulkhead prevented flooding. Rudder and propellers were un-damaged.

Crater 6 × 30 ft. caused by direct hit on this phosphates shed. The roof is out but note there is no damage to the concrete kiln walls.

Hirsch rubbed his chin. "Encouraging, isn't it?"

"Well, they're not hiding anything," Bryant said. "I guess you could look at it that way."

Lewis poked his head in, hesitated, and then came over to the table and sat down. "Gabriel said everyone was here," he complained. He took the *Impact* from Hirsch and paged back and forth through it. "Who reads this rag?" he asked.

He held up for Bryant a photo of a dorsal turret with its front Plexiglas panel blown out. "How much you think they found of him?" Lewis asked. Bryant smiled, some pressure low in his throat. Lewis pointed to another photo, a B-17 with its entire nose missing.

"Flak," he said. "No more Eddy. No more Hirsch. And we come home with a six-hundred-mile-an-hour slipstream through the plane. Gabriel and Cooper's toes are like little rows of ice cubes."

"Any tail pictures like that?" Hirsch asked.

"None," Lewis said. "Hey, here's a shot of *Rabbi Rascal* on her bombing run."

"You know, you haven't quite made being an asshole an art," Hirsch said. "But I got to admire your dedication."

"Hey, fuck you, pal," Lewis said.

Hirsch was quiet, apparently considering the best way to respond. He was not one of the crew's more aggressive second lieutenants.

" 'They Live to Fight Another Day Despite Damage,' " Lewis read.

"I guess the 'They' means the planes," Bryant said.

" 'Rugged airframes can take it,' " Lewis continued, " 'because of special triple support construction.' " He held up a pencil. "Here's your triple support construction," he said. "Plane." He indicated the pencil. He held up his other hand beside it, and made a rapid series of fists. "Flak," he said. He brought the two together, and broke the pencil.

"Knock it off," Hirsch said.

Lewis flopped the magazine in his direction and Hirsch looked at him malevolently.

"What're you lookin' at?" Lewis said. "Fucking ninety-day-wonder Jew second looey."

Hirsch got up and left.

Bryant pulled the magazine over and read silently while

they sat and waited, not talking. Lewis drummed "Sing Sing Sing" on the table with his palms.

Gabriel came in with a sloppy and overweight captain and Bean, Snowberry, Cooper, and Eddy in tow. "This is Captain Ciervanski," he announced. "I trust you'll give him your full cooperation."

Captain Ciervanski set a pad and some sharpened pencils down neatly on the table. He wished them a good afternoon.

"No one's seen Ball or Piacenti?" Gabriel asked glumly. Bryant shook his head. "Now where's Hirsch?"

"He said he didn't want any part of this, sir," Lewis said. "He said he didn't care what you thought."

"That's not really true," Bryant said.

"Well, we'll go on with what we have here," Captain Ciervanski said crisply.

"Sir?" Lewis said. "I didn't know *Impact* did interviews."

"They don't," Ciervanski said. "There's no guarantee this'll run, either. It's a pet idea of mine. It's really up to you guys."

Snowberry gave Bryant an exaggerated shrug. He was *Paper Doll*'s lowest-ranking crew member, a tech three, so it wasn't his place to comment.

"It's a good idea, sir," Cooper said. He so rarely spoke, the rest of the crew assumed in this case he was sucking up to Gabriel. "I think they think back home that guys like Clark Gable are flying the Forts."

"Clark Gable *is* flying Forts," Lewis said. "He's in the 351st."

"Imagine if they knew back home that we were in charge of things?" Snowberry said.

Ciervanski made a show of getting ready, waiting for them to quiet down or for Gabriel to bring them into line. Bryant tried to help. He liked Ciervanski, though they were expected to display a certain distaste for officers.

"I heard from a guy in the 351st that Gable is actually a good officer," Willis Eddy said. "Though he don't actually fly the Forts."

"I heard that," Cooper agreed.

"Which one of you is the youngest?" Ciervanski said. He had apparently given up waiting for Gabriel.

"Snowberry," Gabriel said.

Ciervanski wrote that down. "How old are you?"

"Ah, eighteen," Snowberry said.

"He looks very young for his age," Gabriel said. When Ciervanski looked at him, he nodded helpfully.

"He has a twin brother who's much younger," Lewis added.

Ciervanski scribbled something down and smiled to let them know he was in on the joke. He went on writing.

"Whaddaya want to know?" Snowberry asked. There was a hint of anxiety in his voice—Bryant imagined him envisioning the headline *Underage Gunner Wants to Be in the Fight*—and he raised up a bit in his seat to try and decipher what the captain was writing. "I was born in August nineteen-twenty-something," he said.

Ciervanski asked if his parents were proud of him.

"My dad's dead," Snowberry said. "My mom is, I guess."

The captain scribbled, dissatisfied. "Let me open this up to all the guys," he said. "You boys're just starting out. First real rugged mission recently. How'd it strike you? What're your feelings about combat? What sort of advice would you pass on to green crews?"

They were silent. Gabriel looked at each of them, trying to force an answer.

"I don't think we're ready to be giving advice, sir," Lewis said quietly.

Ciervanski nodded. They could see in his expression the dawning and dismal sense that his pet project might have to be scrapped, or at the very least carried through with another crew. He tried again.

"Are there any outstanding incidents you'd relate?"

"Outstanding incidents," Eddy mused. "Well, once I saw an Arab eat a sandwich made of K rations and shaving cream."

Ciervanski closed his pad, and laughed, which relieved them. "Well, Lieutenant, your boys may be ready for Fred Allen but I'm not sure they're ready for *Impact*. It's like trying to interview the Ritz Brothers."

Gabriel got up from his chair. His face indicated his understanding that his chance to be the skipper of a more famous aircrew was slipping away. He gestured at Lewis. "I think the men are a little, you know, hesitant, sir, and don't want to blow their own horn. Sergeant Peeters here took a 20mm incendiary in the chest, in the flak vest, on the last raid, and lived to tell about it."

Ciervanski looked at him sadly, as if he had offered a bowel movement as news. "All right," he said. "Tell me about it."

Lewis related the incident with no elaboration.

Ciervanski wrote it all down dutifully. "We'll get a shot maybe of you wearing the vest and holding the shell," he said without enthusiasm.

He dismissed them soon after. There had been further silences, additional forlorn questions, spartan answers. Gabriel apologized for all of them. Ciervanski waved off the apology gracefully and said, "Maybe it's tough getting everybody together like this. Bad idea. Tell you what, Lieutenant. I've still got an hour and a half. What do you say I wander around with some of the men in smaller groups and talk to them informally?"

So he ended up with Lewis and Bryant under the nose of *Paper Doll*. Lewis was explaining what he believed to be the weak areas of the Fortress's defensive fire umbrella. Gabriel drifted by in the background, keeping a helpless eye on them, worried, Bryant knew, that Ciervanski was talking to exactly the wrong person.

"Who's that?" Ciervanski asked, pointing to the Plexi-glas nose. "Last-minute replacement?" He chuckled. Audie was sitting upright in the bombardier's seat. Her nose misted the Plexiglas, and her blind and patient lack of comprehension parodied the burned-out look of twenty-mission bombardiers.

Ciervanski offered around cigarettes and then Oh Henry!s. "Look, boys," he said. "I figure the only way this job could do anything more than keep me busy, do anything for anyone at all, is if I try to get the real story out."

Lewis and Bryant pondered that. Above them Audie seemed to be surveying the airfield, chin and tongue bobbing lazily to the rhythm of her panting.

Ciervanski sighed. "Well, I humped all the way out here, talked my CO into this idea in the first place, and chewed up a day and a half on this project. I think when I file this the cream chipped beef is going to hit the fan."

"It may just be us," Bryant suggested.

Ciervanski stood and brushed off the seat of his pants. His belly shook and he puffed. "You boys take care," he said. "Don't take any wooden nickels." Gabriel had seen the leave-taking and was heading their way. "Here comes your lieutenant," he said. "I gotta break the news to him that you guys won't be famous this year."

"I think he already knows, sir," Lewis said.

BRYANT'S FATHER WORKED FOR THE RAILROAD, and had been able to keep his job through the Depression. He didn't share much with Bryant and one Christmas told him, That's all you get; and that's about right.

Once in a while they went hunting in the woods of eastern Connecticut, a biographical detail Bryant could never bring himself to reveal to Lewis. He was never allowed to handle the gun, his father tramping along with the .22 in the crook of his arm, oblivious to the clouds of insects which drove his son into a quiet frenzy of waving and slapping. His father was a poor shot as well, always sending squirrels and opossum skittering out of range with his first attempt. One of the dogs, Toby, or Corky, or the malevolent Snapper, would come along, adding to his father's frustration and Bryant's misery. The one time Tippi, Bobby's favorite, had come, the dog had performed so miserably—not seeing a squirrel it almost tripped over, even after his father had taken the dog's head and oriented it in the right direction— that his father had dragged it back to the car and locked it in for the rest of the day, and Bryant had walked and walked thinking of poor Tippi, shamefaced and only half understanding, gazing out behind the windshield after them into the woods.

When Snowberry felt particularly low he liked to, as he put it, swap dad stories. He said he missed his dad a good bunch. Bryant did, too, he was surprised to discover, though he felt bad he had few stories such as Snowberry seemed able to draw on endlessly, stories of dads and kids having fun. He treated it as a failure of memory when he could and chastised himself for not holding close to the best things now that he was away from home.

"I wish my dad were still around," Snowberry said. "It's tough when you don't have a pop."

Bryant agreed it must be. They talked about the World's Fair, the Trylon and the Perisphere, the Helicline. All the razzmatazz, Snowberry said, all the really wild stuff about how great things were going to be. Snowberry had gone with his father twice; Bryant had visited once on the train with his uncle Tom, the military enthusiast. His uncle had hectored him throughout the trip about the importance of what they were viewing until Bryant had begun to view the whole thing as pretty much ruined.

Everything is progressing, his uncle had said, more than
once. The world was better in every possible way than it was
before, and that was something to think about. They had
seen the GM Futurama three times, despite the lines and the
heat. Bryant had hoarded money his mother had slipped
him—his father had suggested to his uncle that they were
there to see the exhibits, not to fill up on junk—and he
remembered budgeting his time between ice creams more
vividly than the exhibits, even the Futurama, with its vast
plains and miniature cities explained endlessly by a voice
annoyingly like his uncle's. They had to get ready for the
future, his uncle and the voice told him, find their skill, find
their place, because the future was where they were going to
spend the rest of the lives. It had seemed to him plausible as
wisdom until he had thought about it at greater length, at
home, and then he had become annoyed at the obviousness
of it.

The World's Fair had frightened him, with its armies of
everyone excelling or about to excel, with its talk of a future
which seemed so briskly progressive that he'd only be af-
forded minutes to find and fill his niche and hours to prove
himself within it. He had paid close attention to the aviation
exhibits, but had absorbed nothing, really, and was wretch-
edly certain on that long ride back home that he had no
aptitude for it, no aptitude for the future, no place in the
World of Tomorrow.

The immensity of his presumption, he remembered, had
haunted him on that train as it had trundled through Stam-
ford, Bridgeport, New Haven: fly an airplane! Bobby Bryant
bringing in the mail through the winter storms of the Sier-
ras; Bobby Bryant barnstorming to beat the band. Could he
really take these huge metal machines off the ground and
return them as gracefully as falling sheets of paper? His only
comfort, when his fears called his dreams to account, was
that he didn't really see how *anyone* did it.

* * *

He'd developed the courage to mention it once, on a family outing his father had granted his mother. His mother had packed sliced celery and fresh pea pods wrapped in foil, wedges of baloney in waxed paper, and his father's big canteen filled with iced tea, the bags still floating darkly in the cool interior.

They had spread a blanket on a grassy area of Voluntown State Park a short distance into eastern Connecticut, having borrowed his uncle Tom's Ford for the trip. His mother had spread the food out with some joy and his father poured tea into a collapsible cup already sweating with condensation, and gazed at Amy's gingham animal as if clearly not recognizing it but feeling that he should. He was ill at ease on the blanket and wore a T-shirt and black pants belted high on his stomach. Bobby drank the tea and rolled the glass on his forehead. His father after eating had wandered off for a look-see and Bryant had followed. He'd caught up to him standing ankle deep in a pond below a rock fall, in shade deep and cool as his grandmother's sitting room. His father's pants were rolled to the knees, and his legs sloshed gently back and forth in place. Bryant had slipped off his shoes in the hush and edged in, through a stream sheeting water quietly down a rocky grade, the water cold as bone. His feet were prominent and unreal in the lucidity of the water. Bits of glass blinked sunlight back at him from the bottom. He was about to mention the glass in warning when his father quieted him with a hand motion and pointed. Four fish had glided to a stop just next to his ankle, their tails slowly waving like underwater pennants.

Back at the blanket Bryant had been encouraged enough to bring up someone's recent round-the-world flight, and his mother had commented politely that it was quite a feat, though his father had remained noncommittal.

"I'm going to be a pilot in the Army Air Corps," he finally said. His tone struck him as somewhere between

forceful and pitiful. He had considered mentioning the RAF
but had quailed at the last moment.

His father had seemed preoccupied with a nearby pine.
"Isn't that very dangerous?" his mother asked vaguely.

If talk was money, his father had finally said, brushing
those black pants with exaggerated care, he supposed they'd
all be millionaires by now.

"We had a game," Snowberry said, dreamily, "a game we
used to play when we were kids. Mel and I. Mel was a year
older. He's in the Navy now, in the Pacific. We were just
kids. There was a rope swing with a heavy wooden seat,
weathered so that it was that gray color wood gets. We
found out if we lay down underneath it, it cleared our noses
and faces by just a few inches. And I would lie there and
Mel would swing, or Mel would lie there and I would swing,
and you'd look up at the clouds and leaves and branches and
hear it coming and have to look and it would be by, so fast,
so close, you couldn't believe it, each time. At the top of the
swing it was miles away, and then it was back over you, the
grain of the wood whooshing by, and you thought, if I lift
my head, imagine. And you felt the dirt scuffed floury by all
those kids' feet and the ragged dry grass and the sun and the
rush of air from the long swoop of that swing.

"We always went back," Snowberry said, "even when
the ropes were frayed, even when the wood seat split."

During the next few days they were favored with an unexpected guaranteed shutdown—so much for Stormy's highs
and lows, at least for the time being—and Snowberry had
somehow obtained authorization for a base party for the
village children. Naturally, the children would need to be
accompanied, perhaps by unattached village girls. Knowing
it was a squadron tradition, Snowberry had suggested a
Christmas party. When reminded that it was nearly August,
he let on that he knew, but that they needed cheering up.

They'd been able to contact Jean and Robin on the base phone, a lonely and listing booth near the picket post, and both had agreed to come, their voices reflecting first their hesitancy as to how they were to get there and then their amazement at how quickly things happened with Americans. They were running trucks into the surrounding villages, Bryant explained, so it was really just a matter of being there when the trucks showed up and hopping on board. He suggested, at Piacenti's urging from behind him in line at the booth, that she bring friends as well.

After the empty trucks had rolled out to cheers and hoots, the squadron gathered for the pre-mission briefing in one of the huts. The men sat and squatted in rows. Snowberry had pinned a blanket up on the board and had tied rope running away from it in a parody of the red mission yarn and mission board. The rope ran off the board, down the floor, and partially up another wall. Lewis, as the CO, told them with exaggerated sobriety that they had a long one today, and then swayed a bit, slopping something out of a sawed-off can. It spattered on his shoes to much applause. Snowberry played the intelligence officer, and he unveiled maps of a dance floor and the female body. He diagramed the mission route to whoops and concerted foot stamping, and outlined the expected resistance. There would be losses, he assured them. He wasn't going to stand up there and lie. But some of the men would get through.

The men roared. Eddy, who had been drinking since the announcement of guaranteed stand-down, curled forward out of his chair with a crash, and passed out.

"What about flak?" someone called.

The flak was supposed to be very heavy, Snowberry told them. The clap was supposed to be light.

"Remember, men, when you're protecting yourself, you're protecting your country," Lewis said. He slurped from his can.

Snowberry was waiting for attention. "You gunners,"

he was saying. "We need to stress again our desire for accuracy and efficiency." With a flourish he pulled a canvas from the blackboard and revealed a large male organ he'd painstakingly drawn in chalk. Bean cupped his forehead with his hand and Bryant couldn't help laughing. "Now, to illustrate," Snowberry said, "I've diagramed my own situation, much reduced in scale, of course . . ."

"Jeez," Bean said, when the room had calmed down, "I thought this party was supposed to be for the kids."

"Aw it is," Piacenti said from behind them. He jabbed a thumb toward the front of the room. "They're having fun, aren't they?"

Lewis was sitting on the floor with his legs spread, banging his can between them. "He's squiffed," Piacenti said. "Bosto. Plastered." Lewis acknowledged the diagnosis and waved.

They laid in large wooden cases of soda in tall unlabeled bottles and piled up a stash of everyone's candy rations, for the kids to take home with them at the end. The party briefing had broken up at 1400 hours with Lewis and Eddy and three quarters of the crew of *I'se a Muggin'* incapacitated. Snowberry had been fine after throwing up, and was helping with the setups, subdued by the time the first trucks loaded with silent and excited children came rolling in. He had even managed to dig up the Wing's Santa Claus suit, and was wearing it when the first of the children filed into the main hangar they were using for the party.

One of the youngest boys gaped at the five foot, five inch skinny Santa. "Father Christmas?" he asked dubiously.

"You got it right on the noggin, kid," Snowberry said, bustling by with two stacked cases of soda. "Ho ho ho."

Bryant helped Hirsch and another guy with the doughnuts and sandwiches the mess had sent over. "We oughta give out the powdered eggs at these things," the other guy said. "The Alliance'd be over tomorrow."

Two little girls in identical gray cotton blouses with

rounded collars flanked Bean, who was reading to them from a picture book. "Go slow, Bean," Piacenti called. "And let them help with the big words."

There was a small pile of fruit on the table as well, and a tech sergeant from *Seraphim* was holding a tiny boy up so he could see, the boy reaching in wonder for the pile. Bryant set another doughnut tray on the table. "He's never seen an orange," the sergeant said. "Imagine that?" He had handed the undersized fruit to the boy, who was turning it over in his hands.

Bryant felt a tugging at his sleeve and turned to find Colin and another young boy. Colin was wearing a brown jacket with wide lapels and a dark blue tie. The other boy had no tie and a worn and spotless shirt buttoned with such zeal it appeared to be actively choking him.

"Hello, Sergeant," Colin said. "Have we surprised you?"

"No," Bryant said. "This whole thing was just so you could visit." They stood with each other for a moment while Bryant wondered what to do to amuse two little boys. "Have you had anything?" he asked. "We have soda and dough-nuts."

The boys thanked him and Colin indicated they'd get something soon.

Bryant had an inspiration. He led the two of them to the end of the hangar where canvas had been slung over four engines waiting to be overhauled. A small squad of boys and girls followed, but the crew chief in charge hustled over, puffing and shaking his head, before they could get too close, and said, "No soap, kids. Can't touch. Leave the tools alone."

The children seemed unfazed, awestruck simply by the huge canvas shapes. Enough had gathered to make it appear that Bryant was preparing to give a speech.

"Jack-a-mighty, forget security here," the crew chief said within earshot, perhaps even directing the comment at him. "Back in the States we used to say even the lice had to show ID."

Robin was beside him, smiling, and nodded that he should go on with what he was doing. She always touched him that way, lightly, on the shoulder, as if to indicate a subtle favoring of him. He gave her a hug, her skin cool and smooth against his cheek. Colin looked on without approval or disapproval.

"God," he said. "You look great."

"Thank you," she said. She was wearing an enormous red floral scarf and a white blouse. "I hope it's sufficiently in the spirit of Christmas."

"It's great to see you," he went on, searching for something useful to say. "Did you come with Jean?"

She nodded. Jean was with Snowberry at the other end of the hangar, leaning down with her hands on her thighs to talk with a little girl. Snowberry was providing the entertainment, having segued from "The White Cliffs of Dover" to "White Christmas."

"I must say Jean's a bit puzzled by this passion Gordon has concerning Bing Crosby," Robin said. "She says he'll just break into song, at any moment."

"He thinks he sings like Bing," Bryant explained. "We tell him he sings like Hope."

They gathered into the rough semicircle surrounding Snowberry. He was up on a canvas-covered crate festooned with smallish branches painted red and olive green. "But it isn't Christmastime," one small boy blurted. Snowberry winked and swung into the second chorus and began affecting Crosby's sleepy eyes.

Lewis walked by and nodded, wincing as if in constant pain.

"You remember Sergeant Peeters," Bryant said.

Lewis placed a finger to his lips and extended a hand to Robin. "Lewis," he said.

"Oh yes," Robin said apprehensively. "Hello, Lewis."

"Hope you're enjoying the show."

"I am." Robin lifted her hand from his. "Thank you."

"Well, he sounds more like Crosby than Kate Smith," Lewis conceded. "I'm not big on the Groaner. If they ever change the color of Christmas, he's through. Who's the kid?" he added. "Looks like Ned Sparks."

Colin was back. "Hello, Sergeant," he said.

"How you doin', kid," Lewis said.

"Are you a bombardier?" Colin stood straight, arms at his sides.

"Kids." Lewis pressed his fingertips to the sides of his head. "Uncle Lewis has a hangover. We don't want to scream at Uncle Lewis."

"I'm very sorry," Colin said.

"Uncle Lewis was stinkeroo a few hours ago," Bryant explained.

"I'm sorry," Colin said again. "I'm sorry you've been stinkeroo."

Lewis winced, rubbing slowly in tiny circles. "The kid's great," he said.

Snowberry finished his program with a spirited whistling rendition of Al Jolson's "Toot Toot Tootsie," and the children and village girls applauded enthusiastically.

An Irish staff sergeant from *Geezil II* stood up and started on the "Indian Love Call."

"What is this, Talent Night?" Snowberry said. "Siddown." He announced the conclusion of the cultural part of the program—on quite a high note, he felt compelled to add—and set about accepting entries for what he called the Derby, pulling a blackboard over and starting two columns, Rider and Mount. He began the Mount column with his own name, and climbed off the crate to circulate among the children in search of a rider.

"What is it?" Robin asked.

"We race on our hands and knees with the kids on our

backs," Bryant said. "And if I know Gordon, he'll lay out a doozy of a track."

The children milled around chaotically and pairs of names were going up on the board. "How about it, Colin?" Bryant said. "Ready to bring home the Cup?"

"No thank you, Sergeant," Colin said. "But my friend Keir might enjoy it."

Bryant smiled down at the little boy. "Any gum, chum?" he asked. When Keir didn't respond, he added doubtfully, "Is Keir old enough?" He visualized trying to explain a fall to a mother who had never liked Yanks in the first place.

Once the question registered, Keir nodded.

Snowberry laid out the route and they lined up twelve abreast. A wide lane was cleared of everything but grease and oil spots, some of which were clearly considerable enough to play a role. They were to race down to the Wright Cyclones under the canvas and back. To minimize trampling, when riders fell they were out of the race. Bryant instructed Keir to hold on around his neck and lie low and the boy took his advice with ferocious concentration, digging eager fingers into Bryant's windpipe. He was sandwiched between Snowberry, still in the Santa suit, and Hirsch. Piacenti, also representing *Paper Doll,* was at the other end of the line.

Lewis had volunteered to call the start. Snowberry whinnied and snorted impatiently, and his rider giggled with delight. After several intentional false starts Lewis cried "Bang!" and they were off in a tumbling rush, Bryant feeling the shocks in his arms as he jounced forward. There was a good deal of shouldering and the riders shrieked happily as the mounts falling behind grabbed the feet or calves of those ahead and were kicked in retaliation. Snowberry elbowed Bryant and took a big lead heading into the wide curve around the engines, splaying maniacally through the turn like a crab. Bryant accelerated on skinned knees and palms

and lowered a shoulder into the turning Snowberry and
caught him broadside, both riders screaming and laughing,
and Snowberry crashed into the gallery lining the racetrack
and only kept his balance by knocking over two girls and a
gunner drinking soda who'd been facing the other way. The
boy flew off his back but kept hold on his neck, and Snowberry came after him furiously, pawing the ground and gob-
bling distance while the boy clung to his neck like an absurd
version of a weight handicap and tried desperately to regain
his footing and climb back on.

Bryant called No fair! No fair! He's off! but Snowberry
was covering ground like Man O' War, the boy by now more
or less back in the saddle. Ahead of them Hirsch hit a grease
slick with both palms and skidded flat out on his chest before tumbling his rider off to the side, and someone ahead of
him crossed the finish line. With Snowberry almost on top of
him, Bryant gave it a last burst of acceleration looking for
Place or Show, but Snowberry dove in frustration and
caught him around the thighs, spilling the four of them like
colliding skaters short of the finish line.

Robin and Jean helped collect the wounded and dis-
pense Cokes.

"You were marvelous, darling," Jean said, helping
Snowberry brush off his Santa suit. His knees were black
with grease. She wore her red hair swept up on both sides
and her skin seemed thick, like rind. "I thought the way you
stood up to this bully was simply wonderful."

Snowberry brushed his chin with the back of his hand
and scowled in Hollywood pain. "The story you've just
seen," he said, "and the characters in it, are fictional. But
acts of courage such as these are occurring day after day, in
Europe and the Pacific, as Allied fighting men and women
stand tall against aggression wherever it's found and refuse
to say Uncle. Or even meet Uncle. Without their noble inspiration, something somewhere would have been impossible—"

"Such a cynic," Robin scolded. "And hardly old enough to know the meaning of the word."

"I know what it means, Mrs. Weisenheimer," he said. "It means someone who can tell the future."

Audie was cruising the food tables and thumping into the legs consistently, unaccustomed to the new arrangement. She was pulling in a great deal of attention and very little food from the children. She sat and begged from Lewis until Lewis found an egg of unknown antiquity in the bottom of the box sent over from the mess and cracked it over the dog's head. Audie sat unaffected at first, her cloudy eyes like the portraits of Lee or Stonewall Jackson, while the albumen slid mercury-like from the crown of her head. The children loved it. Bryant always found the dog's foolish and inappropriate dignity heartening.

"What kind of person humiliates blind animals for sport?" Robin wondered.

"Tail gunners from Dayton, Ohio, I'd guess," Snowberry suggested. "Who've reenlisted."

Another game evolved while they looked on, a guessing game which evoked great shouts and un-English arguing from the children.

"It was really very sweet of you to do this," Robin said.

"It was Gordon's idea, the whole thing," Bryant said.

"They know," Snowberry said. "I told them."

Jean kissed him lightly on the cheek. "It means so much to the children. I think they see you as superheroes."

"Not a view to which their parents always subscribe," Robin said.

The party was breaking up. They joined the others to help with the distribution of candy and paper squadron patches.

Snowberry handed a patch with a double candy ration to Colin and heaped a banana on the pile in his hands. Colin thanked him so profusely he turned away, reddening.

Bryant loaded Keir up. The boy seemed dazed and his

grip unreliable, so Bryant put the patch and the Baby Ruths in his pockets and let him hold the fruit. He thanked them in a small voice and Robin asked, leaning over him, what he liked best. "Juice from home," he said.

The children were then piled back into the trucks, clutching their loot as though they expected all of this to be rescinded at any moment. Robin and Jean's truck was among the last to leave, and they waved once and disappeared into the interior. The men lingered over clean-up and Bryant took a bucket of water to Audie, who had found a quiet corner and was lapping up some spilled soda she'd nosed out. Hirsch held her collar while Bryant scrubbed. She lowered her head helplessly and submitted, quivering in expectation of further indignities, while Bryant thought of the children's faces.

They endured ground training sessions that were time-filling and redundant. They were mustered out in front of the briefing hut in a drizzle to listen to a lecture on behavior while intoxicated, relations with the locals, and incidents of petty theft. They went back over aircraft recognition, this time with a glum Bean singled out to hold small wooden models at various distances from those being tested. It was especially galling to Lewis that they were still studying aircraft recognition—his suggested technique was to shoot out of the sky anything which wasn't a B-17 that approached within range—and not working on aerial gunnery, or on tightening the combat boxes. The Ju88 ambush on the return flight from Hamburg had spooked the brass, though, so they were back to naming silhouettes in the dark. One of the lowest percentile scores came on what turned out to be a Ju88. The irony put them in a horrible mood.

At the third session a fight broke out between a tail gunner and a dorsal gunner over the real Ju88's—over who should have spotted them first—and the tail gunner, a medium-sized tech sergeant from Peoria named Theobald,

knocked out a couple of the teeth of the dorsal gunner. The
dorsal gunner had gone down on one knee beside Bryant and
Lewis, cupping his mouth with trembling care, and when the
lights had been switched on, Bryant had been arrested by the
two teeth on his desk top like irregular pearls, dotted with
jewel-like blood.

They snoozed through an early morning session on hy-
giene *("Hy*giene," Lewis exclaimed when he saw the topic
posted. "Bean picks his nose and eats it") and tried intermittently to concentrate on an afternoon marathon having to do
with ditching in the water.

The first image which came up on the overhead projector once the room was darkened was that of an entire 17
crew minus pilot and co-pilot crammed into the radio com-
partment, body to body, in crash position. The presentation
was clearly out of sequence, and the image faded from the
screen.

"Fairies!" someone shouted triumphantly. The tail, ball,
and waist gunners' crash positions involved lying on their
sides chest to back, nut to butt, as Lewis characterized so
many military lines, and though the subjects' arms remained
primly at their sides, the crush did make things look comically intimate.

"Is that your hand?" someone else called.

The images reappeared, apparently now correctly ordered. The first sheet read: WHAT HAPPENS WHEN A
BOMBER IS FORCED DOWN AT SEA.

"Not a very military title," Snowberry commented,
next to Bryant.

They were comforted with the next sheet, a navigator
turning rather quickly, Bryant thought, from his station.
NAVIGATOR, it said, calculates estimated position, informs
radio operator, destroys papers, picks up maps, compass,
and celestial equipment, and goes aft to the radio compart-
ment.

The image went dark again and the men groaned. The

light came back on and a pair of small and flustered sergeants began working on the machine.

"Get the same guy who fixed the movie projector," the earlier heckler called. The crews folded their arms and waited with a martyrish patience, griping about the constant snafus and trapped until the whole strip could be shown.

Bean and Snowberry argued about the Conn-Louis fight. Bean had admitted to everyone who would listen that he'd blown "over twenty dollars" on the fluke of Billy's having "walked into that left in the thirteenth."

"Two years and this geep is still moaning about it," Snowberry groaned. "Bryant's the mick. He's the one should be yapping."

"Conn won the fight," Bean asserted. "He was ahead 7-4-1 on one card coming out for the thirteenth."

"Yeah but he got knocked out," Piacenti said. "Lights out. *Capisce?*"

"Nobody beats Joe Louis," Snowberry said. "Joe Louis goes bear hunting with a switch."

An image flashed before them of a bombardier taking aim at his bombsight with his pistol, like a cowboy ruefully dispatching his injured horse, and then it disappeared.

"Twenty dollars," Bean said miserably. "I never bet money. It was a sure thing."

"War," Hirsch said, gazing at the huddled repair attempt going on around the machine, "has got to be one of the most boring of human activities."

The strip resumed and they quieted down, becoming more than a little interested in ensuring that they knew the ways out of a sinking B-17.

At mess Bryant and Snowberry flanked Bean, and Piacenti sat opposite. "You remind me of Peter Lorre, Bean," Snowberry said. "Except he has nicer eyes."

"Why don't you keep quiet?" Bean asked. "And then I could eat in peace. I'm tired of everyone always picking on me."

"Cream chipped beef," Piacenti said grimly. "Don't you just love cream chipped beef? Me, I could eat it all the time."

"Why isn't the food as good as it was in Basic Training?" Snowberry asked. "Why is that?"

No one had any ideas.

"I don't know," Bean said, chewing. Every so often one of the beef strips didn't give up so easily. "I didn't really have Basic."

"You didn't have Basic?"

"No," Bean said, a little cowed. "I got sent to the wrong post because of a typographical mistake. Me and about ninety other guys. The master sergeant didn't know what to do with us, since we weren't supposed to be there in the first place, so he had us on kitchen and latrine detail. We never got Basic, and I know *I* never complained. One day he took us out into the field and showed us his rifle."

"Showed you his rifle," Piacenti said.

"You know, the breech, and loading it, and shouldering it, and all that."

"Are you telling us you only fired a rifle once?" Piacenti asked.

"Well, we didn't get to fire it." Bean took the beef from his mouth and laid it in a strip alongside others next to his plate. "Because then we would have had to use the range and he would have had to explain why and all that."

"Oh, sure," Snowberry said.

"Anyway, he put it on our record that we had Basic Training because of that, but I don't think we did."

"No, I don't think so," Snowberry agreed.

"I'd appreciate it if you didn't tell Lewis that story," Bean said, after they had been silent a moment.

"You don't have a thing to worry about there," Bryant said.

On their leave, they hitched a ride with Army Supply as far as a sleepy crossroads Robin had stipulated and jumped down and gave the drivers the high sign. They stood awkwardly in the sun while the trucks labored and clamored down the curving lane like an embodiment of their own awkward intrusion into the countryside. They were both eager and happy, and took turns pushing each other out of the shade of a reedy beech tree. Snowberry compared the wonders of the upcoming trip to the World's Fair, but Bryant did not carry the joke any farther. They had together that morning gone to the PX and asked the tech sergeant behind the barred window of the pharmacy for boxes of condoms. He had wished them happy flying.

"Aren't you horny?" Snowberry asked. "I'm horny."

Bryant blushed and let on as how this was all pretty old stuff as far as he was concerned. He fingered the package in his breast pocket, amazed that all of this was happening to him.

Snowberry pointed at Robin and Jean, pedaling toward them on ancient red bicycles and raising a low cloud of dust incongruous with their pace. "Here's our World of Tomorrow," Snowberry joked, and Bryant held up a hand in greeting, like a happy Indian, he thought.

It was the beginning of a forty-eight-hour pass. Snowberry and Bryant, thanks to the largesse of Robin Lea and her mother, Elizabeth, were going to enjoy what was for the aircrews one of the more coveted of the officially sanctioned activities: dinner at an English home. Dinner, short-rationed or not, in a setting in some way certain to relieve the sense of being in the service, and the war.

They hugged formally, the girls leaning forward with a cautious hand on their bicycles. Then they walked back the way the girls had come, slipping into single file when the occasional military transport passed. "Hubba! Hubba!" one dope called from the back of a Willys.

"That really burns me," Bryant was going to say, but Robin turned to him and smiled, unconcerned.

The sky was blue and clear and free of the sounds of engines. Robin and Jean were politely happy but also a little jittery and hardly overwhelmed and Bryant wondered if they wondered if they'd done the right thing. He tried to exchange worried or even wounded glances with Snowberry, but his buddy was still cocking his head around, taking in the sights.

At the cottage Elizabeth Lea stood shooing geese. She held a hemp doormat at arm's length and beat it with what looked like a small hoe. She met them at the iron garden gate, repeating their names as she took their hands in a way that was both warm and businesslike, so that Bryant felt both grateful and excluded. She was a thin woman with a posture like a question mark who somehow managed to convey the impression of standing straightbacked with dignity.

There were more, borrowed, bicycles alongside a shed black with creosote—Bryant was heartened to think of the work that must have gone into Robin and Jean's assembly of four bicycles for the afternoon—and the plan was to drop off their things, and tour the countryside as their first activity. They were to go straight inside, Robin directed, and change into their bathing trunks.

They rode out onto the lane in a shaky cluster, Bryant having all kinds of trouble with his bicycle ("Mine's defective," he kept calling, to the girls' delight), the chain slipping disastrously on the sprocket teeth every few revolutions. He was forced to work twice as hard to keep up, but looked up and beamed sweatily whenever they sent a questioning glance back.

They passed a chemist with a kelly green sign, a baker's window with golden and glazed buns. The huddled windows and doors and forehead-low roofs all seemed to him vaguely reminiscent of children's books. They rode through lanes shaded bottle green by overhanging trees, one of which Robin would occasionally single out as particularly old. "She's showing us trees?" Snowberry said as an aside at one point. Bryant kept his eyes on her back, rising and falling gently with the action of the pedals, damp enough now across the delicate wings of the shoulder blades that her blouse was clinging, and he focused on the simple pleasure he derived from that, as they soared down through curves, passing through shaded breezes that cooled his forehead. The leaves on the trees above them turned with the wind like schools of fish.

At a pleasing wide bend in the river they stopped, and rattled their bikes down a short embankment to the water's edge. Jean led them further along a path until a crescent of lawn shielded from the road appeared, and there with a sigh she dropped onto the grass two small satchels that had jounced patiently on the bicycle baskets during the ride. They peeled off tops and shorts and settled down to the water and the sun. The undressing seemed illicit and exciting and awkward, though it was all on the up and up.

"This is something," Bryant enthused. "This is okay." He gave Robin's arm a squeeze. He could feel the sun drawing the smell from the damp earth.

"I love hearing men talk. That's what I miss most," Jean said. Her eyes were closed and her cheeks were pink in the sun.

Robin murmured something reassuring. Her bare arm indolently extended in his direction. Her eyes were closed and relaxed despite facing the sun and her mouth was slightly open. He guessed she didn't feel like conversation. From somewhere he caught the faint and pleasant smell of an oxidized apple. Above them the sun shining through some birch leaves gave them the translucence of fresh grapes.

He thought, I could retire to a place like this, and then

grimaced. Retire from what? He saw himself a fat hatless old man in shorts, still unable to track a German fighter with a Sperry turret. But it seemed foolish and wasteful worrying while on leave with Robin, and he settled to face the sun. It bloomed a luminous red beneath his closed eyelids.

Now I'm thinking about Lois, he realized morosely.

"It's very good to see you, Bobby Bryant," Robin said. She was slowly smoothing her hair back from her ears.

"You look great," he said. "I've been trying to figure out some way of saying it that doesn't sound sappy."

She had a winning way of snorting in amusement at herself. "I'm vain, really," she said. "Comes from my grandmother Janie, I'm told. I'll tell you about her sometime."

Bryant didn't answer. He had the awful feeling at times like this, when he was at a loss for a response, that Robin was inexorably coming to realize that he wasn't good enough for her.

She got up onto one knee, lifting her hair from the back of her neck, and straightened her arms languidly. "I think I'll have a paddle," she said.

At the edge she hunched low and swept water up over her arms and chest, giving a little shake as she did so. He closed his eyes again, and heard the splash of Robin diving in and opened his eyes and immediately she surfaced making crouping sounds. "It's like ice," she was finally able to say.

Her mother had dinner ready when they returned. There was a small pewter pot of horseradish on the table as well, which did not seem to be a mistake, though none of the women used it. Snowberry spooned a small portion onto the outside of his plate. While they ate, Elizabeth recounted in some detail her first sighting of Americans.

"One of them gave Mother a flower," Robin said. "She's been a supporter of the Yanks ever since. I think he in point of fact gave her one of her own bluebells."

"Nonscriptus," Bryant said, remembering Robin's

watercolor, and her mother smiled, pleased that this American had a finer side.

The women talked about where rationed commodities were becoming available. They talked about the war in the village. "We had a Wellington crash nearby some months ago, as well," Robin said. "Near the cottage of an elderly friend. We went straight off to look in on her and we found her drinking port in the front room, with a kettle lid on her head, tied with a regimental tie."

Bryant laughed in a way he hoped maintained decorum. Snowberry grinned.

"She was ready for another blitz, I suppose," Elizabeth said.

After a custard made from white powder from a lidded tin, Snowberry held out for nightlife, so they walked the half mile or so through the cool twilight to the local pub. At the door Snowberry pointed up to the overhanging sign, "Ye Silent Woman Pub." Underneath was carved a decapitated woman. "Very sweet," Robin said.

They sat around a table and listened for a short while to the patrons. Snowberry cleared his throat and smiled and sat up straighter in the chair. "So what did you girls think of a couple of enlisted men asking you out?" he said.

"I put it down to the immaturity and egotism of youth," Jean said.

"You know the British attitude towards the Yanks," Robin said. "Eager blunderers who succeed through sheer weight of numbers."

Bryant could see Snowberry fingering something in his pants pocket and hoped it wasn't the condoms. Snowberry said, "So why date us when the RAF is full of Leslie Howards?"

"Well, you're still to some small degree British," Robin conceded. "Unruly colonials come over to help. There is that."

"And of course, you have chocolate," Jean said. She had large round eyes which frequently lent her expressions a misleading suggestion of credulousness.

"Unruly is right," Snowberry said with enthusiasm. "The other night you should have seen us. We were at The Hoops and from there we flattened this chemist's shop. Looked like someone had backed a truck right through it."

"How does one ruin an entire chemist's shop?" Robin asked. She did not sound pleased.

"We started early," Snowberry said. He slugged his beer.

Robin sighed. Jean sipped the beer. At the bar they were arguing about the quality of the whiskey.

"I guess we're sort of like what you hear about Americans, huh?" Bryant said.

Robin conceded a small smile. "What do the Americans say about us?" she asked. "We're curious."

"There're two theories," Snowberry said. "One is that English girls are as loose as a goose, and that they'll say right out what candy or gum'll get you. The other is that they're just like any other girls, and that any guy who thinks differently is a sap. Lewis is always saying that."

"And to which view do you subscribe?" Robin asked.

"I think you're the berries," Snowberry said.

"A third theory," Jean said disparagingly.

Bryant knew the statement to be only half fraudulent: Snowberry was wild about Jean, probably more than he knew, and had been able to keep his feelings fairly discreet, a trick Bryant envied. But he also had quoted theory number one to Bryant more than once, and liked to say concerning Jean's response to alcohol that after a few drinks the three inhibitions she did have disappeared. The commonly accepted wisdom around the squadron based on both experience and wishful thinking was that if you wore wings, you were halfway home.

"You shouldn't flatter yourself, Gordon," Jean said.

"We're here because you're entertaining, and every bit as generous as you're hopeful." Robin laughed. "And"—Jean touched his cheek—"you're quite handsome, in a younger brother way."

Snowberry grinned. "Now we're getting somewhere."

"If you ladies are golddiggers, why not officers?" Bryant asked. "Why not Lieutenant Gabriel, or Cooper?" He was secretly afraid of just that: officers with more going for them stealing her away.

"Don't give them a choice like that," Snowberry said. "Make it fair. Isn't Gable an officer?"

"I think you've proven quite nicely that enlisted men, with a bit of jerrying around here and there, somehow acquire all the resources available in your Air Corps to officers."

"I think we ought to put our cards on the table," Bryant said. "We think you're the berries, and you think we're tops, too."

Robin smiled. She raised her glass, and they toasted the announcement. One by one they fell to gazing at a poster over the door, of a British Tommy charging forward with a disconcerting ferocity. The caption read, *He's Working for You—Are You Working for Him?* The poster had evidently been torn in half and reassembled. Robin mentioned the connection with the pub's sign. They drank more quickly, looking for the most part at each other, anxious to get out from under the influence of the poster.

On the way back to the cottage Jean and Snowberry held hands. Two children were trying to boot apples soccer-style into a pail. A young woman was peering keenly at the action of a hinge as she swung the door this way and that. It occurred to Bryant as he passed through the village that everyday life was the surprise, not the war: the surprise was in the revelation that all of this life would go on, unconcerned, as he and his friends did what they did every day.

He fancied Robin was thinking the same way. Her eyes were following a low stone wall, and she knitted her brows, as if displeased, the way his father did. Ahead of them Snowberry and Jean were evidently discussing Snowberry's left hand.

"Why don't I ever fall in love at first sight?" Robin asked. She looked at Bryant, who was unable to shrug or smile. The comment seemed thoughtless and deflating. "I suppose it has something to do with my father," she added. "I never knew him very well. Mother used to say he treated us badly when he treated us at all."

"I was never very close to my father, either," Bryant said. But your father's still alive, dope, he thought.

"He was killed in a shipping accident. Did I tell you that?"

"Yes, you did." He wondered what Snowberry and Jean were talking about. "Though that's all you said."

She said, "It all sounds so pathetic and commonplace I suppose I don't often see the point of going into it."

He groped for something that would help. He wanted to know more about her, but was retaining very little.

She smiled for his benefit. "It's funny how everyone agrees on the awfulness of growing up, isn't it?"

He thought he should say something. He remembered Snowberry. "Gordon doesn't. He's always telling me these great stories. I always feel like, God, did I miss the boat."

She gazed ahead sympathetically at Snowberry's back. "Perhaps he's forgotten," she said.

On a low knoll a terrier watched them with the paranoid expression peculiar to the breed. Another dog lay snoozing with its fur poking through the slats of a garden fence, and before arriving at the cottage, he caught a mysterious and fleeting glimpse down a side lane of a small boy in shorts riding a black dog along a winding path beneath silent and dark trees.

Elizabeth had retired, leaving a pot of tea in its quilted

warmer and an overlong note on the dining room table. Bryant had the sudden intuition that she'd been given some sort of instructions prior to their visit. Jean and Gordon went out to the garden despite the dark, and Bryant and Robin tidied up at the strange stone sink. He put away in the cream-colored cupboards dishes or utensils that Robin would then quietly relocate. It began to rain, the sound light on the leaves outside the windows. They heard the heavier sound of running footsteps, and Jean swept back in, with Snowberry behind her. She shook out her hair and Snowberry rubbed his shoulders while Robin circled the room turning out the lamps. Robin kissed Bryant's cheek and Jean kissed Snowberry on the lips and they said goodnight.

"Aw, Jeez," Snowberry said, shivering a bit for effect.

"Let us know if you need anything," Jean whispered.

"I need something," Snowberry said.

"Goodnight," she said again, and the two girls ascended the stairs. Bryant said goodnight and Robin turned on the landing and hesitated, silhouetted in a nimbus of light in the hallway.

Snowberry climbed the stairs himself soon afterwards, disappointed and tired. "I think we probably do worse with girls than anybody in the Army," he said as he climbed. Bryant remained in the kitchen, sitting in the dark and listening to the loud ticking of a clock he hadn't noticed. There was a faint biscuit smell. The rain had stopped and the cardboard blackout shutters rattled faintly against the window frames. In the bathroom he discovered behind the washstand an old corner of National bread, plush with mold. The loo was a separate room altogether, with a long chain hanging down from a flushing tank set up higher than eye level. Bryant assumed it had something to do with gravity. He dreamed that night about a Bing Crosby record with Jesus Christ accompanying on clarinet, and remembered wondering vaguely how sleeping people got their hands on such recordings.

* * *

In the morning when he woke no one was in the house, and in the garden Robin was standing quite still, with a hand cupped and raised over her forearm, her face as placid and beautiful in its absorption as the face of a woman in a painting. Only the tremor of background primroses compromised the stillness. The air above the trees rang with a mysterious bird. The short sleeves of her blouse trembled, and she slapped the insect, and broke the spell.

When he joined her, they sat in wicker garden chairs under the cherry tree she had written him about.

"They've gone for a walk," Robin said.

Bryant rubbed his chin. "Were they trying to leave us alone, you think?"

She sniffed. "Jeannie adores the thought of mad, secret lives of endless trysts and intrigue. I suppose I've let her down a bit on that score. The silly thing is, Gordon seems to believe he's initiating things."

Bryant nodded foolishly, feeling acutely again that he and his friend were overmatched by these women.

An insect thin as a pencil point lighted on his lap. On its back were aqua and scarlet bands as brilliant as fresh paint. An immense white cat perched atop the stone manhole in the corner of the garden, Cardinal Newman's hideout. Robin made birdlike squeaks with her pursed lips. "That's Puff," she said. "Here, Puff."

He asked if she'd been doing any more painting.

"Haven't had much time," she said. "I'd like to go to art college after the war, I think. I was told by a friend I'd be certain to be offered a place." She opened her eyes and turned to face him. "Probably end up doing adverts." Her complexion remained beautifully smooth in the direct sunlight. She seemed pleased by the colors on her arm. She smiled. "What about you, mysterious Bobby? What will you be doing after the war?"

Bryant shrugged. The war had imposed a way of thinking on him, an ability to conceive only in terms of the present. His past was receding, so that calling it forward required ever more effort, and his future was a white wall, bland and abstract enough to discourage speculation.

They had a late dinner, relaxing around a splintery wooden table in the garden with cold meat and pickles. The windows of the cottage filled with the orange and violet of the sunset.

"This is really a beautiful place," Snowberry said.

"I'd like to have you for two weeks," Robin murmured.

Jean gave her eye a delicate rub. "Six would do nicely," she suggested. She crunched a pickle.

Bryant and Snowberry nodded politely.

"You don't seem particularly enthused," Robin noted.

They were awkward momentarily, uncertain what she wanted. "This is great, too," Snowberry said.

"Aren't you always wishing the war would go away?" Jean said.

They were silent. Snowberry looked to Bryant. "I can't say that, exactly," Snowberry said. "There's a lot I hate about it, a lot that's terrible. But in some ways I'm happier than I've ever been."

The girls looked at them.

"I guess it's hard to talk about," Snowberry further volunteered. Bryant felt angry and impatient with the question: they were outside looking in. How could they know?

"I know it sounds terrible," Snowberry said. "I don't mean it to."

After a pause Robin shifted her gaze from Snowberry to Bryant. "And you?" she asked.

"It's bad. It's the worst thing in the world," he said. He wanted to reassure her. He felt the way he had when his mother had discovered him doing something childish and destructive, like vandalizing street signs. He didn't have the words. "But you know. I met you. I got to know good pals I can depend on. It teaches you stuff like that."

She sighed. "I suppose we shouldn't browbeat you so. I suppose we're just trying to understand."

The comment let everyone off the hook, and in celebration Snowberry attempted Crosby speaking: "Well now, little miss, that's the kind of spirit that'll Back the Attack."

"Oh you," Jean said. "It's like having a boy with a drinking problem."

"Now the boys 'n' me would like to bring you a little ditty—"

Bryant slid a pickle in his mouth. Snowberry did a passable Crosby Choking. The girls applauded.

When it was fully dark, they moved the table inside and Jean and Snowberry played cards while Elizabeth listened to the radio. Robin led him out to Cardinal Newman's hideout, claiming there was a phosphorescent glow of some sort emanating from deep within which was visible on certain nights. When they had reached the corner of the garden, they walked forward slowly hand in hand, Bryant setting his feet down with edgy heel-to-toe caution. The ground and the air felt damp. Robin said, "Here," and lowered herself to a crouch and he followed. The earth clearly gave way to a different value of darkness and he could feel and smell the cold cellar air below. His fingertips touched rough stone.

"Do you see it?" Robin whispered.

He considered equivocating and said no.

She leaned back and sighed. "Sometimes it doesn't light up for visitors." Her voice was pleasantly sexual in the darkness. "I can't say I know why."

He settled onto his knees, and judged by the angle of her silhouette that she was gazing at him. He could smell rich earth, rotting leaves.

"Bobby," she said.

He leaned forward and kissed her, in the darkness softly catching the corner of her lips and her cheek.

"I don't seem to like that many boys," she said. "Mother says I seem to think I'm too good for them."

He thought, God, I'm some Romeo. She does everything first. She arranged herself so that his chest formed a kind of a chair back for her. "I think often of my grandmother Janie," she said. "My mother's stepmother. She grew up on a croft, Laghie, in the north of Scotland. I have a photograph of her, windswept and frightened, on top of a carthorse. She kept illustrations of all the birds in the area, and Mother says my artistic ability came from her." She rubbed her eye once, carefully, with a fingertip, reminding him of Jean. "She was always said to be very vain, and sad." Bryant tried to imagine this woman, and saw Robin with her arms folded in a tartan skirt standing in a wagon. "At sixteen she left home and went to Glasgow to train as a nurse. Mother has another snap of her at a cottage hospital. She became engaged to a young man who farmed another croft. Everyone in the family called it a miracle she'd found someone good enough for her. Naturally, he was killed. She never really recovered." She scraped the edges of the man-hole stone with her fingernail, the tiny scratching audible.

"Eventually, she married my mother's father, but Mother says she spoke about that farmer to her dying day as though he were just out of town for a bit, as though he'd just stepped out to the pub. In the cottage hospital photo she's still happy, standing in her stiff white uniform, with such a sad, shy smile. Mother always says, Robin, that's your picture, Robin, that's your smile, until I'm so frightened I can't bear to look at it and have to put it away. The last time I got so cross Mother swore she wouldn't bring Janie up again." She shivered, and patted her arms. "I'm frightened for you, Bobby. I'm frightened for me, as well."

"Don't be scared," he said.

"That's fatuous advice, isn't it?" she said.

He reached his hand down into the hole. The rock wall was cold and lined with water.

Her face was very near his. "You can't separate out the fear," she said. The seriousness of her expression made the possibility of disaster erotic. She kissed him, holding his chin up to hers, with the draft from the hole cooling his legs and feet.

Inside, they curled together into a big wingbacked chair facing the quiet hearth. The arms were doilied where they had gone threadbare. She was wedged in beside him and had her fingers on his throat and her thumb on his collar.

"I was working with the village children," she said. "Did I tell you? A drawing class. One day as something special I brought in a banana. A friend of a friend of Mother's had gotten two from a Yank serviceman. You should have seen their eyes. We all said it together: *ba-na-na.* As if that were a little bit of possessing it. And we all drew it." He touched the fine hairs on her neck, and she took his hand lightly and sniffed his fingertips. "I knew they all entertained the vague hope that it would be shared, or go to the best drawing. I suddenly had this unpleasant feeling of power. I had intended to take it home, but you should have seen their faces. We cut it into sixteen pieces and ate them in tiny nibbles, as I've always imagined one ate caviar."

She turned his head with the gentle pressure of two fingers on his cheek and kissed him. She took in her breath softly. "I remember being saddened a part of their childhood was missing. Perhaps I thought that was the worst thing about war, the way it robbed childhoods. I remembered at their age trekking home past the shops and windows of iced cakes, iced all with lavenders and pale greens."

There was a pronounced thump upstairs and then silence. Some board creaking followed. They caught each other gazing upward and smiled.

"Is that what I think it is?" he asked.

Robin leaned her head against the wingback. "I hope Jean's careful," she said. "You don't suppose Gordon would be careful, do you?"

"I don't suppose so," he said.

"She's had hideous luck with men." She was pressing her thumb into the valleys between his knuckles, one by one.

"You make it sound like a raffle."

"I suppose it is. The great love of her life was a Wellington gunner from Nottinghamshire. She spent two weekends with him and announced one morning she was PWOP."

"Pwop," Bryant said.

"Pregnant without official permission," she explained. "It's an RAF term. We used to joke about it, before it happened. He treated her horribly. Said she wasn't boxing him into anything. Gave her the name of a doctor."

"And she went?"

"The night before, he stayed over, and that morning, *she* had difficulty in getting *him* up. He didn't say anything, made a packet of tea, and ate cake in front of her. Complaining about a hangover. Completely oblivious."

Bryant felt bad for her. "What happened?"

She sighed. "He disappeared during what they called a lull in fighter activity. Jean still visits his mum."

He imagined the two of them chatting quietly before the photo on the mantel, the guy's home clothes hanging in forlorn rows in the other room.

"I'm sorry."

"We talk a lot about living for today, and What Might Happen, and everything feels so rationed we don't want to miss a thing, but we have responsibility, here. We're dealing with people, and it can be very serious. It is very serious."

He swallowed and tried to remain still.

"I don't know what kind of arrangement you have back in the United States with your girl Lois, but I doubt very much it encompasses something like this. You must in some way make clear in your own mind what you think you're doing." She stroked his chest, near the breast pocket that held condoms. He swallowed. "You're no longer another cheery Yank. You're my Bobby, and that scares me." She kissed him on the cheek, holding her lips pressed to it. "I

haven't the words," she whispered, and he felt fear, and
responsibility, and excitement. He wondered if in some un-
guessed-at English way he'd been outmaneuvered or com-
mitted himself. She had his face in her hands, and she kissed
him, and when he relaxed she closed her eyes.

She went upstairs to send Gordon back to his room
when the clock read 3:30 by the light of a kitchen match.
Bryant remained in the chair, too excited to sleep, imagining
she would come back down in a filmy nightgown and a tor-
rent of emotion. After a few minutes the upstairs fell completely silent, and he lingered unhappily on the prospect that
she was still tossing and turning quietly, her resistance
breaking down. He dozed eventually and dreamed of Vera
Lynn singing to him at a barbecue, and when he awoke, Jean
was clinking around the kitchen, making ersatz coffee, and it
was cool and light in the living room. He rose stiffly and said
hello with a weak smile. "Waiting for Father Christmas?"
she asked. She removed the blackout shutters and behind
her, when his eyes adjusted, he could see daffodils under the
apple trees, the lawn grayed with dew.

"They're both sleeping," she said. They sat in silence,
Bryant self-consciously attempting to mat down his hair and
clear the sleep from his eyes. When the water was ready, she
poured the coffee. It smelled like the woods.

"What's the ditty? 'Because of Axis trickery, my coffee
tastes like chicory,' " she said.

He smiled. "It's fine." He was determined not to make
some sort of horrible gaffe by referring to her troubles.

She was listening to the morning noises of the cottage.
"How long has Gordon been having those dreams?" she
asked.

He looked away, embarrassed. "Since a mission we flew
a little while ago. He said they were getting better."

She sniffed skeptically. "I'm happy not to have seen
them earlier, in that case."

"Was he a bother?"

She laughed aloud. "You're a queer one, Bobby Bryant. I can't decide whether you're very nice or very thoughtless. Probably both."

He was taken aback. "Why do you say that?"

She waved him off, her attention returning to the garden. Puff was hunched near the bluebells.

"Maybe she sees something," Bryant suggested.

"Her friend's buried there," Jean said. "A stray. Passed on in her sleep, very mysterious. We buried her in the garden yesterday morning before you came."

Puff pawed at the tilled ground. The loose earth popped and trembled.

"Puff isn't giving up," Jean said.

The cat dug more frantically. Dirt ridged her forehead, above the eyes.

"Jeez," Bryant said. "Kind of morbid."

Puff plunged in and pulled, struggling, and the ground heaved and broke loosely and the weight below came free slightly, a paw showing like a lost mitten. Puff sprinted a foot or so away and turned to watch, coiled. Nothing happened. Puff watched, clumped dirt falling from her head and back like the coating from fried chicken.

Jean watched without expression. Bryant rubbed his nose.

Puff lay in the frosted grass, looking on with complete concentration. They rose finally and went into the garden to retrieve her, scuffing dirt over to rebury the exposed paw. They brought Puff inside and cleaned her with damp soft dress remnants used for rags, and while she lay around licking herself with detachment, the final hour of Bryant's leave passed with the two of them gazing on the yawning cat in glum silence before going to wake the rest of the house so that the boys could get back to base on time.

THEY WERE GOING ON PRACTICE MISSIONS, the CO told
them, and they were going to take them seriously, and if
they didn't take them seriously, they were going to end up
dead. Collisions during assembly were becoming all too frequent as larger and larger bombing groups were attempted
for the raids. Six aircraft had been lost in other squadrons in
the last five days without enemy intervention. Fifty-seven
men. Pilot error and insufficient vigilance, especially in poor
visibility, were the official culprits. The CO demonstrated
with his hands flattened and bobbing closer to one another:
heavily laden bombers momentarily unbalanced by turbu-
lence had little room for safe recovery in a tight combat
formation. At times single aircraft and even whole formations were becoming lost and crossing into the formations of
others in the general pre-dawn chaos. The 341st nearby had
had the particularly humiliating distinction of having to
abandon a mission altogether.

They were going to work on assembly. The assembly
ship was to be the first off the airfield, and would fly to the
designated point and begin firing flares. They were to follow
at minimum intervals and assemble in formation as quickly
and efficiently as possible.

The assembly ship was a battle-weary B-24 called *You
Can't Miss It.* It was bright yellow with huge red polka dots,
and a kelly green tail. The men loved on fairly clear days
such as this to fly right up to it and earnestly ask for radio
confirmation of its status as assembly ship.

If the balloon didn't go up in the next few days, the CO
continued, they could count on additional gunnery training
flights. The standard procedure had been to fly over the British coastal ranges firing away at the targets towed by tired
old RAF Bostons. Now *that* was a job, Lewis said, that had
to be the most dangerous in the armed forces, towing those
targets while planeloads of ginks and shnooks let fly.

Bomber Command, the CO mentioned with exaggerated care, had reason to believe that the gunnery instructors
back in the States had not been as precise in their scoring of
cadet shooting as they might have been. The comment got a
big roar of laughter from the aircrews. A month earlier in
one of those spectacularly embarrassing incidents the Air
Corps seemed able to produce every four weeks or so, one of
the target-towing Bostons had been shot down. The Brit
pilot had hit the silk so angry he had brandished a revolver
at the contrite B-17's that flew past his chute.

Bryant found himself climbing with *Paper Doll* up through
white cumulus clouds and gray sky. Lewis was singing a
parody of "Into the Air, Army Airmen" over the interphone: Into the air, Junior Birdman, get your ass into the
blue. The plane banked sharply and he knew he was supposed to be remaining vigilant in his lookout for the assembly plane and others, but the view through breaks in the
cloud entranced him: visibility distended in a pleasant and
sleepy way by a slight haze all the way to the Dutch coast
and deep into France, the muted colors receding into the
curvature of the earth. The earth closer to home resembled
the subdivided palette of Robin's paintbox. Cooper had
switched the crew's interphone to Liaison, and Bean tuned
them into the BBC, and they climbed higher into the great
chamber of air above the cloud cover listening to an alto
voice singing opera.
    Hirsch spotted the assembly plane and within minutes
they had slipped into a slot above it and behind *Geezil II* and
Leave Me Home, which had achieved its name by three
times developing engine trouble on the transoceanic flight to
England and three times having had to turn back.
    They found themselves enduring the usual casually har-
rowing jockeying and shifting in formation as they circled in
an ever-growing group, the clouds like shoals beneath them.
Bryant could hear the guff Gabriel and Cooper were taking

—Close it up! Close up the formation, goddamnit!—from the pilot of the lead plane.

From above and behind, three more 17's appeared and drifted down to them. Bryant called them in to Gabriel and said aloud, Now where're *they* coming from? They eased terrifyingly close and suddenly everyone in *Paper Doll* was shouting, as if the other crew could hear. Gabriel had no room to maneuver and shouted as much back in response over the interphone when they yelled for evasive action. The closest 17 bobbed higher with an infuriating casualness after having dipped so low that its ball turret had been momentarily level with Bryant in his dorsal. The ball turret gunner had waved.

They had been badly frightened and were glad to be among the first to land, an hour later. They were standing outside of *Paper Doll* waiting for the jeeps when *Lemon Drop* came in with a crushed tail from a collision somewhere in the clouds, its engines straining, the emergency trucks clanging, and *Lemon Drop* swung to the right as it swept in over the tarmac, hesitating with its left wing dipped, and then that wing caught the concrete and the immense plane smashed and concertinaed as they watched, a body cartwheeling out.

The radio operator survived. There was no fire. The plane had shattered into pieces spread over the runway like a junkyard. They had sprinted over to help the emergency crews, and Lewis and Bryant had come across in the cockpit section only the co-pilot's flying boot, wedged beneath a rudder pedal, a bone jutting up from within like the stalk of an immature flower. When the shock had worn off, Bryant's first clear thought, lying on his bunk, was that they were all dying like ants, or pets, or foreigners—they were all dying now as part of a routine.

He lay still. When he woke he was damp. The hut was gloomy and he guessed he had missed dinner. Something nearby smelled like aluminum. On the bunk beside him Snowberry lay face into the pillow with his hands hanging together off the edge like a victim of an exotic torture. Lewis was on his own bunk beyond, shifting his rear to test the sounds of various farts. Piacenti sat upright with his legs over the side and his head in his hands. It looked to Bryant like a training film illustration of Low Morale.

"I want to go home," Snowberry said. His voice came from deep within the pillow.

"For serious drinking the boys had a table the shape of Texas. Cut it out of sheet metal," Lewis said. He had spent his leave with friends in the 92nd. "We were playing Drink the Cities. We were on Galveston or Houston and somebody said, Toast. There was that point when no one knew what to drink to, and some little gunner who'd had his nose smashed over Aachen said, *Yo Momma.* It was just right."

Snowberry had not moved and it looked to Bryant as if he'd stopped breathing. Lewis was chewing on a tightly rolled piece of paper and did not seem to be deriving pleasure from his story. He had a photo of Gene Tierney over his bed, under a handwritten sign that said *Do Not Hump,* and he was stroking her behind absently with his hand in his flying glove. "Now this may be a bunch of guys who appreciate the grotesque no more than seven seconds running in their whole life. But I swear I do love to see the forces come together."

"I was figuring it out, on the ride in," Snowberry said after a silent and dismal pause. "I don't think we can go to chow anymore without fifteen percent casualties."

"The last big party we had," Lewis said, "it was after a big mission. We had WAAF's and WAAC's and Red Cross Girls and Wrens and local girls, you know, nice girls, and they were all standing around or sitting in these little groups. We kept thinking, how'd we get so lucky? Why are there so many girls here? Then it hit us: they were all the dates of the missing guys. We'd lost eight planes. Eighty guys. They're all standing around, all dressed up."

"Big night for sloppy seconds," Piacenti said.

"One little girl musta started getting dressed four hours before she came. She was at a table with some other girls and they were ignoring her, you know, trying to at least have a good time. She was crying. I went over and talked to her."

"I'll bet you did," Piacenti said. He believed Lewis to be a real tail hound.

"I told her it was just arithmetic," Lewis said gently, as if the subject had been inevitable and infinitely dreary. "If each group has to do X number of missions and loses Y number of men with each mission, how soon before all the original men are history?"

"I worry about fire," Piacenti said. "You know, you're caught inside and there's fire."

Lewis chewed and the paper moved around his mouth like a toothpick. "This guy in the 92nd had this photo of all the squadron Forts lined up the week he'd arrived. He showed it to me? All of them are gone now. None left. You ever wonder why they don't have battle-weary B-17's pulling things around?"

He spat the paper high above the bunk in a startling parabola. "It's simple, Dick Ott used to say. You're in a game and you need to score twenty-five. Before you run into the Glass Mountain."

The Glass Mountain was a squadron term for fatal and spectacular disasters in the skies, as in, This or that ship ran into the Glass Mountain. It had to do with the effect achieved when a heavy bomber was hit by flak while flying straight and level.

"Roasting to death," Piacenti repeated. He shivered, and rubbed his neck. "That's what really scares me."

"Think of it like the Brits," Lewis counseled. "You know. They talk about it like polo or something. These are just the single elimination playoffs."

"I was talking to Hirsch," Bryant said. "He was saying nothing was haphazard, you know?, and that if you had all the figures, you could have predicted—"

"*Everything* is haphazard," Lewis said with vehemence. "You don't predict *nothing*. I blow up your house, you tell me which way all the pieces are going to fall."

"But don't you think—"

"Shut up," Lewis said. "You give me a headache. Don't open your mouth."

"I want to go home," Snowberry said into the pillow. "I'm tired of this war."

There was no response. The principal sound in the metal hut became the squeaking of Piacenti's bunk as he scratched himself with an annoying industry. Bryant closed his eyes and nursed his humiliation, imagining Lewis gloating, imagining various forms of comeuppance.

Nothing was on for the next day. In the middle of the night he was aware that Snowberry was awake, and when he got up in dull insomniac frustration to go to the can, Snowberry followed. He sat on the can just for a place to sit.

"Some night," Snowberry said. He ran water on his hands and looked at it.

Bryant was hours past answering. He fancied the water beneath him was rippling quietly in the bowl.

Snowberry produced his little red journal, opening to a marked page. He began reading after settling in with his back to the wall, his lips every so often forming ghostly words. Bryant rose and hoisted his shorts and returned to his bunk.

In the dark, vague shapes telescoped toward and away from him. He followed elusive ribbon-like creatures he hoped were temporary retinal imperfections of some sort until he had to get up, and hissing in frustration he lowered his feet to the floor and padded back to the latrine, concentrating dimly on some notion of a drink of water.

Snowberry was asleep, still seated upright, swaying with tiny starts like a doddering grandfather. Bryant sat beside him and when he didn't wake extended a finger slowly and touched his nose. He didn't stir. He waggled his fingers grimly before Snowberry's face. His journal was opened on his lap. Bryant picked it up and began reading without high hopes. He skipped a section on Frances Langford. The next sections were drafts of letters.

This whole thing has really been something in terms of showing me the world and how different everyone is. Before the service I'd never met anyone from other places and now I know guys from Rhode Island and Ohio, and I've met guys from Texas and New Mexico and places like that. I always think about what Dad used to say about people from upstate and stuff, and I wonder what he would've thought about this crowd.

I eat good. The chow here is really good for the most part though everybody gripes about it all the time. I guess it's something you're supposed to do in the service. You can't believe how important food is here. If Mom knew she certainly wouldn't worry on that score. Guys'll sit around and just talk about eating and never change the subject. Guys are always talking about how their mother made this or that, and everyone listens like their lives depend on it. Sebastian Piacenti, one of our waist gunners I told you about, has this knack for talking about his mother's cooking so that the guys can almost smell it. He went on the other day in the jeeps after a mission about this veal dish with tomatoes that had the guys moaning and biting their hands.

Snowberry then attempted, with limited success, Bryant judged, to recapture some of Piacenti's magic. He skipped ahead.

The guy who wrote to ask for the picture of Sis is Harold Bean. He's got a girl here but I guess things aren't going so well between them, and I was really talking Sis up in front of him one day, so I guess he was sold. He's a nice guy, I think, though Lewis rides him pretty hard. Lewis says Bean raises a crew's buggeration factor—that's the phrase we got from the Brits for chances of something going wrong—but I think he's just pretty much like the rest of us. Maybe more so. We don't want to let each other down, and I think we do a pretty good job.

Lewis thinks Bean's getting jumpy and says you mark his words, he'll end up in a flak home, but I think it's more this thing with the girl, and the rotten luck the squadron's been having. I worry more about Piacenti. I don't know that much more about Bean. He's from Pennsylvania, but I think he told you that. He's a good-hearted guy. He's not a wolf. I think he looks fine but Lewis likes to say he's got a face like an unmade bed. I think he looks like the little guy in Lost Horizons. *You know the one I mean?*

I'm okay. I think we're all pretty blue like I said right now. I've heard some great new stuff from Der Bingle on the Armed Forces Network, and some new Vera Lynn stuff on the English stations. Tell Sis I've been working on the harmonies.

I find myself daydreaming more than I used to, and I have to watch it, or the guys'll think I'm ready for the flak farm, too. I have these other dreams, too, though I don't think they're going to last forever. The guys call dreaming like that pulling a lot of night missions. I have this one where there are German fighters all around us and my turret mechanism is like it has sand in it or something, and the gun controls are all floppy and loose. It gets me in a real sweat.

It seems like what we were taught and everything isn't good enough to handle everything

The entry stopped. Bryant closed the book and woke Snowberry, getting him to his feet and leading him gently to his bunk, as if putting to bed a sleepy child on Christmas Eve.

It seemed to them that it had been decided to keep them flying missions until they were dead. They were informed at the morning briefing that the target of the day would be Kassel, and a lieutenant known to most of them as a good man and a steady co-pilot stood up and said with frightening calm that he was no longer willing to fly these goddamn things, and that he wanted out. When he refused to sit down, he was escorted from the room.

On the hardstand Hirsch and Gabriel alone seemed capable of smooth movement, the rest of the crew drooped and jerked like marionettes waiting for their turn to board. Bean was learning German phrases from the little sheet in his escape kit: *Danke, Bitte. Zug. Schnellzug. Dritte Klasse.*

Snowberry was white. "I'm not gonna make it," he whispered to Bryant. "We were so cocky before. Why were we so *cocky* before?"

Bryant understood, he thought: It was as if the present situation represented an invited retribution.

"This paper pusher I met in London told me, 'You want to make breakfast, you gotta break some eggs,' " Lewis said. He was blowing on his gloves to further dry them out.

"That's what they tell the eggs," Willis Eddy said from within the plane.

Lewis shook his head with the expression of a man with insects on his face. "I clocked him. I got these little marks on my knuckles from his teeth. I hope he gums Farina the rest of his life."

They were thirteenth off the runway, climbing into the lightening sky behind the banking silhouettes of the 17's just ahead of them, and they rose east to the assembly points toward the brighter air. The contrails of the highest aircraft stood out in dark relief.

They flew to Kassel without the usual talk, the periodic oxygen checks the only communication. Most of the way, they had an escort of P-47's with their reassuringly fat milk bottle fuselages, and the leading and trailing elements of the formation far from them attracted the German interceptors once the escorts had sheered off for lack of fuel.

Piacenti called fighters coming up from nine o'clock low and Bryant swung the turret around to catch a glimpse of four Messerschmitts with bright yellow noses pulling up close to one another and breaking formation at *Paper Doll*'s altitude, at the break curling back like the petals of a flower. They swooped out of range after some of the lower squadrons and stragglers.

He spun the turret to follow the action above and ahead and his vision shimmered, as though he had slugged a beer too quickly on a hot day. The diaphragm of his mask felt dank and cold. The bomb bay doors were grinding open and he could hear Eddy's voice calling for steady but it wavered in volume. With concentration and detachment he seemed to understand what might have been happening, remembered a briefing: the A8B masks are prone to ice buildup in the exhalation bags, which unchecked leads to ice in the tube between the bag and diaphragm. He noticed below the fires of downed aircraft and bomb bursts as red peculiar blossoms, and moved to get a grip on his mask but felt like someone chest-deep in muck. Before his eyes colored electric bulbs blinked as sapphire, emerald, and ruby, and he felt his mind becoming luminous with dream; felt, like a drowsy child, ready to accept what needed accepting. He saw his drunk grandmother wandering around in his backyard dazed, impossibly holding a fifty-caliber Browning. With a sturdy and optimistic lack of resistance he slumped from the slung bicycle seat and tore the leg of his suit falling from the turret. He was dimly aware of the iron-cold slipstream blast on his calf. He remembered the creamy blandness of his mother's egg salad, and was surprised to find his leg so tender, so sensitive.

He awoke to find Eddy and Bean working over him, transferring the portable oxygen bottles onto his mask, and he realized he was breathing through someone else's as they did it. They were on their way home, Bean shouted to him. He nodded and waved. He had urinated in his suit and his thighs and rear were cold. The fuselage floor seemed to have the mealiness of wet sand, though he registered that was impossible.

He rode a long while with a kind of animal speechlessness. His mask again iced up and for a stretch Bean sat beside him and worked the only functioning mask on the buddy system, the two of them slumped together in their heavy flight suits as dull as drugged birds. He remembered frostbite and made an effort to move his fingers and toes. He had the weird sense the plane was no longer moving. He tried to keep awake but could not, and curled his toes within his boots as a last measure before passing out.

He was shuttled immediately to the station sick quarters and surrounded by frostbite cases. The sick quarters were four Nissen huts joined by enclosed hallways, discreetly removed by an aspen grove and a hillock from the barracks. He slept for sixteen hours and then sat up and gazed around him. The frostbite cases sat quietly, holding their affected areas like delicate and broken instruments. Their hands and feet changed as they watched absorbedly with apprehension edging on horror, from white and numb to red and swollen to something verging on black. A navigator a few bunks over lay as if dead with his head bandaged completely from the nose up. He'd been there three days and the men called him Claude Rains. Flak had blown out the perspex nose and his goggles had been smashed, Bryant's neighbor told him. "The Doc said his eyes were frozen. Imagine?" The navigator was inert. A boy near the door was shaking uncontrollably. He had a blond cowlick that stuttered and waved like a signaling device.

Bryant was treated for anoxia and mild frostbite, his rear end alternately chilled and burning. It was still white but heading toward pink, his neighbor informed him with an air of certainty. It still burned enough to frighten Bryant, though as far as anyone could tell it was not swelling but recovering. The doctors credited some blankets Bean had stuffed under him.

He was released for dinner and found himself unwilling or unable to talk much with Snowberry or Lewis about what had happened. Lewis had been particularly interested since anoxia was his private phobia, but Bryant was less than specific about whatever early indications he might have noticed, and Lewis clearly decided to pursue the matter later. Bryant found Bean and Eddy and thanked them, but they looked away shyly and protested with shrugs that they found the thanks unnecessary and embarrassing.

He fell asleep quickly after dark and dreamed of swordlike night searchlights picking up a series of placidly floating barrage balloons. There was a wing from the biplane crash he'd witnessed as a child fluttering down like an enormous seed pod and swooping like a pendulum, and he was back in a nature camp he'd attended when he was eight, gazing at a sullen copperhead in a dismal cage.

He was led through a lean-to that molted into a kind of drainage tunnel, and became aware in the darkness ahead of an immense spider with a balloon-like abdomen and a palisade of curled black legs spiky with hairs that were distinct in the gloom. He was on his back and his breath came with his kicking and thrashing and the spider's legs every so often palpated his with a terrible firm gentleness.

He woke to the sound of B-17's returning from their assembly points, a long mission necessitating a pre-dawn start evidently having been scrubbed. There were noises and shift-

ings from most of the bunks. The planes were coming in at
half-minute intervals and the lights reached and spanned,
wavering through the windows and across the barracks, illuminating those who were awake and those who were asleep.

He got up, his mouth sour and dry. On his way to the
latrine he stopped, and could make out in the darkness a boy
in his underwear hunting for something in his barracks bag.
When the lights crossed his face there was a look of pure
apprehension, as if no activity could have been more illicit.
Another boy near the door was chewing the corner of his
sheet.

In the latrine he found a filmy glass and filled it and
drank. The water was cold and when he looked at it, it was
laced with blood, like colored smoke or underwater vegeta-
tion. In the mirror he could see that his gums were bleeding.
The event seemed inexplicable. His teeth were reddening and
he held the glass aloft as if he were offering a toast at a
cannibal feast.

He retrieved his blanket from his bunk and stood outside, wrapped like an old Indian, bare feet cold on the dirt.
Someone else was up as well, smoking just beyond the corner of the hut, but he didn't care to find out who. He appreciated the blanket's warmth and forgave its roughness and
understood that his urges were being narrowed toward the
primal: Safety. Food. Sleep. Farther behind, Robin or Lois.
He stood in the damp early darkness waiting, the great
colored chains of lights floating in. Below them the vermil-
ion lights of the runway markers gleamed and receded. Behind him in the barracks he could hear as a background
murmur the small shrieks and gabblings of battle dreams.
Somebody in another hut altogether was playing a pitchpipe
in sad and unrelated keys.

He walked a little further and climbed atop the hood of
a fuel bowser. There were dull yellow lights on over the
picket post, shuttered in a halfhearted blackout. He could
make out ragged and gaunt dogs moving as shadows in and

out of the illumination, starving, he knew, unsupported by base personnel, waiting for death. One nosed the ground and looked over at him, its tiny pink tongue in the distance visible in the light.

The beams ranging from the towers seemed to be pulling the big ships out of the night, and they dropped and banged like clumsy and lost buses onto the tarmac and swept past him, the turrets gleaming and illuminating shadows within, and then they were gone.

PART THREE

Schweinfurt

Oɴ ᴏɴᴇ ᴏғ ʜɪs ғᴀᴛʜᴇʀ's ʜᴜɴᴛɪɴɢ ᴛʀɪᴘs they had walked and walked through a damp November drizzle, their trail erratic with minor mudslides and gravel, in search of game, without success; Bryant had limped behind nursing a blister, his legs all the way to his calves slick with black mud from falls. They had seen absolutely nothing. His father after the first few fruitless hours had taken to slogging along as if on a forced march, his head lowered. They had stopped for lunch to discover that the rain had ruined the sandwiches Bryant had ineptly wrapped, and his father had swallowed that as well. While Bryant had attempted near-complete un-obtrusiveness, his father had set his .22 stock-down against a forked birch to leave the trail a few feet to relieve himself. Hitting full stream he flushed a huge buck pheasant, which exploded up right before them, and his father's urine stream had looped and written on the air while he'd tried to do everything at once with a hand on his zipper and a hand scrabbling for his gun, and had only succeeded in spraying himself and tipping the .22, which went off in Bryant's general direction. His father ended up on the seat of his pants looking at his hands, his open zipper like a little laughing mouth and the pheasant long gone, a distant flapping among the trees. Bryant hadn't helped him up and hadn't mentioned the waspish sound of the bullet. He had been wise enough, in fact, not to say anything the whole march home.

With a craftsman's care he produced a series of sweat impressions with his palm on the pages of the field manual for the Sperry turret. The moisture made the paper curl.

The summer heat made the great mounded hangars waver like hills in the humid distance. Armorers bandoliered like Mexican bandits with cartridge belts humped their loads across hardstands too hot for England.

Word was Lewis had talked to a guy whose job it was to fill out the Statements of Effects forms for lost or missing airmen. Lewis had caught this guy in one of the huts going through somebody's stuff. The stuff had turned out to belong to a waist gunner from *Boom Town* named Gus Fleener, who had had his left arm taken off by flak over Kassel. They hadn't been able to apply a tourniquet because how do you tourniquet a shoulder? So his crew buddies had made the decision to bail him out and rely on local hospitality to get him to a German hospital in time. He'd gone into shock, though, and pulled his own ripcord, there in the plane, and they'd had to bunch up the chute under his remaining arm and throw him out so it didn't catch on the tail. The belly gunner and tail had reported seeing the chute open but no one was overly optimistic. The wound did not allow for much delay. And they knew enough about the lamentable spread in their bombing patterns to assume what the CO termed "ill will" on the part of the German inhabitants of the countryside. They'd heard stories of hapless chutists being pitchforked, or run down with hoes and sickles.

So this guy went through all of poor Fleener's personal property, the crews heard, making out a list, while Lewis watched: *socks, 4 ea., letters, 8 ea., combs, 2 ea., photos, 2 ea.* Final disposition of this stuff, the guy confided to Lewis, was a touchy bit of work: some poor schmoe's widow, he said, the last things she needs to see are some of these French postcards, or love letters with the wrong names on them. Air Corps policy was to remove the property in question as soon as possible once the airman was known to be missing or lost, so his buddies wouldn't brood any longer than necessary on the loss. The result was the approximate opposite of what was intended. The Statement of Effects man told Lewis wistfully that he didn't make a lot of friends.

Morale dropped as the story circulated. Snowberry at one point mused in Bryant's presence, "Ever notice how morale here keeps going down without ever going up?" Someone posted in the ready room a list headed with the title *What Won't Work,* and filled with items all the way from *"Honey, You Know You're the Only One for Me"* to *Prayer.* Saluting was becoming more overtly a way of saying Fuck You to those who demanded it; the practice had often been considered "chickenshit" by the men in the first place, generally ignored except for the CO, the visiting brass, and formal occasions.

It was no longer uncommon, after missions, to find Norden bombsights, so obsessively protected in training in the States as the secret weapon the Axis would give Italy for, lying in the grass unattended near the hardstands like mysterious, useless gizmos cleared from the attic. Men were becoming geniuses at hoarding small slights. Unpleasant jobs and missions mornings produced a variety of obscure ailments, which debilitated no one and enriched everyone's rotten humor. Everyone had a different method of following what was perceived to be an emerging pattern of sinister design, based on irrefutable omens. Half of three squadrons developed diarrhea.

Bryant didn't and Snowberry did. They sat together watching Tuliese, who had quite a talent with the brush, paint the nose illustration onto *Paper Doll.* Now that he'd finally gotten around to it, there was little enthusiasm among the crew for ornamenting their B-17. Snowberry clutched his knees to his stomach and rocked every so often, glancing at the latrines regularly to assure himself they were there and that he could make it. Tuliese leaned close, giving special attention to the thighs. He was known as a master of shading.

The paper doll in question was a naked redhead vaguely

modeled on Lana Turner. When he'd been informed that Lana Turner was not a redhead, Tuliese had answered menacingly, So what? Everyone had shrugged. She was being clothed with a filmy slip of what was supposed to be a nightgown inadequately covering her private parts. There was an unofficial contest between crews to be the most daring with their nose art, occasionally interrupted by halfhearted cleanup attempts when the brass considered things to be getting out of hand. Bryant thought of some of the flak-smashed noses he'd seen and considered how many hours of loving work were being erased in instants.

Lewis meanwhile was becoming obsessed with speed. His latest idea was the stripping of the camouflage from the B-17's. With the paint gone there would be reduced weight and smoother surfaces, translating into fleeter Fortresses. "I mean, who are we kidding with camouflage?" he said. "They can't see us?"

"You want to fly in a silver plane in the middle of one of those formations?" Bryant asked. "What about just carrying a sign in German that says, '8th Air Force Commanding Officer'?"

"Not just *us*," Lewis said, with the tone of someone teaching the hopelessly limited. "Suppose they were *all* silver. All the planes."

Bryant had no answer. "They'd reflect the sun," he said. "We'd blind each other."

Lewis thumped his cheek with his middle finger and surveyed Bryant a good long time. He said, "Sometimes you make it too easy for me."

And Snowberry, trying not to laugh, imagining no doubt the tremor through his bowels, said, "I think Lewis means he doesn't see the drawback."

Bean received word that his best friend had been killed in the Pacific theater, and he was inconsolable. He did not eat and could barely speak and so worried Bryant that he de-

cided to follow Bean around for a little while and keep an
eye on him. All he was able to get out of Bean was that his
friend had been involved in the bombing of New Georgia
Island and had been trapped in a burning Dauntless. He sat
around the day room feeling useless while Bean stared
blankly at a *Liberty Magazine.* He had tried mentioning
food, and Billy Conn, and home. Bean gazed at the table and
touched an ashtray with his finger.

Snowberry slumped in a chair by the folding magazine
rack. He'd been throwing up for two days now and he
looked drawn. He had his sketchpad propped at an angle
that allowed Bryant a look. The pad was blank. Every so
often Bean shivered and rubbed his arm.

"How do you know he burned to death?" Bryant asked
in a low voice.

Bean didn't seem to hear. He fingered an old snapshot
of his friend that now held a deep bronze tarnish, and let it
drop. He said, "He was my best friend. What're you guys?"

Bryant said, "Look, Bean, I'm going to write a letter,
okay?" He pulled out paper and a pencil to underline his
intention. Instead of oversolicitousness he intended to try
something in the way of Life Goes On.

Bean simply sat, as still as a vacant house.

"I think Bean's stepped off the curb," Snowberry said.
"If you want to know what I think."

Bryant wrote the date on his paper and *Dear Lois,* and a
series of lazy, slanted lines.

Beside him Snowberry noisily began to work and with
quick listless strokes sketched a four-engined plane: a fat
childish cross. After a moment he added a squiggle of smoke
curling upward from the tail. He drew flames as fat parallel
fingers and Bryant said, "Gordon," as a warning. Without
looking up, Snowberry changed the flames to bullets spraying out of a turret.

Bryant wrote, *I guess these sorts of letters are supposed
to go the other way,* and stopped, and then tried, *I'm writing*

because I got myself into a mess that you should know about, and stopped again, and finally wrote, *How are you?,* and decided on that as an opening.

How had he gotten himself into this? What did he want? Lois, and his high school, his town, his friends, all seemed like a half-remembered birthday party. Lois had a right to know what was going on, he told himself, and he felt a loyalty to her that was sincere and nostalgic. But he considered: Could he have written to his prewar self and communicated anything? He thought of Snowberry's fishing trips from the journal, and blackfish rocking gently in the sand with staring eyes and mouths opening and closing as if speech were prevented by this alien medium of air.

Before, he had vaguely hoped for a Dear John letter from her, and had thought melodramatically that he deserved it. Now he was beginning to understand that his country, for whatever its reasons, had informed him that he and his friends were in the most serious way on their own.

He became aware that Snowberry was holding his pencil motionless an inch from the pad, and was staring at it. The pencil point was trembling.

Bryant crossed out *How are you?* and started again.

August 14, 1943
    Dear Lois,
    Things here have not been going well. We have been pushed very hard and have seen many things and the rumors are something big and terrible is coming up.
    I have always wanted to be honest with you so I write this letter. I have been dating another woman here, an Englishwoman, and I don't know how serious it is.
    I didn't know whether to tell you or not but as you can see I decided to.

He folded the paper. A dispatch from the front, he thought. If and when things ever cooled down, and he were

till alive, he would use it. Word was going around about a
colonel in the 379th who had told his crews that the key to
fighting the kind of war they were fighting was to make
believe you were dead already, and then the rest came easy.
Hirsch in line for chow had fiddled with calculating on his
slide rule the odds on their completing their tour alive based
on the squadron's current 6.4 percent loss rate and after
some angry refiguring had thrown the slide rule away. Bean
had left the line to retrieve it, handling it gingerly and reading the cramped lines and numbers as though it might have
made a mistake and could be coaxed out of it.

"He was flying low squadron in the low group," Bean
said. "The guy who wrote me we both knew in school. He
said before it went up, the wing tanks were hit and were
spraying gas all over, that you could see it raining off behind
the plane."

Snowberry dotted his pad loudly and rapidly and made
a peppery trail away from his box plane. "If Piacenti hears
about this he'll never leave his bunk," he said.

Bryant felt some dull sadness for Bean but none for his
anonymous friend. He thought of the grim white-faced officer standing among the wreckage of *Lemon Drop* after it
had crashed, and his order, strident and unnecessary: Get
this cleaned up. A strong sense was growing in everyone that
the dead were just part of the mess.

"He was eighteen years old," Bean said. "Little older
than Gordon. Six months out of flying school."

"Would you cut it out?" Snowberry said murderously.

They sat quietly without speaking. While Bryant
watched, Bean dipped his fingers into the ashtray before
him, distractedly, looking off at something else, and brought
his fingertips, powdered and gray with ash, to his mouth.

When they pulled back the curtain on the mission board the
next morning, the red yarn ran to Paris, and an enlargement
of the target area was headed *Le Bourget.* Snowberry and

Bryant looked at each other immediately and understood. Le Bourget was where Lindbergh had landed after the solo Atlantic flight. Le Bourget had always been for the two of them part of the legend. It was as if they were going to bomb *The Spirit of St. Louis.*

They were going after the depots where reserve aircraft and crews were believed to be. Lewis didn't like it. "Fighters," he said in a low voice during the briefing. "Why are we going after fighters?" Bean sat beside him and registered nothing.

They would have fighter escort the whole trip, they were assured, P-47's all the way there and back. Enough Little Friends for a party.

Lewis murmured about fighter suppression as they filed out: Why were they using B-17's for fighter suppression? There *was* something strange about it: the operations map showed clear weather over most of western Europe, and there were plenty of more important targets spread in an arc across the map. Bombing airfields was not the most efficient use of heavy bombers. The crews didn't complain—the airfields were not as heavily defended, usually, as strategic targets.

"Just do your job, General," Snowberry said. "Nobody said it had to make sense. Let someone else run the war."

"Maybe they want to give us a rest," Bryant suggested.

"I think you hit it," Lewis said. "I'm worried about why."

In the jeep to the hardstand he added, "I don't think it's for what we did. I think it's for what we're gonna do."

In the dark and cold plane Bryant swung experimentally on the sling seat in the turret and eyed the turret canopy critically. He wished he'd overseen the day's cleaning of the Plexiglas; now it was too dark. Gabriel asked over the interphone with some sarcasm if he'd like to be a part of this morning's pre-flight systems check.

They waited two hours for the ceiling to lift so they

might have a safer assembly and finally went off just at dawn, a vivid orange band beneath a purple one behind the darkened and backlit horizon. The Plexiglas surfaces of the ships ahead of them in taxi position glowed with the colors.

They hooked up with a reassuringly large flight of olive green razorback Thunderbolts—as far as Bryant could tell, there were more escorts than bombers—and the gunners joyfully called in each P-47 flight as it slipped into place until they felt they were approaching Paris cocooned in Air Support.

The Thunderbolts positioned themselves above the formations and wove lazy-S patterns to maintain contact with the slower Fortresses. No one in *Paper Doll* saw enemy fighters until the formation made its wide turn out of the echeloned vees into the column of groups that formed the long train for the bombing run. The higher squadron swung in alongside *Paper Doll* and in the process, in a rare instance in which the purest chance crystallized like a well-laid plan, they trapped inside their newly formed defensive box a hapless lone Messerschmitt Me-110 that had magically appeared at three o'clock low just outside Piacenti's window. The unhappy Messerschmitt flew level between them for a long moment. The pilot was gazing over at Bryant like someone about to get it in an old Mack Sennett short. His fuselage was dark gray with a white nose, with what looked like a little green fanged worm on the cowling. And then all hell broke loose, Bryant and Piacenti and Snowberry together hosing the fighter with tracers as the other planes around them opened up as well, the tracer lines converging from all directions like a starburst in reverse. The 110 seemed to stop and rear in mid-air, and pieces flew off like bits of confetti. It turned a baby blue underside to *Paper Doll* and then three tracer streams converged dazzlingly on the same point, like a mirror catching sunlight, and it disintegrated and flew backward out of the formation in a rain of shapes.

Smoke from the guns of the formation all around him trailed back from the bombers in satisfying streams.

"God, that was great," Snowberry said over the interphone.

"That's the best, that's amazing, to get them like that," Piacenti said. Bryant was trembling and overheated. He fired his guns out into space, overwhelmed by how intense the gratification had been, the physical pleasure detached from emotion, from any thought of the absurdly forlorn Mack Sennett face in the canopy before they had let fly. He watched the bombs rain down over Le Bourget, on Lindy's head, and felt as though a part of him were killed off, and had no regrets. They burst yellow and white in the rapid streams of the bombing pattern and the smoke bloomed and spread like stirred-up muck in pond water. "Bye, bye, Bourget," Snowberry said over the interphone, for Bryant's benefit. "Hope the *St. Louis* was off at a dispersal site."

Lewis reported a perfect bombing pattern, and added as an item of interest that somebody's bombs had torn the wings off a fighter attempting to climb beneath them. On the flight home they had maintained perfect formation, the spread of graceful Fortresses ahead and above him beautiful against the sky, and the Thunderbolts had swooped and looped around them after they had cleared the coast, celebrating with their own near-animal grace the ease and success of the day.

There was a minor celebration after debriefing, with Cokes and watery Scotch that Cooper and Gabriel had stashed away. There had been no announcement but already there were signs of another mission the next day, which was supposed to mean no drinking. After their triumph they interpreted that as a little drinking, confined to the afternoon. Gabriel announced to the assembled crew that Snowberry, Bryant, and Piacenti had each been awarded a third of a kill for the Messerschmitt and proposed a toast now that *Paper*

Doll had been officially baptized. Now that the Luftwaffe has felt the sting of our anger, he added wryly. They drank the Scotch and Coke and poured water over each other's heads. It was only late afternoon and the minute amount of Scotch allotted Bryant made him woozy. It tasted like the metal cup.

"I've got an announcement," Gabriel said. "Thanks to the selfless bravery of Tech Sergeant Gordon L. Snowberry, Jr.—"

"L?" Snowberry said. He was rapidly finishing a loose pile of sketches.

"—L. Snowberry, Jr., we were able to obtain gun camera footage of *Paper Doll*'s historic kill today."

Bean looked at Bryant. Gun cameras were altogether glamorous gizmos reserved exclusively for fighter pilots. The notion of *Paper Doll*'s gunners employing gun cameras was akin to the idea of their jousting over aerodromes with the Red Baron or Max Immelmann.

"Gather round. Somebody hit the lights."

It was a sunny midafternoon and they were sitting around crates outside the day room. The crew gathered closer and Snowberry stood before them with his pile of sketches at chest level. On the first was a number 5 ringed with a geometric pattern like a cue number on a film leader. The men laughed.

Snowberry began to flip the pages, rapidly dropping them to his feet, and as the other numbers appeared the crew chanted the countdown, as they did before base movies: 4. 3. 2. 1. The first sketch appeared, a few lines suggesting a B-17 with an oversized tail. The men cheered. The next showed the formation. The next showed a ball turret. The next showed the same ball turret, from a slightly different angle. The men hooted and complained.

The drawings began to change more quickly as Snowberry developed dexterity with the flipping, and the B-17 began to bank—though there was some argument in the au-

dience as to whether it was in fact banking or whether a
wing was falling off—and the Messerschmitt appeared, to a
huge cheer. A close-up of the canopy revealed a fierce-look-
ing Nazi with an eye patch, a dueling scar, and jagged teeth,
and the crew hissed and booed. Across his fuselage were a
string of tiny bull's-eyes that an arrow and tag helpfully
identified as "37 Downed Brit Bombers." In the next drawing the Messerschmitt was approaching the viewer head on,
guns blazing in sunlight-like rays. In the next, *Paper Doll*
was viewed from the beam, with stick figures in the dorsal
and waist windows firing.

"That's Bryant. I could tell by the shape of the head,"
Willis Eddy called.

"And Piacenti 'cause his hands aren't on the guns,"
Lambert Ball said.

More sketches of the firing, the tracer streams double-
dotted lines. Bryant's and Piacenti's guns were missing high.
Snowberry's belly turret, now visible, was firing right into
the cockpit.

A big explosion, a swastikaed tail flying outward with
lines of force.

A final drawing, over which was superimposed THE
END: a cartoon Snowberry curled inside the ball, winking,
holding up an okay sign.

The men booed and threw gear. It did seem to Bryant
as though morale had picked up.

"You gotta be kidding," Lewis called. "I think the only
thing you hit was the Fort opposite."

"Hey, you see the curve in some of these?" Snowberry
rustled around at his feet for the appropriate drawings. "I
got off some classic, classic deflection bursts."

"Hey, the only thing you know about deflection shooting is that you can't do it," Lewis said.

Gabriel had a fat new cigar in his mouth, unlit, and he
grinned around it at them like a proud father.

"Get a load of Billy Mitchell, there," Hirsch said quietly from Bryant's left.

"Gabriel's all right," Lewis answered. Gabriel was hearing again from Piacenti how the Messerschmitt had just appeared, as if out of nowhere. "He's starting to turn into one of those beady-eyed sons of bitches who absolutely hold the course, the kind of guy you want up there. And this movie thing with Snowberry was a good idea. We could use some loosening up."

Lewis stood and suggested a game of Gordon Pong, and over Snowberry's protestations the idea was enthusiastically endorsed by the rest of the crew. Four crates were stacked two on two as a net and Snowberry was caught and dragged to one side. After some rules debate, it was decided that he would not be allowed to bounce once on the receiving team's side.

He kicked and squirmed too much—it was hard to maintain a good throwing grip—so they sat on him and tied his arms and feet. The officers agreed to play, and it was Bryant, Piacenti, Lewis, and Ball against Gabriel, Cooper, Hirsch, and Eddy. The gunners against the ninety-day wonders, as Lewis put it. Bean refused to play.

On the first toss Snowberry shrieked, so it was decided to gag him as well. After a few more tosses the best tactics revealed themselves to be: on the receiving end, spread out and close to the body as it flew over the crates; on the throwing end, try to produce a spin which would overload one end of the opposite line and defeat attempts at a good solid grasp. After one throw from the officers that just cleared the crates—Lewis called net ball but was argued out of it—Bryant commented to the group on the sheer terror in Gordon's eyes, and recommended a blindfold, both as a mercy measure and further elimination of distractions. It was agreed to, and Bean gave up a sock to that purpose when no one was able to produce a handkerchief.

The officers were ahead 3 to 0—they scored when any

part of Snowberry touched the ground as the gunners caught
him, tallying on two real rib-thumpers and a cheapie can of
corn when a limp foot touched—when Lewis abruptly announced Refreshment Break. He poured a bit of Scotch from
an abandoned cup into his Coke bottle and took a slug.
Behind him in a tin lid used as an ashtray Piacenti laid a
CO_2 cartridge atop Gabriel's now-lit cigar and everybody
ducked. The cartridge exploded in a rain of tobacco leaf and
the concussion knocked Lewis forward onto his knees. He
got to his feet grimly amid the laughter, spattered with the
dark bits of cigar and Coke, and shook his head. "I'll have
another, barkeep," he said. "In a clean glass." Complaining
of ringing in his ears, he ended the game prematurely. He
and Bryant sat beside Bean while Piacenti and Ball labori-
ously began to untie Snowberry, who was again showing
signs of life. Lewis offered his Coke and Bean shrugged it off.

"I hate to see a grown man dry," Lewis said.

Snowberry was helping them now with his feet. "You
guys," he said with diffused menace. "You guys."

"What a stand-up bunch of personnel, huh, Bean?"
Lewis said. "Even when the going gets tough, there's still
time for horseplay."

The victorious officers had left. Snowberry pouted
where he lay, rubbing his hip. There were tears in Bean's
eyes.

"I don't know what I'm *doing* here," he said. "What
am I *doing* here?"

Bryant patted his shoulder. Lewis said, "You don't have
to figure it out. Like today. All you have to do is turn on the
Brownings and let them figure it out."

Piacenti had started the jeep and was waving them over.
Gabriel wanted another photo. Piacenti leaned on the horn,
and revved the engine.

"I guess it's my buddy," Bean said. "I guess I haven't
gotten over him."

"He's dead and you're not," Lewis said.

"I feel bad," Bean said.

"Feel good," Lewis said.

"He told me if anything happened to tell his girlfriend the real story," Bean said. "I think about that."

"I think about home, takeoff, assembly, their fighters, our escort," Lewis said. "Flak."

They helped Bean to his feet, and climbed aboard the jeep. At the plane Gabriel arranged them as he had before. Snowberry said, "Why don't you make little white marks on the fuselage over our heads so you can see how much we've grown?" For the photographer, though, he joined with everyone else in pointing to the newly painted iron cross on the nose, and holding up one finger.

Tuliese told them what they had already heard, from a pal of the departed Gus Fleener: the operation the following day was going to be big and unusual. "Unusual" in this case had clearly sinister connotations. Bryant suspected Berlin, and was both excited and panicked. He imagined the Providence *Journal* headline: LOCAL GUNNER A HERO IN HISTORIC FIRST RAID ON NAZI CAPITAL. He had once asked Lewis, Imagine your name in a headline back home? Lewis had responded, Imagine your name on a list in the back of the paper?

Leaves and training courses, they knew, had been postponed. The last few missions had been, Lewis claimed now to understand, morale builders—short and easy with few or no losses. By the time they'd finished chow, there were all sorts of signs that supported the rumors: the beautiful and clear skies, which in the new iconography of the bomber crews meant Danger and Impending Missions; the heavy coming and going at Operations, including a buck-up visit, it appeared, from some major brass; fleets of extra petrol bowsers and bomb trolleys. Spare planes were wheeled to the dispersals alongside the combat-ready ones. Crew lists were displayed an hour after dinner, which struck them as formal and unusual and ominous. Everyone feasible was on the list, including the very newest crews. Lewis joked grimly as he read it that he'd found the names of three of the base dogs, including Audie. They were just to sit around and wait. It was suggested they retire around eight-thirty or nine o'clock. There were hints that roust-up would be earlier than usual.

They sat in the barracks playing cards. They were going to sit and wait for three hours to go to bed, and the theatricality of the unusual preparations made the waiting much more difficult. Hirsch had come out, pale, from a navigators' early evening briefing, and had not answered questions. He had gone straight to another building with an oilskin packet and could be seen through the window, bent over the pool of light on his desk, scratching long rows of figures with his pencil. Guys from *Archangel* and *Cathy Says* told the same story: navigators all over the base shaken and isolated.

Bean was signing his underwear. They found him crosshatching lines on a small pile of laundry and he explained that that was what he was doing.

"What do you think, you're going off to camp, Harold?" Piacenti asked.

"Maybe I am," Bean said, and Bryant understood he meant prison camp.

For a moment he was back in nature camp in Connecticut, with Snowberry sick on Mello Rolls and Bean miserable without his parents. Bean was signing his underwear for prison camp, or as an identification aid (Lewis in talking about antiaircraft casualties had once in his presence made reference to "flak stew"), or because it was a reassuring ritual and maybe he thought the extra bit of caution would help ensure his safety, a gesture of faith in a world that rewarded Preparation and Conscientiousness.

"Maybe you should write your buddy's girl, if you're gonna write her, Bean," Lewis said. "You know. Tonight."

Bean held up a pair by the waistband—GEANT H. BEAN, U.S.AR—Bryant read. Bean's undershorts were strangely oversized and he looked diapered in them. Snowberry called them his Sagbag Underwear. Lewis liked to suggest Bean was hoping he'd grow into them. "I already wrote her," Bean said. "I had to tell her everything I knew."

"Must've been humiliating," Lewis muttered from his bunk.

Snowberry shook Bryant's arm, and leaned close. "I can't sit here," he said quietly. "Let's get out. Let's go down to The Hoops. Some of the other guys're down there. We'll call the girls."

"The girls?" Bryant asked. The idea sounded as bizarre as calling his parents. "They won't be able to come down."

"Willya *try?*" Snowberry said. He was bobbing from foot to foot. "They can try, can't they? We got at least two hours."

Bryant debated for too long and Snowberry whirled and stalked out, and Bryant got up and followed. At the door he looked back. Piacenti picked up a card and eyed it, tantalizing Ball. Bean folded underwear. Lewis lay with his hands behind his head, eyes on the ceiling. God, he thought as he trotted to catch Snowberry, *Ball*. What do I know about *Ball?*

Base preparations over the entire area depressed them further and they were happy to get out onto the lane to the village, away from the activity. Hundreds of Wright-Cyclones were being run up and tuned by ground crews and the result was a wavering roar like an immense child's first tentative attempts at a musical instrument. The sound was cooler and quieter in the lane, a distant racket from another world. As they walked they heard running feet and Colin and his silent friend Keir from the base party caught up to them, and wished them a good evening.

Snowberry quickened his step, and the boys accelerated in little bursts to keep up.

"It's quite busy this evening, isn't it, Sergeant?" Colin said.

"Yes it is," Bryant answered. Ahead of him Snowberry was pulling away and he tried to modulate his speed to keep the group together.

"We understand you need to keep secret about it," the boy said.

"I guess we do," Bryant said. "How have you been?"

"Quite well, thank you. Do you remember Keir?"

"Never forget a face. Or a rider."

The boys were quiet, Keir embarrassed or shy. "Are you off on a walk?" Colin finally asked.

Snowberry came to a stop and turned on them, so that Bryant almost fell over him. "Look, kid," he said. "We're on a secret mission. We got a big day tomorrow. We're not running tours. We're not giving interviews. Comprendo?"

"Gordon," Bryant said.

"Oh for Christ's sake," Snowberry said. "I'll meet you there." He left.

Colin stood as if struck. Keir edged away, flushed, unable to look up.

"Colin, Sergeant Snowberry's got a lot on his mind," Bryant said. He crouched and rubbed his hand in the dirt. It was just his luck that this would have to happen now.

Colin said, "I understand."

Bryant patted his pockets, but there was no chocolate or gum.

"We don't want anything, Sergeant," Colin said. "We don't want anything." Keir had already turned and was attempting to drift away.

"Well, what is it?" Bryant found himself asking with some exasperation. "What is it you want from us?"

Colin pulled further away. "We don't want anything," he repeated.

Bryant stood, angry with his dirty hands, angry that he was alone and Colin was alone on this lane. "I don't know what you want from me, you know?" he said. "I'm not your father. I'm not a war hero. I don't even know what I'm doing here."

Colin backed toward Keir, who had already started for home in mortification.

"We don't want anything, Sergeant," he said. It sounded like a rebuke. "We wanted to wish you luck. We wanted to see you."

Bryant turned from them and started walking. He turned back. Colin had taken Keir's hand and was looking back at him. "Why are you out at this time of night?" Bryant shouted. "Isn't your mother worried? Why isn't anyone taking care of you?"

The boys remained where they were, holding hands, gazing at him, and were still there when he glanced back once more before the curve of the lane pulled them out of sight behind a hedgerow.

He sat fidgety and uncomfortable at a table near a window in The Hoops while Snowberry drummed tunelessly with his little finger and thumb on the table top. Snowberry had reached Jean, and whatever he had told her, she had agreed to come. Robin was coming as well. Bryant wondered irritably how melodramatic Snowberry had been. Snowberry wasn't smiling or crooning. He was all business. He'd opened one of his condom packages and was snapping it back and forth between his fingers like a rubber band. He'd gotten them each a beer and they were either too nervous to drink or were waiting for the girls.

Snowberry stopped drumming. He rubbed his eyes with his balled fists and Bryant felt as if he was keeping a younger brother up. Snowberry widened his eyes comically to regain focus and said, "Are you thinking of proposing to Robin?"

Bryant stared at him, and shook his head. "This was your idea."

Snowberry shrugged. "I just figured," he said.

The girls arrived forty-five minutes later. The beers remained untouched. Bryant had spent his time musing on the convexity of the surface of the beer in the glass. Snowberry had gazed off toward the bar. Their spirits had deteriorated further.

"How long have you been waiting?" Robin said after they'd crossed to the table. "We were able to get a lift in an officer's car. Very nice young man, who claimed to be a war correspondent." She offered her hand and he squeezed it. Jean gave Snowberry a kiss on the cheek and he looked at her morosely.

"Are you keeping up with your drawing?" Robin asked him.

"No," Snowberry said. To mitigate the rudeness he added, "Are you?"

Robin shook her head. It occurred to Bryant that the girls didn't have beers, but he was unable for the moment to generate the sociability necessary to volunteer to get more. The two beers sat between them like curios they were jointly examining.

"Is it going to be so very bad tomorrow?" Jean asked.

"No," Snowberry said. "There's a lot of big talk, though. Bryant here is excitable. Me, I've got no worries."

Jean appropriated Snowberry's untouched beer and took a sip.

Robin said, "Is anyone going to offer to buy us drinks?" and Snowberry seemed to come to himself, but instead of rising moved Bryant's glass in front of her.

"Well," Robin said quietly, looking between them, and placed her hands on the table.

"What I miss is reading," Snowberry said. "I used to read a lot."

Jean agreed. "A number of us have been exchanging books," she said. "People are reading everything and anything."

Bryant nodded and no one carried the conversation forward.

"I saw a wonderful bit scratched on the wall of the loo here," Jean said. "Did I tell you? It said, 'Good girls go to heaven. Bad girls go everywhere.' "

When the boys didn't laugh, Robin said "Well" again and shifted in her chair, and Bryant understood that what had been anxiety and sympathy was turning into frustration and resentment. He sat up, smiled ruefully for them both. "Well, heck," he said. "If it is a big deal, we'll probably all come back officers. That's the Air Corps. Everyone moves up."

"That's right," Jean said. "I expect you two will be running things before too long. Especially our young Gordon. In two years he has a chance to be quite an officer, that's my guess."

Gordon said, "In two years I have a chance to be nineteen."

They were silent. He rarely mentioned his age; never around the girls.

He added: "Like Billy Conn used to say—I got my whole past ahead of me."

"Billy Conn," Bryant explained, "is a boxer Harold Bean's always talking about."

"Well," Robin repeated, this time cheerfully, "I suggest we either all go for a walk, or call it a night. What do you say?"

Bryant was grateful for the idea. He was finding Snowberry oppressive, though he was behaving the same way. And he did feel that this was an opportunity to transmit something of how he felt to Robin.

They walked hand in hand. A few steps ahead Jean stopped to kiss Snowberry, and they passed them.

They sat beside a low stone wall. On the opposite side of the lane a cow gazed at them, scratching its chin in slow strokes on a wire gate. They heard a convoy of fuel bowsers coming from a long way off, and didn't speak until they had passed. No one driving the trucks understood gear shifting and one by one they rounded the corner and ground noisily up the slight hill.

"What a nice image for things right now," Robin said. "These cows with their mild eyes watching all this Yank bustle."

Bryant suggested quietly that she might draw it.

She leaned his head closer with her hand. Her hair smelled of fir needles. "Oh, I'm not much use with lorries and big machines," she said. "A lot of clank and precious few beautiful lines."

He imagined her rushing to get dressed, hurrying into the night with almost no notice. "I'm sorry I've been jerky," he said. "Thanks for coming out like this. I guess I'm just scared I'll let everyone down. Scared I really don't belong here, that nobody realizes that."

It was dark. The shine on his boots interested him. Robin stroked his arm and tried to reassure him. As she spoke he grew less sure of himself, less sure of his ability to perform.

They could make out Snowberry and Jean thirty or so yards down the lane.

"Is Gordon all right?" Robin asked.

"He and Bean," Bryant said. "They're unhappy."

"Just the two of them?"

He shrugged and made an amused sound with his tongue on his palate. "We all are."

They sat in the dark and something twittered from a house eave behind them.

"I used to have dreams about you," she said. "I used to dream the war was over or everyone had quit or one thing or another and you were living here. In one you were a tax assessor, of all things."

He looked at her.

"Now I'm all dreamed out. They've stopped. That's

hat Janie had said, you know, from one of her letters to my
reat aunt: I'm all dreamed out. She wrote it late one night
t the cottage hospital." She sighed, and bit her little finger
ghtly. "I think at this point you need a child's faith," she
aid. "I don't think I have that. Gone with the lavender
ing, or something of that sort, I suppose."

They sat a bit longer. He had shifted to a cross-legged
osition and his foot was asleep.

"How fitting," she added, with some anger. "How fit-
ng, Bobby Bryant, that your aeroplane should be called the
ortress. Defended on all sides." She stood.

"What do you mean?" he asked, looking up at her in
ne dark.

"I mean I'm quite exhausted, thank you, trying to get
nrough to you, trying to get you to volunteer something. I
ame all the way down here, Bobby, and you sit there."
ryant stood, and shook his leg. It was not the best move.

"I say to myself, be patient with him, Robin, think of
is position, he's just a boy at any rate, how can you know
hat it feels like? But Bobby, is it really so very *hard?* Is it so
ard to be straightforward with me? To tell me how you
el?"

He felt himself becoming angry and half understood the
pportunity to avoid the question. He resented her the way
e resented Colin. He had never been happier anywhere
an he was with her, and he remained standing apart from
er, shaking a sleeping leg. She waited, and he didn't come
p with anything to say.

"Bobby Bryant," she said, and he knew how much he
ad hurt her. She touched her forearm with an open palm,
s if he had hurt her there. "I have to go."

Halfway to Snowberry and Jean she turned and said
ehemently, "You had better not get killed. Don't let me
ear that. You had better not get killed."

On THE WAY BACK DOWN THE LANE in the dark Snowberry with his hands thrust deep in his pockets golfed a stone twenty or thirty feet with a left-footed swipe and asked, "So what happened to you?"

"We had a little fight," Bryant said. "This has been some night."

"Big night before a big day," Snowberry said bitterly.

They walked on. Snowberry lined a rock off a postbox with another kick. He and Jean had not parted on the best of terms, either. "She said I was a spoiled brat," he said. "Just out of shorts, and that I wasn't going to give her the runaround. Then she turned on the waterworks."

"She's had some tough breaks," Bryant commented.

"Ah, God," he said. "Lewis warned me." He bent over to discover why a stone he'd kicked hadn't moved. "I shoulda known better. The thing is, she's great."

From somewhere around them a dog growled. They could see nothing but a few lights.

"I don't need that right now," Snowberry said. "I don't need a dog bite."

They waited, and then went quietly on. Bryant said "What do you think about Bean?"

Snowberry made a dismissive noise that sounded like spitting. "Don't you get it yet?" he said. "It's all of us." Down one of the turnoffs a horn blared and wavered. "Lewis is right. We're *not ready* for this. There's something big tomorrow now, and we're not ready. We were taking that picture today and falling all over ourselves for downing that poor sorry bastard and it hit me: What are we ready for? What happens when we run into a shitstorm? On the run to Kassel they went through our formations like shit through a goose. I never even got my guns on them."

"You sound like Lewis," Bryant said. The conversion was not reassuring.

Snowberry snorted. "You should start thinking for yourself, and stop worrying about who sounds like who. How long has he been trying to tell us all this stuff?"

Bryant resisted the notion that Snowberry had reached a level of awareness that he had not. "I don't see it that way," he said stubbornly. "I don't think we did so bad at Kassel."

"Oh, yeah. Well. You didn't even make it that far. Kayoed by the oxygen mask."

"Don't be a little asshole," Bryant said. The "little" was a measure of how wounded he had been by Snowberry's crack about the mask. "What good does it do to talk like that?"

"Look at this hand," Snowberry said. Bryant couldn't see it in the dark. "Christ."

"Oh, God, let it be a milk run," Snowberry added, minutes later, in a small voice. "Oh, let it be a milk run."

He lay on his back and thought of his father.

It still seemed impossibly early. Somebody in the latrine was scrounging magazines from the trash drums. Lewis was where they had left him. Ball was asleep. Piacenti was playing solitaire, possibly; the cards were in unsteady rows beside him on the bed and Bryant could hear the faintest tapping as he laid one upon the other. Bryant had asked, on one of those interminable hunting trips when the plodding or the sun or the rain had finally angered him into courage, why he could never carry the gun, even when his father was obviously tired.

You can't carry the gun, his father had answered. You're a danger to yourself with a pointed stick.

The day he was to leave for the induction center, his mother had wrapped some pears and an apple together in a waxed-paper bundle for the train, and had urged him to say goodbye again to his father, waiting on the porch. His uncle Tom's final words to him had been an admonition not to

forget the following advice for getting by in the service: If
you can move it, pick it up. If you can't, paint it. If it moves
by itself, salute it. Jeez, Bryant had thought. Here I am going away to something like this and that's the best he can
do? His father had been facing away from the house, gazing
out over the clotheslines crowded with wash below.

"I should go if I'm going to be there by two-thirty,"
Bryant had said, thinking, Turn around. Tell me I'm doing
the right thing. Tell me you're proud of all this. An inverted
bright red shirt on the line waved, bye bye, bye bye.

"I've tried with you, Robert," his father had said.
"Your mother and I have tried. We hope you're doing the
right thing."

He remembered lying on a cot in Florida with all those
mosquitoes, thinking, You son of a bitch. If I ever get famous I'm gonna claim to be an orphan. He groaned aloud.

"Easy, trooper," Lewis said from the opposite bunk.
"Save your energy."

He hadn't been good enough for his father. He hadn't
been good enough to fly. He hadn't been good enough to
make bombardier, or navigator. He was an aerial gunner,
and a flight engineer, and no one thought he could hit a barn
at six feet and Tuliese didn't trust him near the engines. He
tried to calm himself with images of his own competence
and grew frustrated. He tried to see himself again pouring
fire into the hapless Messerschmitt they'd shot down, and
saw instead the elusive lines of the others flashing through
the formations, defeating easily the fastest manipulations of
the turrets. He saw the cartwheeling *Lemon Drop,* with that
poor schmoe's foot, and the Fortress from the Hamburg mission sailing into the hill. He lay under the sheets covered
with sweat and dreaded the moment Lewis would notice his
terror.

After a while he sat up. His feet hurt. His head
pounded. The hut was darker and the sweat smell was sti-
fling. Nearly everyone was awake. He could tell by the

breathing. A little army of insomniacs, all listening, waiting, paying close attention to the night. He got off his bunk and started to walk and a voice said, "Watch the glasses, bub." He headed for an upright shape on Lewis's bunk. It turned out to be Snowberry.

Lewis was lying as he had been hours ago, hands behind his head. It seemed to Bryant a feat of some sort.

Snowberry whispered, "Somebody can't sleep," and Lewis grunted. Bryant slowly crouched beside the bed. They were quiet, and he felt like an intruder.

He became aware of another sound, a quiet and asthmatic sort of sniffing. Snowberry's head was turned from both of them and he was crying.

Lewis wasn't saying anything. Bryant was at a complete loss. He grimaced when he felt his own mouth trembling. Snowberry stopped for stretches, and swallowed, or made little *tsking* sounds with his tongue on his teeth. He did not rub his eyes or nose. Lewis seemed to be helping, though he didn't move.

When Bryant's knees hurt enough, he stood. Snowberry was still turned away. He crossed quietly to his bunk and climbed back into it, pulling the sheet up to his chin, remembering his grandmother in the doorway. He did not look back over at Snowberry and Lewis. He stared at the ceiling of the hut, which rippled in the darkness. He thought, *tomorrow is just another mission,* and, *you need to sleep,* and he closed his eyes to the ripples and to calm himself thought of Audie sitting blind and imperturbable in the Plexiglas nose while Ciervanski took her picture.

Someone hit the lights and he came out of what seemed a daze thinking something was wrong. He squinted and opened his eyes to slits and his watch said 1:15 a.m. All around him men were groaning and cursing. Snowberry was sitting upright already, blinking painfully. Lewis said, "Oh

my God," at the extent of his fatigue and the inhumanity of
the hour.

With a refined touch of cruelty the orderly on wake-up
duty read the bomb group's timetable instead of repeating
up-and-at-'em exhortations: breakfast, 0200; briefing, 0300;
stations, 0515; alert, 0530; taxi, 0540; takeoff, 0550. "0550,
gentlemen," he repeated. "Let's go." He wasn't going. He
would be filling out forms and loafing around the day room
for the next twelve hours while they did God knew what.
Men swung without looking when he shook their covers,
and near the door a gunner stood and shoved him with such
force he cleared a bed and landed on his back. He lay
stunned and winded with his arms and legs in the air like a
baby's. His breath returned with the sounds a long-distance
runner makes.

"Hey," he said, scrambling to his feet, alert for a general uprising. "Hey." He was used to verbal abuse, and his
voice registered his acute sense of the unfairness of physical
abuse. He negotiated his way to the door and turned, a hand
on the frame. "Stay in bed. See if I care. I hope they break
all of you." He turned off the lights and left, affecting triumph, but everyone was up.

They dressed. Bryant had saved for this mission a fresh
pair of long underwear. The idea was to have something to
absorb the pre-takeoff sweat before reaching altitude and the
paralyzing cold. The hope was that the wait before takeoff
would be short, to minimize the soaking the underwear had
to absorb.

Bean was powdering his feet. Bryant borrowed some of
the powder without asking. He pulled on his beat-up GI
shoes. That was the prevailing wisdom: in case of hard luck,
something comfortable enough to walk miles in, and dirty
enough not to arouse suspicion.

Bean and Lewis, Snowberry and Ball were all without
discussion putting on their best Class A uniforms—olive
drab, pressed and folded wool—beneath their flying suits.

Ball carefully straightened a leg and his pants fell as if new,
creaseless, to the shoetops. Bean was straightening his cuffs
with a special slow care. Even Lewis was working on his tie,
struggling slightly with the knot: none of them held any
hope that this would be a normal mission, and they were not
going to be killed or captured in the worn General Issue they
usually wore.

At breakfast the coffee kept coming, and was served in
thick white mugs that were pleasing to handle and drink
from. Every cook in the squadron was on duty, and they
were asking the men in line how each wanted his eggs done.
There was ham and corned beef hash and bread and a little
butter. They sat before their trays staring at the excess in
wonder and fear. The place was packed with crews, including guys they recognized who had to have arrived within the
last week, some of whom looked younger than Snowberry.
Bryant thought: Suppose we're in formation next to some of
these guys?

Ball was evidently thinking the same thing. He said,
"Man, if we're incompetent, what does that make *them?*"

Everyone was talking about Berlin. Bryant was able to
eat all of his hash and none of the eggs. Beside him Lewis
and Snowberry ate without speaking. Bean sat before his
plate and did not move. Piacenti drank three mugs of coffee
and went back for more.

In the briefing room there were not enough seats, and men
were leaning against the walls. One young staff sergeant who
looked as if he were wearing his father's jacket sat on the
floor next to the door, his eyes half closed and his mouth
ajar. The extra people crowded toward the front, peering
closely at the sheet covering the mission board in an attempt
to see through it.

"The pulley," Snowberry said. They were squeezed into
the second row. The pulley was near the top. All the yarn
had been used. They looked at the bare metal spindle with

the hope there had been some mistake. "Christ, where're they sending us?" Lewis asked. "Arabia?"

It took some time to get everyone quiet enough to begin. "I know a guy," Lewis said wistfully, "flew fifty missions, two whole tours, and never fired a shot."

The Ops captain stepped up to the sheet. He put a hand on it and looked at them.

"Can you imagine milking something like this?" Snowberry said under his breath. If they could have killed the Ops captain at that moment, they would have.

The sheet was pulled back. The red yarn went all the way through Germany nearly to the Austrian border.

The room was in total shock. The Ops captain who'd pulled the sheet stood quietly beside it, hands clasped, and leaned forward and gazed at it again, as if wondering if the silence were due to an empty board.

The room exploded. There were protests and loud exclamations. One group was booing. Everyone was shouting questions. Bryant sat silently and thought, What idiot dreamed this up? Lewis said clearly through the noise, "Look at the map. Their entire fighter strength has to be within eighty-five miles of that course. How many fucking fighters do you think that is?"

Snowberry was white. "How can we go that far without fighter escort?" he asked.

It took five minutes to calm everyone down. The briefing continued.

"*Schwein*furt," Snowberry said. "I've never *heard* of it."

A major whom Bryant hadn't seen before centered himself beside the screen, eclipsing the captain. "The primary targets," he said, lowering his volume as the crews quieted, "are the three major ball-bearing factories at Schweinfurt."

Bryant and Bean looked at one another. What was next? Zipper factories?

"Bomber Command tells us that this is the most important target ever attached by aircraft. This is the big deal, gentlemen, as you can see."

He pointed to the board, as if there were something further to emphasize. "Now this is a revolutionary way of employing the strategic bomber, and you men are the first to be a part of it; we will mount a sustained attack against one especially vital industry, rather than spreading ourselves thin over a number of targets. Schweinfurt is what we call a bottleneck target, gentlemen. Nazi fighters—and a whole hell of a lot of other things in Germany—run on ball bearings. Hundreds of ball bearings, thousands in one plane alone. Seventy-six percent of those ball bearings, seventy-six percent of all the bearings in Germany, come from Schweinfurt. Get Schweinfurt and you get seventy-six percent of the bearings that make the Focke Wulfs and Messerschmitts go. I suspect that that is an item of personal interest to you men."

"Ha, ha," someone said from the back of the room.

The major continued.

"There will be, simultaneously, a mission against the Messerschmitt factory at Regensburg." He pointed.

"Probably the second most important target ever attacked," Piacenti whispered.

"The second most important target ever attacked by aircraft," the major said. A sheet was pulled back from a second smaller board and the Regensburg mission was outlined. The men stared. The number of planes now involved in this joint mission was staggering.

"The Messerschmitt factory produces some three hundred fighters a month, a full thirty percent of the total. The idea, gentlemen, is to break the Luftwaffe fighter arm. To break it for you men, and to break it in preparation for the planned invasion of Europe." He paused. "I don't think I'm giving too much away to tell you men that," he said.

"Couldn't we just keep going after airfields, like Le Bourget?" Piacenti asked quietly.

The screen came down. They were shown photo blow-ups. They were given details of the three targets. The impossible German names for the factories they shortened to KGF, VKF 1, and VKF 2. They learned that *Kugel* meant spherical in German.

They felt worse receiving elaborate explanations. It seemed un-military and un-Army for their commanding officers to be so willing to confide in them. They did not expect to know precisely why they went on missions. There was not going to be a vote. They nursed the possibility that they went on some of the missions because somebody somewhere simply felt like sending them. The major spoke again of the critical concentration of ball bearings.

"We got 'em by the *colones,*" Piacenti said.

"Have you ever heard such dog shit in all your life?" Lewis said. "After we do this, all the machines stop. Germany surrenders."

But they were incompletely focused on the importance of the targets. What most interested them was the length of yarn line. Their fighter escort range, drawn in an arc through the Netherlands with a blue pen, covered a forlorn fifth of the distance.

The line-up of formations and squadron positions was still concealed. It made a great deal of difference in the defensive boxes whether they were in the center, or on the leading or trailing edges, where the heaviest casualties were.

The crews were waiting for that unveiling. They had quieted and sat in orderly rows and everyone behind Bryant looked too young. The crew of *Murder, Inc.* had that stenciled over their left front pockets. Bryant was reminded of a school assembly.

One of the *Murder, Inc.* gunners, a skinny Polish guy named Skink or Strink or something like that, caught Bryant's eyes with his own. "It just goes to show you," he said, across the intervening row, "how important the little ball bearing is to our mechanized world."

Bryant stared at him a moment longer, and turned back around.

"Who *is* that guy?" Lewis asked.

"Now we'll talk about the opposition," the major said.

He pointed to concentrations of black X's—their symbols for German airfields—lining the yarn route, little visible manifestations of bad news. "Men, we're going to be straight with you. There's no hiding the fact that these raids are going to be hazardous."

"That's why you're going to be straight with us," Snowberry said audibly and bitterly.

"Mission planners have been able, as you can see, to choose routes avoiding the worst of the flak areas, and both targets have never been attacked before, so they're believed to be lightly defended." He indicated the blank spaces at the bottom of the map surrounding Regensburg and Schweinfurt. "In addition, Bomber Command has planned diversionary raids on German airfields at Bryas, Lille, and Poix, and the railway yards at Dunkirk and Calais. We've never even flown this far into Germany before, so they're obviously going to be surprised." His pointer stopped and tapped along the yarn up near the Dutch border. "The problem is that fighters are obviously going to be the danger of the day. I'm not going to mince words. We're going to be flying through the most heavily defended sectors of the German Air Defense and deep into their homeland."

"Oh, mince, mince," someone said.

"And the length of the mission prevents any elaborate zigzagging or avoidance of these areas."

"Some fucking colonel thought this one up," Lewis breathed. "Some fucking desk-bound colonel of a bastard."

"The Regensburg force is not coming back. They are going on to temporary airfields in North Africa. We, on the other hand, are going to turn around, and come back through those same defenses." The crews were noisy with anxiety again. "The expectation is," the major said, getting

louder, "that the Regensburg people, going through before
us, will catch most of it going in. And that we'll catch all of
it going out."

The men sat. This was worse than they could have
imagined. Bryant absorbed the information that followed
with less than perfect concentration.

"We'll be routed through that part of the German
fighter belt with the greatest density of units, all capable of
immediate or near-immediate response." Snowberry bit his
lip and winced. The sound carried. "Now the German units
likely to come into action first will be the *Gruppen* of
Jagdeschwader 1 and *JG 26* stationed in Holland and northern France. There's also evidence of the recent movement of
units into this area—*JG 2* and *JG 11.*There's further evidence that *JG 3* was pulled recently from the Russian front.
We haven't been able to locate it." Bryant swept his hair
back with both hands, both palms. "Now we should expect
trouble from these airfields: Woensdrecht. München-
Gladbach. Deelen. Leeuwarden, and Schiphol. We believe
they won't be at full strength, and we believe they won't be
well coordinated. They'll use up valuable flying time, besides, trying to establish a height advantage and an up-sun
position for attack. Gunners should be ready for the head-on
stuff, and the stuff out of the sun. And pilots remember: they
always look for the group with the loosest formation. They
look for the raggedy-ass guys. You fly like assholes and
they'll shoot you a few more."

He paused, and a few people coughed. "The toughest
opposition should be between here and here—the coast and
a point halfway to the target. After that, you should run into
only a few twin-engined jobs, night fighters pressed into day
work. It's hoped that the interior will be largely empty of
fighters."

Bryant and Lewis looked at one another in amazement.
"Sir?" someone asked. "Doesn't anybody *know?*"

"Intelligence is sketchy on that score," the major said. "All we have is our best guess."

Lewis was in the blackest despair. "Shithouse mouse," he said. "Look at that line. You know how many *Gruppen* that has to be? Every Kraut in the West has to have a shot at us. We're going to fly over everyone but the Red Baron."

"Now there's plenty of fighter support, as far as that goes," the major said. "Eight Spitfire squadrons from the RAF will take us as far as Antwerp and then turn us over to two P-47 groups that'll take us all the way to Eupen."

"All that way," Lewis muttered. "Isn't that a big deal."

"They'll pick us up around Eupen on the return. Questions?"

"What're you worried about?" Piacenti whispered to Lewis. "We get fighter escort the whole way. Ours all the way to Eupen and theirs all the rest of the way." Lewis snorted.

The room was quiet. The entire row of gunners ahead of Bryant had their arms crossed, and their heads sunk down into the fur collars of their jackets.

The major looked through his notes. "Because of the importance of the strike, we've ordered a maximum effort. That means whatever individual extra planes are available will be added to existing formations whenever possible. The availability status for the 1st Bombardment Wing, including our group, is 238 Forts. We're planning on sending 231 of those." The crews gave a surprised "whoa!" "And using the other seven as 'air spares' to replace those aircraft forced to turn back early on with mechanical problems."

The formation and squadron position charts were then unveiled. There was a roar of disapproval. Their group was in the lead low position of the formation, which meant the lowest part of the front of the giant arrowhead the twelve groups and 231 planes would form in the sky. Lead low and lead high, because of the head-on nature of the German interceptor strategies, were the coffin corners.

The crews gradually stopped making noise and sank into a profound depression. "As you can see, we drew a hard ride," the major said. He was clearly frustrated with the atmosphere. He continued with the route briefing, taking it in stages: from point A to point B, there were these things to consider. "Now from point E to point F," he said, "the force—"

"Them that's left," Skrink or Strink said behind Bryant.

A different weather officer took over, poor Stormy left in the wings, even more useless than usual. Whether he was on someone's shit list or this was just standard operating procedure for such a big mission, they didn't know.

"You guys'll recognize this," the new officer said, pointing to the weather chart. "A low pressure system went through Denmark last night and is heading north and east up the Baltic. An associated cold front is swinging eastward right across the map, north to south. That's why it's so foggy right now."

He hit the lights from a switch near the front and a projector beamed upon a screen to the left an oversimplified diagram of cumulus clouds piled layer upon layer. There were conflicting wind arrows with velocity figures aimed at one another and a series of temperature and visibility estimates at all possible flying altitudes. Hirsch scribbled everything down on a little white pad, though later they'd be picking up mimeographed summaries of all of this, and it looked less than helpful to begin with.

They were told that this mission would take place exactly one year after the first 8th Bomber Command mission, when twelve B-17's had made the run to a marshaling yard at Rouen. The information was intended to boost morale. The men clapped glumly.

They were given some final instructions: Fly their formations like it was a Presidential Review. Conserve ammo. Fill holes that appear in the formations as quickly as possi-

ble. Keep your guns loaded and stay alert all the way back—
remember the Ju88's. The major finished up with a joke
about Nazis slipping and sliding in droves for days after this
on scattered ball bearings. Ball smiled. Lewis said, "That's
the Nazis, boy. Kings of comedy."

They were given a final exhortation: If they were successful, what they had done would significantly shorten the
war. The briefing ended.

Bryant fell in behind Gabriel filing out. Gabriel touched
with his finger the small airplane representing their squadron on the squadron position chart, and traced a path closer
to the defensive box of the others, like a small boy attempting voodoo. They were on the far end of the low group, a
position they could safely term the worst draw of the worst
draw. Their major hope, as far as Bryant understood it, was
to minimize vulnerability by making sure the planes ahead
of them and in the center maintained a tight formation. If
the formation strung out, they would be left fat and inviting
and alone on the extreme edge of the "wheel," overworking
their engines to hold position with each formation turn of
two or three degrees.

Gabriel grabbed a guy ahead of him Bryant recognized
as the pilot of *Lucky Me!* and warned him about dragging
his ass this time. "You don't stay tight, I'm gonna go around
you," he said. "You remember that."

They filed by Stormy at the door and turned their
watches over to him. Hirsch kept his and a spare besides.
Stormy was visibly suffering. They understood he hurt but
found it difficult, considering their situation, to generate major league sympathy. Snowberry gave him a tight smile and
pumped his hand.

"I wish I could go instead of you guys," Stormy said.

"I'm with you," Snowberry said. Ball gave Stormy the
last watch and he slipped it into an open spot on his arm,
and ran his forefinger from wrist to elbow over watchbands.

"Boy, if we go down, Stormy's rich," Ball murmured, eyeing the arm over his shoulder.

"What're you, kidding?" Hirsch said. "Some of those watches, I think they came out of cereal boxes."

They picked up their exterior flight clothing, parachutes, and oxygen masks. They went to the armament shops to be issued their fifty-caliber guns. They looked their individual guns over with agitation, some breaking them down right there and reassembling them. Any jams or sticking, anything less than smooth operation, was cause for bitter arguments with the armorers. Bryant checked his on the canvas engine tarps the line crews had left on the grass beside the hardstand, remembering Favale and the Texas sun at Harlingen. There were fights of near-riot intensity over ammunition: everyone wanted as much as possible, to hell with conservation, and some crews were stealing from the next plane over if the other crew was late arriving. There were extra supplies coming by truck, they were assured, and it was up to the individual captains to decide how much extra weight to take on. Gabriel decided by one-man committee on ten thousand rounds per station, which they loaded in huge wooden boxes all over the plane, like haphazard cargo. Bryant had expected Lewis to argue passionately for limitless ammo, but he had not.

There was no point, he explained, when Bryant asked about it. They were watching the crew of the plane next to them skirmish with another crew further down the flight line over a box of ammo left under the tail. Someone was brandishing a piece of cable like a whip and it snapped and cracked authentically. The plane they were fighting beneath, it occurred to Bryant, was startling and incontrovertible proof of a maximum effort: a real lemon that had aborted every mission flown so far, and had never dropped bombs on its target. It had been renamed *No Way*. They had assumed before it had appeared next to them looking shaky and ready to go that it was to be cannibalized for spare parts.

"We got the 2,780 blues," Lewis said. He had apparently not finished with the topic of extra ammo; 2,780 was the number of gallons of fuel the B-17 held. "We got the fuel. We got the bombs. We got all this ammunition, we got the ten of us. Takeoff in that situation is a real interesting proposition. It's like I strap twenty-seven gallons of fuel to your ass, fill your pockets with lead sinkers, and ask you to jump that fence."

They watched Ball and Piacenti heft a box into the waist.

"No, I'm not gonna argue for more weight," Lewis said. There was a crash from within and Piacenti said, "Lift it! *Lift* it, for Chrissakes!"

"Imagine all the bullets that are going to Schweinfurt?" Bryant said.

"I know." Lewis headed for the hatch near the tail. "We may not hit any fighters, but we sure might knock a few cows silly."

According to Hirsch it was coming up on 5:15 a.m. Bryant climbed aboard and went through the flight engineer's panel with Tuliese, and then ran through his checks with Gabriel and Cooper. Finally there was nothing more to check, and Tuliese turned the plane reluctantly over to them and climbed out. Bryant could see him gazing back at *Paper Doll* like someone who'd left family heirlooms in the hands of vandals.

Ball and Lewis were up beside him, for no reason, it seemed, before going back to their stations. Ball hesitated at the catwalk over the bomb bay, waved, and held a thumbs-up signal. "I guess it's like it's in the hands of God, now," he called.

"God didn't pick Schweinfurt," Lewis said. Ball stopped halfway across the catwalk and knitted his brows to indicate he hadn't heard, and then his face brightened and he pretended he had, and he nodded.

"Idiot," Lewis muttered. He shook Bryant's hand. He

crossed the catwalk to the radio room and shook Bean's
hand. Bean removed his headphones for the occasion but
Lewis didn't say anything, and disappeared through the
door to the waist.

Bryant climbed into his turret sling for a quick test and
raised his head into the Plexiglas. The black guns and the
glass encased him like a pickle in a jar. He connected his
interphone. Cooper was already checking the stations over
it, and he gazed ahead at all the dark bustle. The clouds
were surprisingly thick and low; it was like being in a vast
room. He noticed without enjoyment the beauty of the lights
of the trucks and the tower spindling out and intersecting,
and the arrayed red and green lights of a runway full of
B-17's.

Willis Eddy seemed to be filing or sawing something up
in the nose, the sound coming rhythmically over the interphone as a background to his voice. "Anything's better than
a month of going after U-boat pens," he said. "The way I
figure it. Solid concrete."

"What are you doing?" Gabriel asked him. "What's
that noise?"

The noise stopped.

"0530," Hirsch announced.

The ceiling had lowered still more. North of the tower
the clouds were dropping and were now so low that the term
"ceiling" seemed a little foolish.

"This is *fog,*" Eddy called from the bombardier's perch.
"What're they talking about, no fog?"

"Stormy," Bryant lamented. "What happened?"

"It's always the weather nobody figures on," Gabriel
said. The lights all around them were reflecting in carnival-
like patterns on the cloud wall above. The grayness drifted
in to the point of easing *No Way* into a shadowy uncertainty
beside them.

"We can get up in this," Cooper said. "But I hate to
think about assembly."

"We try to assemble in this," Lewis said from back in the tail, "we're gonna have a few unplanned mergers."

"It just came over," Gabriel said. "We wait."

They piled out and sat or lay around the hardstand on excess equipment. Bryant sat on a coil of rope. Snowberry sat on a squat twelve-gallon drum of hydraulic fluid. Ball settled in Indian style against an empty fifty-caliber box and was eating his candy. Piacenti wagged a finger and warned him he'd wish he had it later.

Audie appeared out of the fog, nosing her way over. Bryant said, "Hey, Audie, where you been?" and the dog's tail wagged and she padded gingerly over to him. She lay down to wait with them, her muzzle tucked between her front paws. Bryant gave her one of his Baby Ruths. She chewed exaggeratedly, the caramel sticking to her molars.

Bean was down on his hands and knees as though he had lost something or was studying the surface of the hardstand. He threw up, bracing himself with his hands spread wide, and shuddering, and then made an effort to clean it up.

"National League," Snowberry said. His hands were together between his knees and he was looking out toward Bryant. "Goobers Bratcher. Chops Broskie. Played for the Cards and Braves. Skeeter Scalzi. The Giants. Bunions Zeider. Spinach Melillo, Inky Strange. Podgie Weihe. Yam Yaryan."

Bean rose and worked his way unsteadily down to the nose. He sat by himself.

"I think Bean asked that girl to marry him," Piacenti theorized.

Lewis was flicking small stones into the mess Bean had made. "That's one way to solve your problems. How do you know that?" They all gazed at Bean, a small Buddha out in the fog under the nose, crosslegged in his heavy jacket.

"He showed me. He gave her a ring I think he got at Woolworth's. Probably turn her whole arm green."

"Jeez," Ball said, wrapping the end of his Oh Henry! and repocketing it. "Married. Jeez."

They were silent. Someone slammed a hatch door violently way off in the fog.

"American League," Snowberry said. "Inch Gleich. Bootnose Hoffman. Whoops Creeden. Boob McNair. Ping Bodie."

"Ping Bodie," Lewis said. "I remember Ping Bodie. Somebody once asked him what it was like rooming with Babe Ruth. He said, 'I don't room with Babe Ruth. I room with his suitcase.' Ping Bodie."

Bryant gave Audie another pat and got up and went over to Bean. He sat beside him and Bean nodded and rubbed an eye with the back of his hand. Bryant wondered whether or not to congratulate him. Bean was looking out into the fog, concentrating on something. *"Habe,"* he said. *"Ich habe ein . . .* injury," he finally added. "I don't remember the word for injury."

"How you doing?" Bryant asked. "You all right?"

"Oh, I'm okay," Bean said. He sounded tired and sad. "I just hate this waiting."

"It stinks," Bryant agreed. "You know what Lewis is always saying—as long as it keeps happening quickly."

Bean seemed further discouraged and Bryant regretted bringing Lewis up.

"You know, in some way, this is just worse odds," Bean said. "We're all gonna die, you know, someday, and anything could happen. This is just worse odds."

"That's a good way of thinking about it," Bryant said quietly.

"Except it doesn't help," Bean said.

"I have some extra candy," Bryant said, although he didn't. "Want some?"

Bean shook his head. "You know, I don't really think about getting killed," he said. "I'm scared of getting hurt. I can imagine disappearing, or not being around anymore. But I don't want to feel it. Imagine how some of those guys felt?"

"A lot of guys say that," Bryant murmured. "Me, I worry about dying, too."

"The one thing I can't figure," Bean said, "through all of this, is why Lewis signed up to go through it again. Even Lewis."

Bryant thought about it. A jeep swept by, the mist soupy before its headlights. "He told me once he'd rather listen to us idiots talk about the war than the idiots back home," he offered. "So I guess he wasn't happy there." It sounded obvious and lame.

"One night he had this horrible dream," Bean said. "You know, like Snowberry has. We were alone in the hut, sacked out early. I woke him up. I asked him then. He said, 'Harold, it's a shithouse bind. You become a real American by fighting in another country.' Then he tried to go back to sleep."

"What'd he say after that?" Bryant said. "Was that it?"

"I said, 'So then what?'" Bean continued. "And he said, 'So then you lose that America.'"

Bryant looked back over his shoulder at Lewis. He was a ghostly form in the fog, part of the equipment he leaned against.

"Gabriel's come out," he said. "Something may be up." He stood.

"Let me know," Bean said. He continued to look off into the grayness. It was lightening, and closer to the ground visibility was better.

Back with the group Gabriel and Hirsch had more news. "It's postponed again," Gabriel said. "But we're still on station."

"What time is it?" Lewis asked.

"After six," Hirsch said. He returned to the plane with Gabriel. Tuliese had come back and was poking distractedly at the number four engine from below.

Lewis resumed what he had evidently been talking about. "They want to pull off a big one. They need to pull off a big one. Put up or shut up time. I think it's like they been comparing the losses to the accomplishments and we're not doing so good. Maybe this whole idea of bombing during the day is hanging on this."

"Maybe it should," Snowberry said.

"Maybe. I myself think the RAF have got it knocked, going at night. Everyone bombs a field and comes home happy."

"It's a helluva way to run a war, this daytime stuff," Piacenti said. "Shoot your way in, shoot your way out."

"That's the idea of the Fort to begin with." Lewis tapped his head ironically. "All it is is a fat-assed bird with a lot of guns all over it. Put all the guns together. That's the idea. Who needs fighter help?"

"Yeah," Snowberry said. "Who needs fighter help?"

"It's a shitty idea," Lewis said. "But they want to make it work. Someone wants to make it work. You telling me they wouldn't have come up with a long-range fighter by now if they had wanted to?"

They thought glumly about the Air Corps' neglect on that score. Snowberry was wearing his World's Fair button.

"This is Charge of the Light Brigade stuff, is what this is," Lewis added.

"Bean's doing German up there," Snowberry said. "I can hear him."

Lewis snorted. "At this point I just want to hit the ground alive. Let's start from there, and worry about *sprechen sie* later."

Tuliese had a panel off and was fiddling. They listened to the *click-click-click* of his spanner wrench. "They should cancel," Lewis said. "They have to cancel. The Regensburg people have to be running out of time. They have to get to Africa in daylight. I can't see how they can send us up in

this. We haven't exactly lived and breathed instrument flying."

Bryant reflected on the relative laxity of the base and
Lewis's anger at their free time and the base CO, the car
salesman from Pocatello. He understood this was what
Lewis's anger had meant. They were not ready for this. He
hoped the car salesman from Pocatello understood that and
passed the information along. They sat, and waited. Ball
finished the rest of his candy. Bean lay on his back under the
nose like someone wishing to be run over. The darkness was
completely gone now, and from moment to moment the
clouds inched a little higher in an irritating meteorological
tease.

There was another delay, to 0715. And then, while Bryant
was urinating off behind some oil drums, Piacenti tapped his
arm and told him of another delay, of nearly three and a half
hours.

Lewis was aghast when he got back to the plane, and tried to
get Gabriel to listen to him. *"Three and a half hours?"* he
was saying. "What about the Regensburg force? They
couldn't be waiting that long."

"I don't know," Gabriel finally snapped. "Who are you,
Bomber Command? Maybe they are waiting. Maybe they're
scrubbed and we're not."

"Sir, isn't there someone we could ask?" Lewis pleaded.
"Sir, do you under*stand?* If they went off, then the Germans
can catch them and rearm and refuel for us. Sir, *they can go
after us both* with everything they've got."

"Peeters, shut up," Gabriel said. "You're gonna have
everybody shitting their pants before we even take off."

Lewis stepped back and looked at him. "Yes sir, thank
you sir," he said. He sat down and put his hand in Bean's
old vomit. "I'll have more faith in the Army, sir."

Gabriel shook his head and walked away from him,

standing with arms folded where Bean was lying. Bryant said to Lewis, "That's the worst possible case you're talking about. Things aren't that bad."

"I'm beginning to catch on," Lewis said. His eyes were glittering. "I'm the one who gets to figure this all out, and then no one gets to listen."

They remained where they were. It was hot. Everything was ready and there was nothing to do. They hated the Army, hated the mission, hated the wait. At eleven o'clock Lewis announced they had now been up nearly ten fucking hours and they hadn't started the mission yet. They had been at the planes for almost six hours. No one around Bryant had spoken for two hours. Bryant was talking to himself in discrete little snippets of conversation. He had no idea how long he could wait like this, but he did know he was approaching some sort of limit.

The sky had cleared a good deal. They were perhaps waiting now for the more western bases to clear. No one mentioned the Regensburg force, and there were no official announcements on the subject. Most of their gear was strewn around them. A jeep arrived, and an officer climbed out and conferred off to the side with Gabriel. When they parted Gabriel, with a look of regret, waved them into the plane, and they stood and wrenched on their outer layers while the jeep tooled off. They climbed in in small groups, officers near the nose, gunners and radio operator through the waist. Bryant was the last aboard.

He sat on his sling and swayed like the boy on Snowberry's swing. The air was cooler. His neck prickled. The turret retained its factory smell of gasoline and leather and steel. It was too recently off the assembly line to have lost it, he understood, and it struck him how little time had been involved in all of this—sign up, show up, train, arrive in England, end up here, doing this. He shook himself, frightened all over again. While the first B-17's of the flight line ran up their engines, turning over the huge Wright Cyclones with a roar, he ran through his training manual's profile of the perfect gunner, reciting silently from memory: the perfect aerial gunner, when he was six, his father gave him a .22 and taught him to shoot it at a target. At nine, he was ranging the hills and woods near his home potting squirrels until the pointing of his rifle was as natural to him as the pointing of his finger. At twelve, he got his first shotgun and went quail hunting, duck hunting, grouse hunting, and learned the principle of leading a moving target. He learned instinctively that you do not fire at a moving target, since it will no longer be where it was, but ahead of it, and learned too that his gun is a deadly weapon, to be respected and cared for. When such a boy enters the Air Corps, he has a whole background of aerial gunnery in him before he starts, and he has only to learn the mechanism of the new weapon, and the principles of shooting down the enemy airplanes are exactly the same as those of shooting a duck. Such a boy, with such a background, makes the ideal aerial gunner.

He closed his eyes. His throat seemed constricted and he wondered if he was getting the mumps. He visualized Messerschmitts as tow targets, Focke Wulfs as fragile and static ducks.

A bird stood on the canopy of the dorsal gunner in *No Way,* to his right, feathering wingtip feathers slightly in the gathering slipstream from the plane's engines. Bryant thought, This must be the way it is before a stupid attack, when you know it's going to fail and it can't help but fail but you can't change it or run away; you can only be a part of it, and help it to fail.

Over on *No Way* the dorsal gunner was rotating his turret and elevating his guns to dislodge the bird, which turned slowly and imperturbably with the rotating canopy, the black fifty-caliber barrels flanking it in a paradox of power and impotence.

No Way WENT OFF AHEAD OF THEM, the huge tail swinging around like a monstrous and slow weathervane. Bryant
could see on the small blurred face of the tail gunner his
irritation at the danger and probable stupidity of all this. He
swiveled his guns at *Paper Doll* angrily, like the butt of a
joke, a man in a tiny car fitted with towering and foolish fins.

Bryant watched them go off tail-heavy and wallowing,
only slowly achieving any sort of grace, and then looked on
blankly as his own ship began the rush forward. The end of
the paved strip was happily vague in the fog but he could
feel when they had been on earth too long, and started
counting, and it seemed far too late when he felt the bump
and lift and sway of *Paper Doll* finally letting go and straining upward. The wings tilted and wobbled under the weight
and the trees marking the end of the base appeared and
rolled by beneath, and that gave way to undifferentiated
gray, and then they were climbing and banking to the right,
although he couldn't be sure. No one spoke. All four engines
sounded good. He watched for lights, for the black shapes of
other Forts, though by then it would be too late. The engines' pitch seemed changed and enclosed, a roar in a bath-
tub. The gray began to thin and strand and suddenly they
were out and into a brilliant blue, the sun flooding across his
canopy and the ship's upper surfaces, and all around him
was the awesome boys' war spectacle of the entire group's
B-17's rising from the cloud blanket, like a horizon of magically appearing good guys, all sweeping into the clear and
cold sunlight.

They were to form up as a squadron seven miles north
of the field. The earliest planes to arrive began circling at an
agreed-upon altitude and subsequent arrivals formed into
their three-plane vees and slipped into place to join the slow
wait. With the twelve-plane squadron finally assembled, they

began climbing to the south to find the larger group. Hirsch announced they were eleven minutes late.

The larger group was not where it was supposed to be. Bryant circled his glass dome, scanning the blue and finding nothing. Gabriel asked Hirsch peevishly if *they* were where they were supposed to be, and Hirsch, though he wasn't lead navigator, confirmed it testily. After the pre-takeoff wait the delay was particularly irritating.

They crisscrossed a good bit of England searching. With every change of direction there were groans over the interphone. Willis Eddy every so often asked Hirsch to identify various towns. Hirsch pointed out Peterborough and Oxford, and then stopped answering. A pond or lake below was a luminous light blue. Bryant imagined Robin seeing these colors, and missed her. Eddy speculated on the interphone as to the identities of subsequent villages until Gabriel told him to pickle it, and Cooper asked for some semblance of interphone discipline.

With the rest of their squadron they circled, scanning the horizon for the larger group.

"What's a silage?" Willis Eddy asked. His voice in Bryant's ear suggested a casual curiosity that made Bryant wish Eddy would lose consciousness until the bomb run. He lifted his earpiece away and cleaned an ear with his little finger, his glove under his arm, and resettled the earpiece.

"A *what?*" Gabriel was saying.

"A silage," Eddy said. The formation banked and they banked with it. The horizon lifted and swung and their starboard wing rose to the light. "S-I-L-A-G-E. Like on a farm."

"Jesus Christ," Gabriel said.

It's where they keep the animals at night," Lewis called in. "What's going on up there?"

"I thought that was a barn," Eddy murmured.

"Eddy, the next thing I hear out of you better have to

do with the bomb run," Gabriel said. "You keep interphone discipline like Gracie Allen."

"Jeez Louise," Eddy said. The interphone was silent.

No Way was not far off their port wingtip. Their dorsal gunner rotated slowly, as if satisfying himself the bird was gone. Bryant remembered the potato farms in Barrington he'd been taken to see, a Fourth of July he'd spent in Tiverton, hot and dusty and enjoying a sticky strawberry soda while a parade went by. Small parade by Providence standards, with dogs sprinting along the route barking at the bands. A barnstormer had been promised in a local field and had indeed shown up, but had spent all of Bryant's visit tinkering with an engine that seemed disappointingly small and ill-kept. *Mother of Jesus,* the barnstormer kept saying in exasperation. Afterwards Bryant's father had sardonically commented on the miracle of the airplane, although his uncle Tom had been more enthusiastic later when Bryant had reported on the trip. The barnstormer's machine had resembled the biplane he'd seen disintegrate as a small child and he'd come away impressed with the flying machine as an amazingly complex assemblage of interdependent elements, all capable of failure. That any of them flew and returned their pilots to earth safely he found a notion to marvel at. He'd started studying engines not long after that. He hadn't been very good—"Just *watch,*" he remembered his father saying more than once, like Favale, like Tuliese—but he had been dogged.

Despite the radio silence imposed on him, Eddy was the first to call in the larger formation of Fortresses, turning like slow birds off to the north at an unexpectedly high altitude. They climbed to rendezvous, and in a group slipped into their position as lead low squadron.

There was something matter-of-fact about the spectacle, having to do with the bland impossibility of the sheer numbers of planes. Above and behind him B-17's extended into the sky with the dazzling and fraudulent abundance of replicating images in facing mirrors.

He could see Bean amidships peering upward out of the radio operator's oval window. Bean saw him and waved and pointed. He realized with awe that the bomber stream extended farther back than they could see.

"I guess the theory is, the Germans just don't have this many cannon shells," Lewis said finally, from the tail.

Bryant adjusted his mask and thought again, unhappily, about the brevity of his training—who was to replace who as formations of this size got thinned out or broke down? did anybody really know?—and swiveled his turret to face forward. His mask was wet. His toes were ominously cold. It was August. In September of the previous year he had first set foot in an airplane of any kind.

He swayed on his sling, squeezing his oxygen hose every so often as a hedge against ice buildup. He felt the cold through the sheepskin and felt the hollowness and fragility of the airplane carrying them. He thought of Lewis, whispering to Snowberry during the night in an effort to calm him, the words frightening Bryant, at least, still more. All we have is that thin metal can. We can't run and we can't hide. We just do our job and do right by our buddies and tighten up our ass and pull our knees in and hope for the best.

The leading aircraft of the 231-plane formation left the English coast at a little promontory of Suffolk that Hirsch identified in passing as Orford Ness. Snowberry repeated the name with distaste from the ball turret below and then was silent. They were over water at 1:17, just about two hours after takeoff. Hirsch called it in. Bryant thought of Stormy with all those watches. They left landfall at 14,000 feet and climbing, in a bomber stream sixty miles long and drawing closer together. The sea crossing was scheduled to take thirty-five minutes.

"Where's Der Bingle?" Lewis asked about halfway across. "Don't we get Der Bingle anymore?"

There was no answer from the ball.

"Oxygen check," Cooper said. "Ball turret?"

"Ball turret," Snowberry said. "Okay."

Cooper reeled through the others, Bryant included. They rode on grimly. Bryant switched off his interphone. " 'I'm going to buy a Paper Doll that I can call my own,' " he sang softly, " 'A doll that other fellows cannot steal.' " Around him the force was closing up. He could see the smoke and the shuddering from the planes to his right as they tested their guns. The racketing started on their ship and he shook in his sling when the ball and waist guns let go. He charged and cleared his own, aimed off into space, and squeezed the triggers, the roar shaking him and the tracer lines corkscrewing down and away. The waist and tail were firing, he could feel. Eddy and Hirsch up front on their single fifties. He smelled the cordite through the mask, the pungency tainting the cool oxygen. Fireworks. He flashed back on cans blowing into the air, cats shocked by porch to porch lobs. The smaller smoke bursts from the other planes' guns trailed backward as lesser echoes of the enlarging contrail streams, all of the lines unfurling behind, striating the sky. The sight gave him the proud and uneasy sense that the whole attack, the whole formation, was indifferent to stealth or surprise, and was serenely intended to overwhelm the air defenses that lay ahead.

In their shallow elements of three the wingmen floated slightly above and behind their element leaders, trying to keep wingtips level with the leader's waist gun positions. *Paper Doll* was an element leader, flanked by *No Way* and *Archangel*. Above them in a vee were *Geezil II, Leave Me Home,* and *Dog Star.* Immediately behind them were *Quarterback, Lucky Me!,* and *Boom Town. Plum Seed* flew between them as a loose egg, a spare. Element leaders maintained formation by keeping watch on squadron leaders, squadron leaders on group leaders, group leaders on combat wing leaders. There was, Bryant assumed, an extensive chain of succession worked out, in the event of what the CO called unexpected visits with the Glass Mountain.

Gabriel was correcting their course with the most discreet calibrations, the adjustments rippling through the following planes. He was flying well, and Bryant appreciated it. If the lead planes flew erratically, they forced a constant seesawing of position, with the ships sliding and sideslipping to hold their distances, which exhausted pilots and gave everyone else shortened breath, as well as shaking out the formation into a pattern too loose for adequate defense.

They did their share of weaving, but Bryant imagined the strain on Cooper and Gabriel, hauling their heavy plane around for hours with their hands and feet, and marveled at their endurance and ability. *No Way* and *Archangel* stuck right to them. Everyone was good. They were going to get through this.

They began the serious looking, for their escorts, for interceptors. Bryant divided the sky into eighths and searched each with something he hoped was methodical precision from horizon to azimuth. A scratch on the Plexiglas between the guns kept him occupied for minutes. His eyes hurt and rebelled at focusing and refocusing on nothing and his concentration waned and returned.

They turned a few degrees and he permitted himself a look down, at blue waves, the threads of whitecaps, a tiny boat. Eddy called out the Dutch coast landfall ahead and through the haze of the distance the edged pale green emerged, resolving itself as they drummed nearer into three large islands near wide river estuaries gleaming in the sun. He saw drifting motes which had to be shipping. One of the islands reminded him of Florida.

"Fighters, fighters, fighters," someone shouted. It was Piacenti.

"Escort," Lewis said. "Escort, sir. Three o'clock low."

"Jesus," Gabriel said. "Piacenti, you know?"

"Sorry, sir," Piacenti said.

A group of them swept by in two diamond formations, green and brown Spitfires with their red, white, and blue rondelles flashing underwing. The crew cheered. They waggled their wings as they passed and climbed up and away from them, seeking altitude and a station well ahead of the bomber stream. The American P-47's remained closer when escorting. The Brits believed it more useful to break up attacking German formations at a greater distance. The crews liked to see fighters nearby, and preferred the American strategy.

"Fighters! Fighters!" Eddy called, but Bryant could see nothing. A moment later a Spitfire flashed back past them, chasing something.

"Something's wrong with *No Way!*" Piacenti called. "They got fire in the number two and three—"

Right beside him *No Way* was battered and smashed across its cockpit, the windshield shattered and the two inboard engines feathered and flaming. The co-pilot climbed out his window while Bryant watched, a guy named Pease who Bryant remembered hated the powdered eggs, and he waved his arms in the slipstream as if to deflect it. He let go and hit the horizontal stabilizer on the tail, and tumbled away.

"Jesus God," Gabriel said. "What happened? Anybody see it?"

No Way nosed smoothly up with the inboards still flaming and then sideslipped like a leaf and turned over. They could see the tail gunner trying to get out and through the smoke he did, the chute blooming open. The gunners started calling together, a chant, get out, get out, get out, and while they watched two waist gunners and someone else cleared. A wing separated at the root near the fire and trailed away, easy as a veil, and it began spiraling. Bryant lost it as it fell away behind them. Lewis and Snowberry called out another chute. When they banked he picked *No Way* up again, fluttering toward some rolling hills. A slope rose to meet it and it exploded, the thousands of pieces filling the air like silver dust.

At Antwerp the Spitfires heeled about and flew back the other way, having waited as long as possible for the P-47's to show up and carry on the escort. The P-47's did not show up. Some of the Thunderbolts assigned to the rear of the formation arrived, Lewis was able to report, but there was no sign of the groups charged with their protection at the front of the stream. They waited and searched and cursed. Piacenti suggested from the waist that they were all back in their bunks, having sex with each other and farm animals.

They flew over dark green forests dotted with red and white farms and silver and blue lakes. There were a series of small villages forming a loose chain along tan roads. The sky was piercingly clear. There were no Thunderbolts. To the right a cluster of the gray and tan lanes converged on a town.

"Eupen," Hirsch announced. Bryant felt his forehead cool and could see the planes in the formation above and behind them edging closer together, closing up the box. He swiveled his guns to the front and ran his gloved hands over the charger assemblies to reassure himself. He kept his turret moving from side to side, metronomically, to keep the fluid warm for smoother tracking. He could feel his fingertips and palms.

"I know what I hate about this so much," Snowberry said over the interphone. They could hear him charging his guns. "No one is ever glad to see us."

"There they go," Lewis called. Bryant twisted around in his sling. The Thunderbolts in the rear were peeling off, their wings flashing sunlight, their fuel already exhausted.

Gabriel's voice was constricted and the interphone buzzed and popped. He said, "It won't be long. Call 'em out."

"Here they come," Eddy said. "Here they come."

Bryant picked them out as well, miles away, hundreds of insects rising in the heat. From all around them in a crescent to the south the flattened specks were lifting off the pale landscape and wheeling toward them, and Bryant and everyone else swung their guns around like talismans. They floated higher, spreading across the sky.

"Ladies and gentlemen," Piacenti said over the interphone. "The shit is about to officially hit the fan."

THE ENGINES THROTTLED SLIGHTLY BACK, Gabriel slowing speed to allow the following planes to pack it in and close the formation further. *Plum Seed* slipped into *No Way*'s slot and together with *Archangel* swung close enough to hit with a rock. The specks grew larger and Bryant recognized the fatter noses of the Focke Wulfs. Someone said, "Here they come." There was a chorus in Bryant's ears over the interphone: Here they come.

They were above the bombers now, and swinging out in rows in a descending arc toward the leading elements of the stream, their formations perfect, coming on in groups of five, wingtip to wingtip.

Bryant called them in as they flashed through the upper groups, giving the numbers, reeling off line after line as they passed through firing. Eddy mentioned that the higher groups seemed to be getting the worst of it, and the sixth line to disengage dropped lower, and came for them.

Gabriel was shouting reminders on the interphone as they closed distance and everything accelerated, and he began slewing the plane slightly to the left and right in formation to present a more difficult target. He was warning Snowberry and Bryant at the same time to be alert, telling Eddy in the nose to call the break, down or up, to let everyone know instantly whether they'd decided to sweep over or under *Paper Doll*'s vee. They grew like nightmares because of the combined closing speeds of the head-on attack, hold-

ing fire as they swelled in Bryant's Plexiglas vision: no move,
no flickers or razoring lines of light, just the configurations
from the aircraft identification charts on a collision course.
He urinated, pissing the fear out, he hoped. His thighs
warmed and then cooled and he felt the wet on his calves.
He chose the central Focke Wulf and it grew and shook in
his gunsight, the canopy glittering and malignant like the
eye of an insect. He started firing and the plane shook and
his tracers spiraled outward at the line, and Eddy and
Hirsch started firing, and the wings of the fighters flashed
and threw light, their tracers expanding magically and ra-
diating past as if *Paper Doll* were flying into a garden sprin-
kler, and his own guns were drowned out by the high-
pitched hammering of their pass, all of them skidding side-
ways as they roared by, firing in short bursts, and were gone.

"Hits?" Gabriel yelled. "Any hits? Everybody okay?"

Another line had detached ahead. "Twelve o'clock!
Twelve o'clock!" Eddy was calling.

"Bryant! Bryant! Bandits coming down on you twelve
o'clock!" Hirsch shouted. Someone else cut in about another
bandit at ten o'clock.

The Focke Wulfs were growing in a line of seven with
wing roots and noses winking light at him as they closed.
They shot through the vee ahead and above them, firing all
the while, and the intensity of the head-on attack was such
that Bryant could see the entire vee ahead go sloppy, and
Eddy screamed, "Breaking high! Breaking high!", and there
was a white flash on the top corner of the cockpit over
Cooper's seat and the Focke Wulfs broke over them, still
firing, the center plane rolling and sweeping over their nose
upside down, filling the sky over Bryant's dome, shaking
him and all of *Paper Doll* with the enormous air compres-
sion, the German's eyes in the Focke Wulf's black cockpit
flashing into Bryant's, the oddly shaped goggles and brown
leather mask distinct and shocking. Then it was gone.

"Jesus Christ," Bryant said hoarsely. The cockpit metal

ahead of him and to the right was twisted upward where the white flash had been, and a thin wire trailed back in the slipstream. He could feel the cold now, coming over the co-pilot's seat onto his legs.

"Cooper's okay," Gabriel said in response to someone's question. "He's a little shook up. They enlarged his view."

"Did anybody see that son of a bitch who just came over?" Lewis asked from the tail. "I think his wingtip hit my guns on the way by."

Behind *Archangel*, *Quarterback* was washing around in formation. Its upper turret was a red smear, cracked and jagged. One of the gun barrels stuck up at a bizarre angle. The flight engineer climbed out of the smashed shell like a bloody chick, dazed perhaps by the explosion. He held on and swayed, impossibly, against the force of the air. Bryant felt acutely their interchangeability. That was *Paper Doll,* this was *Quarterback*. Someone in *Quarterback* was trying to pull the gunner back in. The gunner held a finger into the battering slipstream like a man testing the wind and reached back for his parachute too late, as if remembering something, and was blown away behind them, out of sight.

"Who's that? Who's that?" Snowberry called. Bryant looked right and left and caught a column of smoke diagonally looping away beyond the tail.

"It's *Boom Town,*" Lewis called. "Charley Rice. Three out. Four."

Bryant remembered Hallet, fighting with him after the cat throw.

"Stop counting," Gabriel cut in. "They're coming around again."

Way off to their right the Germans were flying alongside, passing their formations easily, pulling ahead to come around in more head-on passes. Bryant watched them all stream by outside of the group's range, lining up like kids at the city pool to use the diving board, running along the edge after a dive to get back into the forming line.

They flew into the far distance and massed, wheeling, and a fraction detached, seven, and turned toward them. Others swept out at the higher squadrons.

The new group closed like the first without firing, sliding from side to side slightly as if they were projectiles out of control or a squadron of drunks, and Gabriel said, "Smart bastards, smart bastards," and Bryant understood from an earlier briefing that the sliding represented their keeping watch in case any of the bomb group's escort were still around, and knew then that these were veterans, old bomber killers, and felt himself wanting to urinate with nothing left and whipped his guns from one target to another, and at the very last moment they started firing, yellow and white lines looping past his turret like liquid light, and his tracer lines ratcheted out and too low and they roared overhead still in line, firing at the Forts behind. He skidded his turret around to the rear and fired short bursts but they were gone and pieces were flying from bombers way behind them in the stream.

Subsequent lines were sawing through the upper squadrons. A bit of debris with something fluttery on it went by his turret from above.

"Oh, God," Eddy was warning. In the distance Bryant could see below the massed fighters slow sprays of specks lifting off postage stamp airfields, new planes rising all along the corridor ahead.

"Look at them all!" Snowberry said. "Look at them all! There's a jillion of 'em!"

Lewis called in the lines that had gone through and were regrouping behind the formation. Piacenti called in the groups to the right passing them for another head-on attack. Snowberry and Eddy were trying to estimate the numbers ahead.

"Get off the goddamn interphone, everybody off the interphone," Cooper said. "It's like a Chinese fire drill."

They were momentarily silent, watching the filling sky.

Bryant could feel in the silence a dawning awareness on everyone's part that something had gone, and was going to go, very wrong.

"Glad to see you're still with us, Lootenant," Lewis finally said from the tail.

More lines of fighters were separating out toward them from the groups ahead. Bryant registered the formation above him closing up, filling the gaps left by the last passes, and he watched two lines of seven Focke Wulfs and Messerschmitts apiece bear down on them and felt keenly the isolation and helplessness of this kind of war, hanging there in his sling and aluminum capsule, as exposed, as far away from a place to hide his head, as anyone could be.

He could see growing to the left of center in his gunsight the narrower nose and longer wings of a Messerschmitt, the pale blue of the spanner visible even at this distance. The lines came on with the Focke Wulfs echeloned behind and above the Me-109's, and they all opened fire together. Bryant was reminded of plugging in the lights on a Christmas tree. He was hearing hits on *Paper Doll* and other rows of fighters were detaching from the mass and coming on, one after the other, and Bryant fired and fired, worrying now about overheating guns, trying hard to keep his bursts short. *Paper Doll* rocked back and bucked with all the forward firing guns going, the notion of ammo conservation gone forever.

The sky went white from a blinding flash and above him a Fort's tail flew upward alone from a huge fireball, the concussion shoving *Paper Doll* down and the explosion audible through their headphones.

The fighters went through ragged and uncertain, disconcerted by the light and the blast. The tail had fallen through the formation without producing a chute and there was nothing else left. Whoever they were, Eddy called, they musta taken a shell in the bomb bay.

Hirsch seemed the first to recover and was shouting in new lines.

"Get your nose up! Nose up!" Snowberry was calling in frustration. "Give me air!" He could see the oncoming fighters but couldn't fire, with *Paper Doll*'s nose above him too close to his aiming point. "Give me air!" Snowberry was calling and Bryant was firing and firing and the three-Fort vee in front of them went yellow and white and jerked upward and Bryant was blinded. He could feel the whole ship rock backward violently in the shockwave and when his vision returned with ghostly afterimage colors all three planes that had been flying in the vee ahead were gone. *Paper Doll* was wallowing stupidly along, nosing around for something to follow. Bryant could see the dorsal gunner in *Plum Seed* beside them with his hands on his head in a melodramatic gesture of shock and surprise.

"They're all gone!" Snowberry cried. "They're all gone! Where are they?"

"Christ amighty," Gabriel said. "All three of them just like that."

"What? What?" Lewis shouted. "What happened?" Bryant could imagine his frustration, as tail gunner in an endless series of head-on attacks.

"They got the whole element in front of us," he told him. "One swoop."

"Who was it? Who was it?" Lewis called. He had friends everywhere in the formation.

"*Banshee. I'se a Muggin'. Training Wheels,*" Gabriel said.

Lewis was silent. Eddy was screaming at his guns. Snowberry was crying and asking for air, a clear shot. He said Gabriel was an idiot and they were all going to get killed.

A beautiful and horrible diamond of fighters swam free ahead in a long loop and dropped deftly and in perfect order down toward them, resolving itself into a line staggered up-

ward in altitude, each following plane higher than the one
before it. The effect was that of an immense javelin or spear
coming through the formation. Bryant's arms hurt and his
eyes hurt and he tracked and sighted and fired with a furious
haste and effort as pass after pass became simply horrible
and intense work. The casing shells overflowed from the
huge metal chutes flanking his legs in the turret and rang
and clattered past his feet to the floor of the fuselage, spilling
further down the companionway to the hatchway door below to Eddy and Hirsch's stations.

There were further explosions from ahead and above,
and a man went spinning by his turret, a startled look on his
face, knees up as if executing something tricky off the high
board. A hatch door flipped by, and a flak helmet.

"Four o'clock!" Piacenti cried, "High!", but when he
looked there were no fighters up there but two B-17's inexplicably together, frozen in contact for a moment as they
collided, until they exploded in a long liquid tongue of fire,
wings and control surfaces spinning outward.

The fighters behind them were banking around to return. The fighters ahead were circling to gain altitude, a few
minutes away. Cooper called in a lightning oxygen check,
station by station. *Quarterback* beyond *Archangel* was
streaming gasoline from its number three engine, the sheets
of fuel fluttering into rain as they left the wing. Every so
often pieces flew from the shattered dorsal turret.

"Man," Piacenti said from the waist, evidently getting
an eyeful. *Quarterback* could not keep up. "We're a losin'
ticket," he said. Bryant flashed on Snowberry's journal and
its warning about Piacenti.

"Close up! Close up!" Gabriel was calling to
Quarterback's pilot. It drifted further back, and soon hung
distantly off *Archangel*'s tail, Lewis reporting as it slipped
still further back. From the belly Snowberry called in other
losses in a congested voice. *"WAAC Hunter,"* he said. *"Pad-
dlefoot."*

Bryant looked up and back into the main body of the formation. Prop wash from the massed planes was deflating and collapsing the small parachutes that were drifting downward. He watched one of the white ovals puff and fold and thought, *Survival is out of your hands.*

"More more more," Eddy said. "And my fucking gun is shot."

The fighters ahead seemed to have misjudged the necessary altitude and were hurrying down to them, having wasted precious fuel. There were limitless fighters, Bryant imagined. They were all going to go down, one by one. The question was really the order. They weren't going to get back. What he wanted at this point was to reach the target.

They came through in waves, steady lines, and in the chaos Bryant and Snowberry and Eddy and Hirsch and Piacenti and Ball and Bean and Lewis lectured and jabbered, shrieked and called out fighters, and hit almost nothing. Something nearby exploded with splintered pieces slashing outward, end over end. A Messerschmitt of a startling green appeared following a palisade of tracers to Bryant's left. A Focke Wulf came in from abeam and stalled, and falling away raked their belly, and he could feel the hits banging into them. "Son of a bitch!" Snowberry was screaming. "He was *right there!* Son of a *bitch!*" And they were gone.

"Comin' around," Piacenti called. Someone whimpered.

"They came a long way," Lewis observed. "I don't think they got too much juice left."

They came on loose, every man for himself, maybe without the fuel to form up, some from the side and even the rear, and Lewis finally had something to shoot at. A Messerschmitt sideslipped by upside down, shooting at *Archangel,* and above them in a higher squadron Bryant saw an engine torn off and tumbling backward, the Fortress wing folding and shearing away. While he was watching, something else—a Messerschmitt?—collided head on with another Fortress, half rolling into its nose and shattering pieces outward before both planes exploded and the belly turret and its mount fell away free like a small barbell or a baby's rattle.

He slewed his turret around and a Messerschmitt was on him in a quartering turn, the nose flashing, and the yellow dazzles of 20mm bursts walked toward his turret, one two three four five, banging the ship, and stopped, and the cowling and wingtip flashed by.

"Bryant!" Gabriel called.

"Bryant's hit!" Ball said. "I saw the guy go past."

"I'm okay," Bryant was able to say. He felt like a ventriloquist's dummy.

"Frankfurt! Frankfurt!" Hirsch was clicking the call button on the interphone in his excitement and it sounded like chattering teeth. To their left the sun showed silver and wide on two huge rivers, the Rhine and the Main. The whole formation was turning north and east toward the Initial Point.

The fighters were gone. Hirsch called in a time check. It had been more or less thirty minutes since Eupen. Bryant found that impossible to believe. Snowberry said, "You shoulda kept a better watch. You shoulda given that one to Stormy."

Behind them Lewis was counting chutes. Bryant said, "The top squadron in the lead high group is gone, near as I can tell. Completely."

"The 525th," Gabriel said.

Quarterback had drifted out of sight, straggling back beyond the rear group. In that direction they could see on the curve of the earth a series of small fires generating spiraled pillars of black and gray smoke. The sky between the pillars seemed filled with confetti and litter, the hundreds of white American and occasional pale yellow Luftwaffe parachutes mingling and floating down like a chaotic air-

borne invasion. A Fortress miles away caught fire and fell
from its vee, a quiet bundle in the sky.

"They're pruning," Snowberry said, and his words affected them all. "They're pruning the 8th Air Force."

Bryant remembered himself and checked the functioning of
the four engines on his flight engineer's panel, checking as
well the fuel transfer, in case Cooper and Gabriel had forgotten. His rear end hurt and he was glad to be out of the sling
seat. Hirsch announced they were passing over the IP and
after a beat Lewis asked what it was.

"Dink town," Hirsch said. "Gemünden, it's called."

"Just wanted to know," Lewis said. He sounded miserable.

Bryant debated whether or not to get back into his turret and decided against it, in case there was trouble with or
damage to the bomb bay doors. He'd hooked into a walk-
around oxygen bottle and the rubber of his mask was cool
and sloppy with sweat. He plugged in his interphone at the
flight engineer's panel.

"Now hit the target, you son of a bitch," he heard Gabriel say to Eddy.

It felt as if they were accelerating, though he knew that
wasn't the case, and he imagined the flat and featureless
landscape preceding Schweinfurt that he remembered from
the briefing, imagined the flak batteries minutes away with
infallible Nazis loading up and calibrating their elevations.

"What do we do if they're using smoke?" Gabriel
asked, more or less talking to himself.

The interphone crackled, and they could hear Eddy
hesitate. He said, "They told us that if the lead couldn't see
the aiming point, we'd go for the housing and try for some
skilled workers. We're gonna hit something, I'll tell you
that."

You better believe it, Bryant thought. The notion of
bombed civilians at this point did not concern him. People

down there were being blown up. People up here were being blown up. Everyone down there had something to do with the attempt on his life. He felt the sway and lift of short-term changes in direction, and knew the combat boxes were breaking up into their small component groups for the bomb run. The bombardiers of all following planes, Eddy included, would release on signal from the lead.

_ He could hear a distant thrumming and some faint booms. "Flak," Hirsch called in. "Looks like one seven triple zero. Which is our altitude. If anyone's wondering."

The ship jerked upward and Bryant banged his head. There was another shock and the musical sound of fragments splaying over the plane's metal skin. He was happy to be inside and closed in, happy to be unable to see the sky.

There was a huge boom and the plane bucked and reared upward and then mashed back to level flight.

"Guess they don't want us at their steel balls," Eddy murmured over the interphone. Bryant could hear his concentration.

"Everything's fine," Gabriel said. "Snowberry, did you see that burst?"

"It was purple and red in the center," Snowberry said. "I don't know how it missed me."

Gabriel was skidding the plane a few degrees every so often as a last attempt at evasive action before turning the plane over to Eddy. Bryant felt the torque and gravity shift in his feet on the metal floor. Eddy called in the takeover, and flew them on the Automatic Flight Control, making careful and minute adjustments. Bryant imagined him hunched over the Norden bombsight the way Robin hunched over her drawings, her lips bunching and pursing, her eyes shifting in concentration.

The rate of climb indicator on the far right of his panel began to flutter. He called in the information to Gabriel.

"Stay off the interphone," Gabriel said. "We're fine."

There was a creak and a growing roar and he felt from

his position at the panel the circular buffeting of the changing air pressure. Back through the companionway the center of the plane was filling with light, glared highlights curving around the black cylinders of the five-hundred-pound bombs. The bomb bay doors were grinding open and the noise from the blast of air was an environmental force that surrounded the particular and thin noises from his interphone. He looked down through the companionway and out into space and saw a golden and green landscape with low drifting white smoke crossing to the southeast, the beginnings of the defensive screen the town was pinning its hopes on. The sky below was pocked and dirtied with smallish flak bursts. There was glare beyond his vision and shrapnel tinkled on the open doors.

His interphone was unplugged and he had no warning of bombs away. They shifted and dropped from sight in a single spasmic load and the whole ship rose beneath him from the enormous loss of weight, the horizon through the bomb bay doors ducking and sweeping upward.

Below them the first salvoes were hitting and he could see each as a rapid series of flashing bursts turning dark red and then black as the smoke billowed and mushroomed like underwater murk.

He watched longer than he should have before climbing back into his turret and strapping himself in.

They were turning, flying in circles around the flak while they waited for the hundreds of B-17's following to bomb. Bryant was not a bomb jockey but he had the feeling that their bombing pattern had left a good deal to be desired. He plugged in his interphone cord.

Gabriel was telling them all to look. Bryant imagined him grabbing Cooper's arm, pointing to the bombing pattern. "Willis! Mr. Eddy!" he said. "What do you think? Are they nailed or are they nailed?"

"Hard to say, sir." Eddy was cautious. "*Some*body was way off. See all that stuff to the north?"

"I hope we got an orphanage," Lewis said from the back. "Kids with toys in their tiny hands."

They maintained a steep bank, Bryant's knees against a shell chute in the turret. "I don't think we hit anything," Eddy said glumly after a pause.

No one commented. Whatever had happened was no one person's fault and there were more than enough extenuating circumstances. "So much for pickle barrels," Piacenti commented.

Archangel was pulled in tight behind their starboard wing, and *Plum Seed* was drawing closer on the opposite side. The flak stopped abruptly, the sky sweeping clean ahead of them, signaling the onset of fighters, and through the charging of the guns Snowberry asked over the interphone in a small voice if they were going to be leaving anytime soon, and if so, when.

It became quiet. The flak had seemed harmless, defensive gestures the Germans only half meant but felt they should make. They flew north and west, for the Rhine. The plains gave way to hilly wooded areas dotted with orange and yellow.

"You guys should see the foliage," Snowberry said. "In August, yet." They could hear him rotating his belly turret.

Hirsch wondered aloud if they were exactly on course. Bryant knew that he considered himself privately to be the equal of the lead navigator. As far as Bryant understood, he was alone in that view.

"In my opinion," Bean ventured in a shaky voice, "this was an *extremely* difficult mission." He had been quiet so long Bryant for one had forgotten about him.

"Bryant," Gabriel said. "Eddy's gun."

Bryant pushed the interphone to Call, embarrassed. He had forgotten. "Eddy," he said. "Is it burned out?"

"It's just sticking." Eddy grunted. "Goddamn thing almost got me killed. I'm pointing it like it's a magic wand, like it's going to do something."

"You keep swiveling it around, even when it's out," Gabriel said. "You let it hang down and it's the dinner bell."

"I'm not stupid," Eddy said. His Gary Cooper voice had returned to maintain dignity but he sounded hurt.

"Try playing with the retainer on the solenoid," Bryant said. He waited.

"Yeah," Eddy finally said. "So what? Wait. Hirsch's got pliers."

"Make sure he keeps his gloves on," Gabriel said. "Or doesn't have them off for long."

"I think it's working," Eddy said. "Who'd a thought it?" Bryant was relieved and proud and thought, *Who's* not a good flight engineer?

"You know the force is split," Lewis reported from the back. "The second combat group has to be fifteen miles away."

"Maybe our group broke too soon," Gabriel said. "Maybe we got a chicken colonel."

Bryant turned his turret to the rear. The other group was a pattern of staggered dashes, just visible flying through intermittent cloud.

"Someday they may know what they're doing in this war," Lewis said. "Right now they have only the slightest fucking idea."

"Does anybody know how many we lost?" Lambert Ball asked. He, too, had been quiet.

"Everybody shut up," Gabriel said. "No more casualty lists. We got enough to worry about."

They could hear from the tail Lewis counting softly, the numbers just whispers, counting with the interphone on. Piacenti crawled to all the gun stations with a walk-around oxygen bottle, divvying up whatever ammo was left. Bryant showed him how to feed the coiled belt he'd brought into the turret, and when they were set, Piacenti made a circle with his thumb and forefinger and disappeared.

The front of the plane was silent. Eddy and Hirsch in the nose, Gabriel and Cooper in the cockpit, and Bryant on top were searching for fighters. Ahead of them lay the corridor of their losses on the way in, the fires still burning and visible beneath the columns of climbing black smoke. They passed into it.

"It's like training, in Florida," Eddy murmured. "Navigating by beacons at night."

They all recognized the similarity. "We could follow these home," Gabriel mused.

"This stinks," Snowberry said. "We shouldn't have to do this." The port wingtip brushed through one of the smoke columns. They seemed to be only creeping along, as if flying into a terrific headwind. Snowberry said, to himself, "I'm only seventeen years old." Someone asked testily why they were dragging their ass.

"Look at them all," Snowberry said. His voice was filled with regret.

"Keep watch ahead," Gabriel said.

Snowberry said, "You know, it's like you expect guys to get it. But not so many. Not everybody."

"We're comin' up on the Rhine," Hirsch announced.

Bryant turned his turret a final time to the rear, gazing back at the tall anvil of black smoke over Schweinfurt, now fifty—sixty?—miles back.

"Dots. Bandits. Fighters," Eddy called. The dots in the distance spread into even lines, and they knew they were in for it again. Bryant had gone back to believing he was going to get home, and here all these dots were, coming hard, to make sure he understood that that was not going to be the case.

The air around them started to fill with small detonations and flashes and tracer lines began to lariat by, and a B-17 above and to the right turned almost immediately and

plunged away out of sight, as if suddenly aerodynamic principles had failed it. The interphone was impossible with
chatter and in the chaos that followed all the o'clocks were
called out. A Messerschmitt spiraled by wing over fuselage,
tumbling out of control. He saw a B-17 upside down and
when he looked again it was gone. Something of a shining
aquamarine sailed past, striking the turret and leaving a
clouded white nick in the Plexiglas, like a distant cumulus.
He fired snarling into his mask, slewing his guns around
with the rage of a pestered animal, and shouting unintelligible things. There were hits all around him on *Paper Doll*'s
fuselage, hits like dropping bricks down the cellar stairs, or
pouring loads of stones into metal garbage cans. There was a
stream of incoherent jabbering and Ball broke in and said,
"That's Piacenti. Don't pay no attention to him."

   The air exploded over the right wing, an orange sheet of
flame. Bryant looked and there was fire buffeting from the
nacelle of the number three engine. What looked like water
or mercury was washing from the wing, and he realized as
the olive skin curled and withered that what he saw was the
aluminum itself, melting and spraying backward. He felt his
turret overheating and understood it was his imagination.
For all his fear he registered engine fire procedure, and he
thought: Rev up the rpm's. They accelerated, Gabriel a step
ahead of him, and the fire continued. Gabriel and Cooper
closed the cowl flaps and the fire went to blue and then thin
gray smoke, though the smoke kept coming. The propeller
feathered and stopped.

   "Fuel shut off," Bryant said to remind them. "Fire ex-
tinguisher valve."

   "Both," Gabriel said. "We appreciate the thought."

   He clambered down to his panel behind them to work
with Cooper transferring the fuel from the tank of the dead
engine, and scrambled back into the sling once Cooper had
confirmed his readings.

   He settled himself in and swiveled the guns and everything went white and the plane tipped and there was a whooshing vacuum of air and he felt as though he'd been hit across the ribs and arm with a metal pole. In another part of the ship there was a scooping, thunderous sound, and he felt the whole aircraft slide across to the right. He gazed at his right arm and hand and was vaguely aware of Gabriel trying to get through to him, and he could see nothing but the discreet mouth of a tear along the forearm of his jacket, but the pain beneath it fascinated him, immobilized him. He thought of acid poured along his arm, searing invisibly in a chemistry accident. There was a strange unreality to all of this, not having been touched despite all those close calls and then this violation out of nowhere, like the villain in a movie reaching into the seats to knock his teeth out.

He felt a tug on his leg and looked down to see Cooper, the worry evident in his eyes over the oxygen mask. Bryant smiled reassuringly, though Cooper couldn't see, and made a thumbs-up sign. It must have had the desired effect, because after a wary pause Cooper patted his knee and left. He focused on the interphone and said, "No problem."

Static popped when Cooper, back in the cockpit, plugged his interphone back in. "The turret all right?" he said. "It don't look like it."

He looked around himself, woozy and relaxed. The charging slides were smashed, as if someone had taken the edge of a shovel to them. The feed chutes were severed. Oil was jetting up delicately from somewhere and spattering like soft rain on the sheepskin of his collar. He had the unpleasant sense that his forearm was open, cold air on bone. His glove was sodden with blood and when he squeezed, it bubbled over his wrist. He thought, Will this be like the oxygen?, and was drunkenly proud of his courage in the face of his wound, and then said What? at Gabriel's shouts of bandits, bandits coming down from above.

"My guns're through," he said, as if wanting to get that clear.

"Goddamnit, *track* 'em!" Gabriel screamed. "They think we're dead meat." Hits banged along the side of the fuselage, a horse cantering on sheet metal. He understood, and swiveled the turret. A Focke Wulf was arching by and he tracked it across their beam, and then let it go, and picked up a looping Messerschmitt. Another went by overhead and he followed it easily. "Lots of kills," he said. "I got lots of kills."

"At least they're less ballsy now," he heard Cooper mutter. He tracked another, the outline shifting and slipping out of the cracked gunsight. He was scaring Germans, pretending to shoot, playing at war in the middle of war. Then the oil got worse and glazed his goggles, and he climbed tenderly out of his sling, nauseated from the smell and taste within his mask.

He recognized Hirsch in front of him on the walk-around bottle, his eyes peering at Bryant as if looking for something. Hirsch was making lowering motions with both hands, gesturing Bryant to the fuselage floor beside the turret base. Lightheaded, Bryant complied. His arm was raised and cold and Hirsch was picking at it with a jackknife. The jackknife seemed incongruous. Cooper appeared beside him and took over with the knife and hacked expertly up his sleeve, the sheepskin parting yellow and thick like whale blubber. Hirsch unzipped the first aid kit and held the sulfanilamide powder up for Bryant to see. He saw his arm exposed for the first time. The skin was whitish and sheared back and blood matted blackly around it, bright red here and there. Hirsch started sprinkling the powder, and Bryant watched as it crenelated the edge of the wound. They wrapped the arm in a temporary bandage, which felt cool and clean and kind. There was some hammering and Bryant was annoyed at the noise. Hirsch disappeared. Cooper nodded sternly and thumped his good shoulder and left as well. The plane rocked and stumbled.

His head cleared a little. He pushed the interphone button.

"Thanks, everybody," he said, stupidly. "I'm okay."

"If you're okay get back up in the fucking turret," Gabriel said. He sounded absolutely harassed. "Cooper says it's just your arm."

He struggled to his feet. "I'm up, Skipper, aye aye," he said.

The plane hit a wall and he catapulted into and off the panel before him, ending up on his side. They were diving. The floor rose up past him. There was a cannonade of frigid air, and things flew past him toward the bomb bay. He covered his head with his hands. He crawled around on his knees to the flight engineer's panel, and then they pulled out of the dive and he fell back onto the floor.

The interphone was skewed on his head and when he righted it, it was filled with panicked shouts and babble.

"Get me out of here! Get me *out!*" Snowberry was shrieking. Lewis was demanding to know what was happening. Gabriel was shouting Bryant's name. Bryant acknowledged. The airstream through his position was strong enough to lean against.

"Goddamnit! Get down to the nose!" Gabriel shouted. "Somebody get down to the nose!"

The plane was more or less level. Bryant hooked into the portable oxygen bottle and heard Gabriel tell Snowberry to keep his goddamn shirt on, for Chrissakes, nobody was going anywhere, before he unplugged the interphone and climbed cautiously down through the companionway.

It was much too bright. Just below Gabriel and Cooper's seat level there was nothing but space. The nose opened outward into air like a wide-mouthed chute, flapping wires and cables. The legs of Hirsch's seat remained in a grotesquely twisted bulkhead. His gun mount flapped backward. There was nothing in front of Bryant.

Hirsch's interphone outlet hung loose above his head.
He plugged in. It sparked and crackled.

"They're gone," he said.

"What do you mean, they're gone?" Gabriel said.
"Where'd they go?"

"They're gone," Bryant repeated.

"Jesus Christ, did they bail out? What?" Gabriel asked.

"The whole nose is gone," Bryant said.

Snowberry said, "Oh, no." Lewis cursed.

"Do you think they got out?" Gabriel demanded. "Is
there any blood?"

Bryant looked. It was impossible to tell. His hands and
feet were freezing. "I don't see any blood," he said.

"Their chutes?" Cooper tried. A fighter flashed by, bi-
zarrely close without the mediating Plexiglas. "Are their
chutes gone?" Bryant's eyes were tearing even behind the
goggles. Lewis and Snowberry were firing and Gabriel was
jerking the plane all over the sky.

"I'm coming down," Gabriel said. "Take over,
Cooper."

Bryant waited for him, suffering with the cold and edging out of the companionway both for his own protection
and so that his pilot might get a look. Near his foot was a
shattered rack for holding Hirsch's pencils. Gabriel crawled
down and mimed something Bryant couldn't understand.
He stared dumbly at his pilot until Gabriel in exasperation
poked into the companionway. When he returned, he gestured that everything in front was gone. Bryant gestured
that he knew that. Snowberry's guns were still going. Cooper
was shouting over the interphone, "Get back up here, you
guys, no one called time out here."

THE FUSELAGE BEHIND THEM ROCKED AND twanged like
a banjo, yawing to the left. Snowberry shrieked, the sound
blizzarding into static on the interphone, and didn't stop.
Get it away! it sounded like, *Get it away!*

Bryant was up onto the platform behind the pilots' seats
and through the passageway to the bomb bay catwalk,
squeezing past the narrow V-shaped support beams in his fat
flying jacket like a child desperate to get through some ban-
nisters. In the radio room Bean had climbed onto a box, an
ammo crate, to get better tracking angles for his gun out of
the slanted overhead window. He took off his mask in alarm
when he saw Bryant, his face painted with brass dust above
the mask line from the cartridges and so much firing. He
pointed at the bailout signal as if to indicate he hadn't seen it
and Bryant shook his head, and indicated Bean's walk-
around bottle and the hatchway to the waist. They stepped
through it, Bean following.

The waist was empty. Cold air was blasting through an
open hatch, and they hunched in the narrowed cylinder of
this tapered part of the fuselage and pointed for each other
at the escape door, which had been jettisoned. Piacenti's and
Ball's oxygen masks were still plugged in and hung floppy
and inverted along the wall, like bats.

He connected his interphone at Piacenti's station to tell
Gabriel, and Lewis already had, having called in their deser-
tion after the chutes had streamed out past him. Lewis was
still cursing and Bryant took the earpiece from his ear for a
moment. "Both of them?" Gabriel was asking.

Lewis said something about that filthy wop bastard and
his pal. Snowberry broke in in explosive bursts when his call
button could override Lewis's and gasped and made noises
impossible to interpret. Lewis said, "Bryant, are you checking on the kid?"

Bryant and Bean moved with peculiar and mechanical

quickness, shoulder to shoulder, the seals of their masks
trembling. They hunched over the ball turret and hand-
cranked it around to position the exit door inside the fuselage, and yanked it open. Blood sprinkled upward from the
change in pressure.

"He says he's gonna puke," Gabriel called. "Get his
mask off."

They pulled him out and he seemed to uncoil raggedly
from the tiny sphere. Bean was lifting weakly under his
shoulders and Bryant tore off Snowberry's mask, the vomit
looping and threading from his face. His head was moving
from side to side and he slapped at his thigh. His pant leg
was badly holed at the knee like a boy's old pair of jeans, and
beneath the dark and soaked edges of sheepskin the kneecap
slid free and flapped like the lining of a pocket.

Bryant felt his stomach rise and squeezed his hand over
his mask. Bean had not slowed and seemed to be systemati-
cally checking him. His left hand was smashed and the glove
was flat and mangled. Blood scattered in cold and coagulating droplets wherever he'd been, wherever he gestured. He
coughed and choked and brought his good hand to his
mouth to clear away the mess. Blood flecked and painted
Bean's goggles.

They stuffed a blanket between his head and the bulkhead and wrapped his feet in another. Blood dripped from
his nose and he looked childlike. He was whispering something and they both looked at his parachute, hacked by
shrapnel. He whispered and they understood it had to be.
Don't leave me here, and Bryant shook his head, twice, to
indicate they wouldn't. Bean cupped his chin and Bryant
wiped his mouth and they hooked him into Piacenti's air.
Bean's gloved fingers sorted through the first aid kit. Blood
bubbled and froze around the seal of Snowberry's oxygen
mask and Bryant scraped at it with the double-seamed fingertips of his gloves. Bean laid the morphine syrette on the
tumble of the blanket and exposed the wrist of Snowberry's

good hand and gestured for Bryant. Snowberry's head thumped the bulkhead in pain. Bean held the wrist as level and as still as possible. Bryant jabbed it with the tiny needle, anywhere. Snowberry jerked, as though that had been the worst of all.

He tried to remember what else was necessary. Bean had clearly moved on to the knee. He remembered bored NCO's modeling splints and neat bandages in training lectures. He had Snowberry's flight jacket zipped open and could see a soaked area the size of a baseball on his left side. He looked at Bean and Bean looked back helplessly, his gloves under his arms, his hands in the wet of Snowberry's knee. Paper bandages flew from the kit. Bryant found some cloth, bunched and folded, and eased it onto the spot. He held it there until Bean lifted it from his hands and set it aside and moved to expose the wound with a surprising and gentle assurance. Snowberry's knee was already wrapped, poorly but vehemently.

Bean gestured to the ball, and Bryant understood. In the hatchway to the radio room, Cooper, too, was pointing at the ball. They were taking additional hits, and he saw a pattern of daylight through the fuselage, a magical and artificial Big Dipper.

He removed his parachute and climbed gingerly into the hatch, his rear dropping low, his legs spreading and curling upward into the gun charging stirrups. He didn't fit completely, and the contortion was painful on the back of his neck and his hamstrings. He felt Bean close the hatch door behind him, heaving the metal door shut against the pressure of Bryant's back.

He got his hand on the rotation mechanism and swung the turret around so that he was curled more or less upright, head and feet up, rear down. He sighted out a circular Plexiglas panel between his legs. He adjusted the reticles of the gunsight for range with a left foot pedal. Tracking and firing involved the same grip handles as the dorsal, above his head instead of in front of him. The jetstream whistled through jigsaw holes along his left side, and below and beside one leg, like paint, he had to contend with a large frozen smear of blood, hampering visibility. His knees flanked his ears. His fingers and eyes moved along the guns on either side of him, checking for damage. A fighter swam up over his crotch from the world below, lining up for a free pass at their underside. He swiveled and aligned the shot delicately and let go a burst that surprised the German pilot but was too low. The sky cleared a little and he experimented, to get the hang of the turret's play. The rotation mechanism seemed more sensitive than the dorsal. He plugged in the interphone. Something else passed by and he fired at it, unused to the way the targets appeared so quickly from his blind spot above, and the cartridge cases tumbled and spilled over him. When he could, he slid them out the slots for the gun barrels.

A straggler trailing smoke thousands of feet below and behind them was swept over by a swarm of single- and twin-engine fighters, the spurts and blips of hits at that distance registering all over the wings and fuselage. All four engines caught fire and the plane broke up gently and silently into smaller pieces.

"We got manifold pressure problems in the number two engine," Gabriel said. Bryant could feel the shaking, their engine trying to tear itself out of the wing. They'd have to shut it down, but with only two engines left they weren't going to keep up with the formation. The shaking stopped, and he could feel the airspeed drop.

Behind them twin-engined Me-110's trailed along out of range with the intention of executing stragglers. They had a choice in *Paper Doll* of bailing out or hitting the deck, trying to get back flying the lowest possible altitude, hedgehopping home.

Gabriel asked for a vote.

"Our waist gunners already voted," Lewis said.

"I'm asking you guys," Gabriel said. "Our navigator's gone so I don't know exactly where we are. But it ain't friendly."

Bean was not on the system; still treating Snowberry, Bryant assumed. Bryant said, "I say we stay. Snowberry's chute is bad news. He won't survive a jump, anyway."

Gabriel waited. The plane was falling back now, and Bryant imagined *Archangel* and *Plum Seed* leaving them behind, the tail gunners in each regretting *Paper Doll*'s misfortune.

Lewis said, "What are we gonna do? The kid can't go. We gotta count on the flying ability of our Looeys. And me and Bryant and Harold Bean to keep them off our back."

"Big cloud to our left," Gabriel said. "I'm gonna use it to get down."

The mist of the cloud edge began to stream by Bryant's ball position, giving him the sense of dry immersion, and another straggler below them suddenly rose upward dramatically but Bryant understood that it was *Paper Doll*, going down. Lewis said, "I say we divvy up Ball and the wop's stuff when we get back," and Bryant thought about them, drifting down to the ground, killed or taken care of, and imagined Piacenti grinning and burying his parachute. He thought of Snowberry and hoped he was sleeping.

The cloud was raveling white, as bland as thick fog. The cloud would hide them all the way down to the ground, he hoped. The walk-around bottles were probably exhausted. It would be good to get off the oxygen for everyone's sake, especially Gordon's.

The plane banked lightly and Gabriel announced he was heading west, to avoid the mission return route. "Maybe we'll avoid everyone heading to the main force," he said. "It's such a mess maybe we'll get through. Maybe we'll have lost those 110's with this cloud."

"Oh, Jeez," Cooper said.

Bean came over the interphone. "Gordon's not so hot,"

he said calmly. "He's throwing up and throwing up as fast as I can clear it. I took care of his knee and his hand but I don't know what happened to his side. Maybe it's his stomach."

"Don't let him drink anything," Gabriel said, help-lessly.

"I got him wedged in so he won't bounce around much," Bean said. "I think he's sleeping."

"You better get back to the radio room," Lewis said. "You're the only gun on top, now."

"Yep," Bean said.

They racketed on in the white fog. "Keep going, cloud," Gabriel said.

"But stop before the ground," Cooper said.

Then the clouds were gone and green hillsides were coming up at them. They rose and soared over one, register-ing the successive images: the spilled stones of some fence mending, bright green clover in the sunlight, an open-mouthed boy with a staff.

They dipped and followed the land, a high-banked stream and tall blue firs going by. "Well, we got a nose open like a funnel and two engines out and enough holes in us to make a watering can and if our airspeed drops any more we'll be taxiing home, but I don't see anybody behind us and I think we slickered 'em," Gabriel crowed. "Lewis? See any-thing?"

Lewis was silent. Then he said, "Not yet."

"You guys can come off oxygen," Gabriel said. "In case you didn't know."

Bryant pulled off his mask. The cold air streamed over his mouth and cheeks and nose like home. The hillsides and thickets rolled and pleated beneath them, bright with clarity in the sunlight, *Paper Doll* towing its shadow across the landscape. They were close enough to see the gravel on hill-side trails and paths weaving beneath them and the cool, bottle green depths of a shaded pool overhung with thick trees. A white and black goat on an outcropping watched them come and ducked awkwardly, leaning backward on its haunches and keeping its front legs straight.

"It feels good to be off oxygen," Gabriel said.

Bryant said, "The lieutenant can say that again."

"I think I know what I'm doing," Gabriel said. "I'm going by the sun."

They'd begun following a stream, slipping lower as the cool spruce and fir tips rose past Bryant's position, the steeply banked forest blurring by, and Bryant watched as the blue and white water unreeled beneath him, changing features and speeds, rocks, whitewater, snags, clear cul de sacs, and around a bend he was over a fisherman, a big leather rucksack at his hip, ripples drifting outward from his legs, his thin rod the wisp of a line.

The stream banks narrowed and drew together and a fir branch whistled by his turret. Others slapped and grated their wingtips, and Gabriel gave a northerner's version of a Rebel yell. A huge fir rose from a grassy bend and they lurched upward, the sound of the branches on their starboard wing like someone crushing kindling. "Whoa, Nellie," Gabriel called. The stream opened out dramatically into a river, the water silver and smooth beneath, and they turned with it to the north, the prop wash from the lowered outboard engine fluttering the surface of the water. They roared by over a sailboat, collapsing the sail, and past docks and swimming floats, the white figures bobbing or pointing in shock as they careened past. They passed a humped yellow-green bank edged with willows and he could see picnickers and the red and white squares of blankets dotted with food and drink and that same crescent of lawn and remembered Robin, and swung his barrels harmlessly at everyone who pointed or ran.

Gabriel ducked still lower, and Bryant sped along in his glass ball twenty or so feet above the waves, catching a faint mist of spray kicked up by the props. Something rang faintly on the fuselage but he'd seen no one on shore fire anything.

A woman on a float directly below them capsized as they thundered over. A small red dog ran to the water's edge and threw himself in.

"Oh God," Gabriel said, and ahead of them the river opened out into some sort of inland port, and there were two long gray ships in their path, the decks busy with superstructure and the tiny figures of running men, and delicate barreled guns swinging about to face them.

"It's the German *Navy,* for Chrissakes!" Gabriel said, and yanked the plane into a hard bank just as the naval guns opened fire with theatrical booms and huge geysers erupted around and behind them. He banked them the opposite way, trapped into going right over the ships, and as they spanned the distance Bryant sighted along the superstructure and opened up, able to watch in the river surface his hits skip and spray upward across the bow and along the deck, a crew member leaping and pedaling an invisible bicycle into the water. The ships' guns thundered and then they were over, *Paper Doll* jerking and someone screaming on the interphone, and Bryant spun the turret and kept firing, the naval guns turning slowly to retrack, Lewis's twin fifties clattering now, too, fountaining water around the ships. They banked away from the river and were skimming farmland, scaring livestock.

Gabriel was sobbing and cursing. After a moment they heard another voice on the same line, and Bean said, "They got Cooper. It came in the same hole the other shell made."

Gabriel was still crying. "God, I just bent over to get the trim tab," he said. "God, I just bent over."

"I'm going to stay up here with him," Bean said.

"Are you sure he's dead?" Lewis said.

"He's a mess," Bean said. "He's all over the steering column." His voice was flat and high with shock.

Ahead jumbled shapes and lines rose from the landscape and converged.

"Town! A town!" Bryant said. "You see it?"

Gabriel and Bean took them down the main street at full throttle. Wagons swerved from the road and collided. A woman cleaning windows toppled outward and he flashed past and missed what happened to her. The huge wings filled the street with shadow from side to side and the sense of power was exhilarating, the greatest rush of adrenaline of all. They went by a pack of dogs turning over onto their backs in supplication, a railroad crossing, three boys on bicycles all wearing red, gaping.

Lewis was firing back down the center of the street. Bryant began firing, too, for Cooper, turning his guns this way and that and ripping up the windows and housefronts in long ravaging bursts. An elderly and fat man with tiny glasses glinting white emerged ahead with a long rifle and lifted it to them, and he slewed the turret ever so slightly and triggered a burst and folded the fat man in half, his arms waving from a puff of red mist.

They were out of the town but still over the main road, the telegraph wires below looping up and descending with each pole, and there were hedges and then an expanse of tarmac with white numbers and aircraft, camouflaged in gray and green and marked with black crosses.

"We're over an airfield! We're over an airfield!" Lewis cried, the first to understand, in the tail. "Get us out of here!"

Gabriel and Bean banked them sharply to the left and Bryant could see spinning away thirty feet below airfield personnel running in all directions, flak batteries swiveling uselessly around as they tried to get the barrels low enough. A Fiesler Storch, a single-engined observation plane as delicate and awkward as a chicken, with a huge ribbed window along its side, turned violently away from them, apparently in its landing pattern, and as it swung behind them Lewis opened fire, his tracer streams lashing across its length. It dove immediately into the ground and exploded and its engine went shooting up over a little hill into some trees.

There were more fields of tan and green lines of cultivation spanning quickly away behind them and he hoped they were safely away from it but Lewis called, "Trouble. Bryant, get out of there, and get to Bean's gun."

Gabriel was steady enough now that Bean was able to come all the way back and help Bryant out of the ball. With the hatch sprung he unfolded painfully out into the waist and flexed and rubbed parts of his legs as he scrambled back to the radio room and Bean's gun.

Closing fast behind them from above was a black Dornier 217, a night fighter, maybe, clearly all the airfield had around with everything else out intercepting the returning bomber stream.

"Let it close, let it close," Lewis said. "I'm dangling my guns."

The Dornier started firing early and inaccurately— filled with trainees, Bryant registered—and it closed in until the faceted Plexiglas nose filled his gunsight and he let fly. Lewis had opened up with his twin fifties as well and the three streams of tracers hesitated and flexed and then converged across the Dornier and disintegrated it, the wings and tiny pieces spinning end over end after them as if continuing pursuit.

"We did it!" Bryant called. "We did it!"

"Me-110's!" Bean called. "Head on. Treetop level."

The hits smashed into them along their entire length from wingtip to wingtip, it seemed, and Bryant fired as they flashed beside one another over his position, their bellies pale gray and then gone. Lewis did not fire. Bryant could see them hesitate, and then not bank around.

"They're not coming after us," he called in. "I think they're out of gas." It was, he realized, probably the only reason they'd been returning to the field.

The interphone sputtered and gasped.

"What happened?" Lewis said, his voice faint.

Gabriel chattered and snorted as if he was trying to

clear something from his throat. Bean said, "Bobby, you better get up here. Some control wires are flapping around behind me."

They were hydraulic lines. He found them fluttering and whipsawing right beside his turret, back behind Cooper's seat. He could make out Gabriel's head but did not want to see Bean or what was left of Cooper. The hydraulic fluid which allowed operation of the brakes and flaps was slipping away, streaming yellow and thick from the broken lines. He pinched the feeder tubes shut with pliers, and needed more fluid to keep the pressure in the system up. He broke into the flight rations behind Gabriel's seat, and found a can of apricot juice. He used that. He wrapped the pinched areas with electrical tape.

"Don't use the brakes or flaps until the very end," he called to the cockpit, to whoever was flying.

The hydraulic fluid had leaked through his hacked jacket to his bandage, and stung. He looked back down the catwalk toward the radio room, empty, and the waist with Snowberry beyond. His mind unclouded like washed glass, the pain stinging and clear in his arm, and he understood that they weren't getting back, that this had been more malevolent than they could have imagined, and that he had been, finally, adequate, sort of, with no one to see.

Lewis's final words struck him and he called Lewis, but no one answered. He climbed back through the bomb bay, through the radio room, past Snowberry, who seemed drowsing as he went by, boots splayed out like a lazy hillbilly.

There was a hatchway to the tail and he crawled into it on his hands and knees, squeezing forward past the assembly for the raised tail wheel. The flexing sheets of steel in the huge hollow tail above him echoed and lightly boomed with a drumlike sound in the wind. The cables along the narrow fuselage were severed, and he was relieved—the interphone was out, and the wind streamed through jagged holes generated from the head-on attacks. In the darkness his gloved hand slipped on ice except that part of the ice was sticky and he knew it was frozen and coagulating blood. He could see light beyond the armored headrest and the glass was smashed outward, sharp-edged and spread with crystals of blood. "Lewis," he said. "Lewis."

There were shell cases everywhere, in some parts six inches deep. The sighting glass on the machine guns was shot out. The ammunition boxes were torn and splintered. There were holes through the seat back, from the Me-110's head-on pass, he knew, and Lewis's head was back against the headrest but his middle had been destroyed and thrown forward all over the guns he had held.

Bryant had to back out, without turning around, and he was crying, his gloves smeared and gummy with blood, his head down and his rear edging tentatively back until he was out of the hatchway at the end of the waist, curled against the door, crying.

He pulled himself over to Snowberry, who looked on without expression as his head jiggled with the plane's motion. He lowered his face close and Snowberry looked into his eyes and bubbled some blood from his mouth. He was white and an eye drifted. He reached up and squeezed Bryant's nose feebly. Bryant understood he was dying. He opened the box of flight rations left for the waist and found an Oh Henry! He held it close to Snowberry's face and unwrapped it, holding the pebbled bar up for him to see. He broke it in two, and let Snowberry inhale the sugar smell. He put half in Snowberry's mouth. He put the rest in Snowberry's hand, and sat with him. Snowberry gave a little artificial grin, showing teeth.

Bean peered close to Snowberry and then tapped Bryant to get up, gesturing toward the waist guns. He picked up the flight rations, puffing, and threw them out the escape hatch.

He unslung the right waist gun from its mount and cleared an ammo belt and threw that out as well.

Bryant understood that they were lightening the load and stood and fumbled with the other gun. Bean threw out tool boxes and ammo boxes, and started work on the support housing for the ball turret itself. The ball could be jettisoned and was safer off in a rough landing.

He led Bryant by the hand away from Snowberry to the radio room. Bryant watched him broadcast an alert to British Air Sea Rescue. He saw ocean waves outside the small side window. He helped Bean heft the stacks of transmitters and receivers and tuners back to the waist, and they heaved them out. It took three trips. When they left the radio room, the red warning light was on, signaling them to destroy the radio.

In the cockpit when they returned, the air was unbelievable on the broken open side, Cooper's side. Gabriel was talking to himself. He told himself that the hydraulics were inoperative and most of the electricals were burned out. He said the inverter was shot and the trim tabs jammed. He said they were losing altitude and their airspeed was way too high. He said they should get Snowberry, because they were going to put it down in the Channel. He saw Bryant crying and he waved him violently away. "A lot of good that does," he said, nearly hysterical. "A lot of good that does."

They went back to the waist and hefted Snowberry. His head thumped and bobbed against Bryant's chest and they had an impossible time on the narrow catwalk, tipping this way and that, catching limbs. Bryant's arm was open again and streaming blood and he was faint. They managed to lay Snowberry down beside the dorsal turret and Bryant's flight engineer's panel. There was nothing to wedge him in with. Bryant leaned into the cockpit and saw above and beside them two Spitfires, watching them lose altitude, trying by example to nurse them back.

Bean stayed with Snowberry, wedging himself in to

cushion the blow for his friend. Bryant assumed Cooper's
seat when the steering columns began to shake, the great
posts with their horseshoe wheels impossible for Gabriel to
control alone anymore as the last of the hydraulics went and
Paper Doll dipped lower, and lower, and the gray and rough
waves loomed up like harsh and jagged pavement, and Gabriel wrapped an arm around the column, trying to bring
them in along the troughs of these waves, trying to keep
their nose up. And Bryant held on and mimicked his pilot
and fought what was out of control, wanting despite everything to believe the nose would stay up and the fuselage
would hold together, wanting to believe in Air Sea Rescue
and the Spitfires' silent assurance, wanting to believe that
Hirsch had jumped, that Eddy had survived, that Snowberry
hadn't suffered so; wanting to believe even then in their ability to deal with the uprushing stone ocean, rising now in all
its detail, filling his field of view.

WAR

The glory,
the horror, the
excitement of men in combat
—all captured in these unforgettable
works of fiction and non-fiction:

☐ **BATTLE FOR HUE, TET, 1968** (NF)
by Keith William Nolan 10407-6 $4.95

☐ **BODY COUNT** (F)
by William Turner Huggett 11392-X $3.95

☐ **DELTA FORCE** (NF)
by Col. Charlie A. Beckwith
and Donald Knox 11886-7 $3.95

☐ **THE DYING PLACE** (F)
by David A. Maurer 12183-3 $3.50

☐ **FRAGMENTS** (F) by Jack Fuller 12687-8 $3.50

☐ **GOODBYE, DARKNESS** (NF)
by William Manchester 13110-3 $4.95

☐ **MISSION M.I.A.** (F) by J.C. Pollock .. 15819-2 $3.95

☐ **WAR STORY** (NF) by Jim Morris 19362-1 $3.95

Dell At your local bookstore or use this handy coupon for ordering:

**DELL READERS SERVICE, DEPT. DW1,
P.O. Box 5057, Des Plaines, IL. 60017-5057**

Please send me the above title(s). I am enclosing $_____. (Please add $1.50 per order to cover shipping and handling.) Send check or money order—no cash or C.O.D.s please.

Ms./Mrs./Mr. _____

Address _____

City/State _____ Zip _____

DW1-4/88

Prices and availability subject to change without notice. Please allow four to six weeks for delivery. This offer expires 10/88.

THE WORLD
AT WAR

Experience the convulsion of total war with these riveting World War II nonfiction titles.

☐ AMERICAN CAESAR
  by William Manchester   30424-5 $6.95
☐ CONGRESSIONAL MEDAL
  OF HONOR LIBRARY
  World War II—The Names,
  The Deeds (A-L)   11454-3 $3.95
☐ CONGRESSIONAL MEDAL
  OF HONOR LIBRARY
  World War II—The Names,
  The Deeds (M-Z)   11457-8 $3.95
☐ GOODBYE, DARKNESS
  by William Manchester   13110-3 $4.95

Dell At your local bookstore or use this handy coupon for ordering:

DELL READERS SERVICE, DEPT. DW2,
P.O. Box 5057, Des Plaines, IL. 60017-5057

Please send me the above title(s). I am enclosing $_____. (Please add $1.50 per order to cover shipping and handling.) Send check or money order—no cash or C.O.D.s please.

Ms./Mrs./Mr. _____

Address _____

City/State _____ Zip _____

DW2-4/88

Prices and availability subject to change without notice. Please allow four to six weeks for delivery. This offer expires 10/88.

Special Offer
Buy a Dell Book
For only 50¢.

Now you can have Dell's Readers Service Listing filled with hundreds of titles. Plus, take advantage of our unique and exciting bonus book offer which gives you the opportunity to purchase a Dell book for *only 50¢.* Here's how!

Just order any five books at the regular price. Then choose any other single book listed (up to $5.95 value) for just 50¢. Use the coupon below to send for Dell's Readers Service Listing of titles today!

 DELL READERS SERVICE LISTING
P.O. Box 1045, South Holland, IL. 60473

Ms./Mrs./Mr. _____

Address _____

City/State_____ Zip _____

DFCA - 4/88